Naked Edge

Rocky Mountain Romance

By Charli Webb

Charli Webb

"You're the only boy I've ever loved. And the only man I ever will." — Skylar

This book is a work of fiction. Any resemblance to real persons, living or dead, is purely coincidental.

Copyright © 2013 Charli Webb

All rights reserved.

ISBN: 1494327597
ISBN-13: 978-1494327590

~***~

What early reviewers are saying about **Naked Edge**...

"I didn't want the story to end. Loved it from start to finish."

"I couldn't put it down! 5/5 stars. Can't wait to see where Charli goes from here."

"Naked Edge fills a gap that I didn't even realize I had in the New Adult books I've been reading...I felt for Skylar and Rowdy. I cheered for them. I ached for them."

"If Rowdy is out there somewhere, please let me get stranded on the side of a mountain...Good lord that man is yummy, and perfect. Yup. Perfect."

"Naked Edge has a great balance of angst and love, longing and affection, sexy and scary to satisfy most romance reader's needs. If you like your romance with less angst and more drama, this book is for you."

"Naked Edge is one of those amazing stories where you want to be friends with the characters."

"The sex scenes got me hot and bothered. I was definitely in the mood after the passage was over."

This book is dedicated to Aria Grace for inspiring me to write with courage.

Chapter One

Skylar

I wipe the sweat off my brow with the back of my hand. Even with the windows open and the ceiling fan set on high, Boone's house is a convection oven. It's at least ninety degrees in here. I know it's a 'dry heat,' nothing like the sweltering humidity of New Orleans. And it could snow tomorrow. But anyone that claims you don't need air-conditioning in Colorado is a freaking liar. "Call him again."

"I've already left two voice mails and a text."

"Please, Boone." I slip my hand into the front pocket of my jeans and wrap my fingers around my rescue inhaler. The fan churning dust in the air isn't the best thing for my asthma, but it's my burning desire to see Rowdy Daletski that's got my chest trapped in a giant vise. "I need to talk to him."

"It's been four years, Sky. Things change. People change."

"Is Rowdy involved with someone?" The vice tightens.

Boone grimaces, confirming my worst fear.

"Is he married?" Please, god, don't let him be married. Anything but that. I'll fight for him if he's engaged, but I won't break up a marriage.

Boone leans against the rough-rock fireplace. It's the end of May but there's still a pile of ashes under the grate. He traces a finger over the dusty frame of Aunt Lori and Uncle Will's wedding picture on the mantle. "Rowdy hasn't spent more than a few hours with the same girl since you left."

I can't help the relieved *oh* that escapes with my breath. I press a hand over my pounding heart and smile.

"Skylar." The hardwood floor creaks as Boone crosses the room to sit beside me on the old leather couch. "That's not a good thing."

"Of course it is." It takes a second for his words to hit me. "Wait. Are you saying shy, sweet Rowdy's a *player*?"

"Your disappearance, as devastating as it was for all of us, wasn't the only trauma Rowdy suffered that night."

"What happened?"

"That's not my story to tell." Boone closes his eyes for a second then gazes at me with profound sorrow. "Even though it wasn't your fault, when Rowdy needed you most, you weren't here. He's still trying to put his life back together and there're more than a few missing pieces."

"I can help him—"

"You aren't listening to me." Boone takes my face in his hands and forces me to look at him. "Rowdy's with a different girl every night."

I pull Boone's hands off my face and stand up to pace across the worn carpet runner in front of the couch. The rabbit-shaped stain where I spilled a pitcher of cherry Kool-Aid ten years ago tugs at my heart as I remember how Rowdy peeled off his shirt and tried to soak up the crimson liquid. He was so afraid I would get in trouble. I also remember the little round scars all over Rowdy's back. He's the one that got punished when he went home with a stained shirt.

"So he dates a lot of girls. So what? That's better than being tied down with a girlfriend." Or worse. "I didn't expect him to become a monk after I disappeared."

"Rowdy doesn't date girls. He fucks them."

"He's not like that." I can't keep my voice from trembling. "We were friends for years before we were a couple and then it was another three years before we made love."

"Rowdy uses women to deal with...stuff."

My hands curl into fists. Every time Dennis got caught with another woman, he'd blame it on stress and his 'addiction.' I still can't believe Mom let him get away with that. "Is Rowdy a sex addict?"

Boone laughs then covers it with a cough. "Rowdy's a slut, but I wouldn't go so far as to call him a sex addict. If it makes you feel any better, I don't think he even looked at another girl until after Mom and Dad died. I know for a fact he didn't start drinking until then."

I sink down on the couch next to Boone. "Rowdy's drinking?"

Boone takes my hands and gazes at me with wide eyes. "I still love him like a brother, but Rowdy's not the right guy for you. Not anymore. Please tell me you haven't spent the past four years locked away in your room, pining after him."

"I grieved for Rowdy as if he'd died when I was forced into WITSEC. But I didn't waste away like some tragic heroine in a fairy tale." I tug my hands out of Boone's grasp. "We'd only been in the program a little over a year when Mom got diagnosed with cancer. I felt so guilty for wallowing in self-pity when she was fighting for her life. I had to move on, for her sake as well as mine. I didn't think I'd ever see any of you again. I started new hobbies. I made new friends. I even tried to fall in love with someone else."

"Tried?"

"It didn't work." I couldn't force myself to love Ethan any more than I could force myself to stop loving Rowdy. "When we learned that Mom's last round of chemo failed, I started making plans to leave New Orleans."

"Did you tell her?"

"I didn't tell anyone until after her funeral. Not even Ethan."

"Ethan?"

"My ex-boyfriend." I press my palm over the ache in my chest. Even though I was never in love with him, I care about Ethan, deeply. You can't be with someone for as long as we were together and not care about them.

"How did he take your decision to move?"

"Not well."

"It sounds intense."

"I broke his heart, Boone. I didn't mean to, but I did."

"Does he know where you are?"

"No." I blink back tears as I relive our emotional farewell. "Ethan only needs a few more credit hours at Tulane to graduate, but he would have dropped out of school to follow me."

"Maybe you guys can patch things up once he graduates."

"He needs to forget about me and move on."

"I'm so sorry, Skylar." The tenderness in Boone's voice is nearly my undoing.

"It's okay. I'm okay." The familiar surroundings comfort me. "I can't believe I'm really here."

He slings an arm over my shoulders and gives me a sideways hug. "I can't believe you talked the witness protection people into letting you move to Eldorado Springs."

"I didn't." I take a deep breath and let it out slowly. "I opted out of the program."

Boone grabs both my shoulders. "Are you in danger?"

"Mom never married Dennis so she and I were never in any danger." I take a deep breath to fight the ever-tightening sensation around my lungs. "But, I didn't know that until I met with our WITSEC Inspector to submit my relocation request."

"What happened?" Boone's fingers loosen their grip, but he doesn't let go.

"Taking Mom and me with him was part of the deal Dennis made with the Department of Justice." I dig my fingers into the knotted muscles of my jaw, trying to unclench my teeth before I crack a molar. "When Mom chose to enter the program with that scumbag, I got dragged into it as well."

"You could have stayed with us."

"I would've if I'd been given the choice. But I wasn't." Mom's betrayal is still too raw. I don't want to talk about it anymore. I don't know how to deal with all this rage on top of her death. Anger and grief is a confusing, toxic brew. I can't believe Mom destroyed my life to stay with that cheating, lying, murdering son of a bitch.

I can't change the past or bring back the dead. But I've been given a second chance with Rowdy and I'm not going to waste it. It's time to quit feeling sorry for myself and start living again. I stand up and square my shoulders. "Let's go climbing."

Boone arches his eyebrows. "Now?"

I can't think of a better way to begin the process of reclaiming my life. "Why not?"

"Well, for starters," Boone ticks the reasons off on his fingers. "You just got here. You aren't acclimated to the altitude. You don't have any gear. And it's hotter than hell."

"We don't have to climb The Naked Edge our first time out."

"Why don't I take you to the gym where I work? It's a great way to get back into climbing. It's air-conditioned. It's safe—"

"I've done nothing but climb in gyms for the past four years. I need a mountain. I'll even settle for The Governor's Climb. It's what, a five point two? Single pitch? Please." I'm not above begging.

"You've been working out at a climbing gym?"

"Three times a week." I flex my arms to prove it. "And I brought my gear with me."

Boone arches an eyebrow, obviously not impressed by my firm, but extremely lean, biceps. "Fine. But The Governor's Climb is for pussies. Think you can handle The Bastille Crack?"

I throw my arms around his neck. "Thank you!"

~***~

I grab Boone's wrist before he can take me off belay. "I'm tired of shooting pictures of your butt. Let me lead this pitch."

"No way." His grin morphs into a frown, making him look more like Uncle Will than the fun-loving cousin I grew up with.

"Come on. It's only a five point four. I want to get a shot of your face just before you summit." I also want more of a challenge. Adrenaline is my drug of choice and rock climbing is my favorite way to get it. Pulling the crux on the first pitch gave me my first hit. Just getting to it is a bitch, especially for someone with a small wingspan like me. And it's dangerous. People have died attempting it. It gave me a good rush but it's long gone.

I stare down the sheer, red face of The Bastille, trying to psych myself out a little. South Boulder Creek looks like a discarded shoestring. The cars in the parking lot look like toys. The climbers at the base, waiting for their turn on the wall, look like ants. And none of it looks real.

The sky is a brilliant shade of turquoise. Even though the sun's heat beats down on my shoulders and radiates off the red sandstone cliff, the scent of evergreens gives the air a sense of sharpness.

It's peaceful up here. Too peaceful. And it's killing my buzz. Leading a climb is much riskier than seconding it. "Have a little faith, Boone. This isn't the first time I've led this pitch."

"It's been more than four years. And trad climbing The Bastille is a lot different than sport climbing in a gym."

I pat the rack of gear attached to my harness. "I'll sew it up so tight it'll be bombproof. I've got this. I wouldn't ask to lead if I couldn't handle it."

He finally nods, one quick dip of his chin. "All right. But I want you clipping in every five feet."

I scamper up the chimney, placing nuts and cams like a damn gumby. But if that's what it takes to make Boone feel comfortable, I'll do it.

I'm almost to the top when I decide to exit out a little to the right, over a small roof. It'll require a short traverse, but it's a much more challenging climb.

I shove my last cam into the crack then top out. I want to get some shots of Boone coming out of the chimney but I can't do it from here. I call out for more slack and edge my way back over to the left and build an anchor.

When Boone gets close to the top, I yell at him to wait. "I'm going to lock off the belay."

"Did you say 'off belay?'"

"No." I probably could have worded that better. "I'm using a mule knot so I can go hands free for a second."

I snap off a half-dozen shots. Looking at Boone through the lens gives me the emotional distance I need to see him as something other than my goofy cousin. Even if we weren't related, I wouldn't be attracted to his Abercrombie blond-tipped hair, honey-brown eyes and pretty-boy face. I prefer a more rugged, darker, masculine look. A more Rowdy Daletzki look.

"Skylar? What the hell did you do?" Boone's obviously not happy with the way I ran out the route.

"You're the one that insisted I place pro every five feet. I ran out of cams."

"No. I mean the traverse." He points at the rope that's angled sharply to the right. "Jesus."

"Hang on. I want to get a few more shots."

"How much longer?" Boone dips his fingers in his chalk bag then switches grips and shakes out his right arm. "I'm getting pumped."

I loosen the mule knot then brace my feet on the edge and lean out over it.

"What are you doing?" Boone's voice is tight, higher pitched than normal.

"It's okay. I've practiced this stance a hundred times." It was in a climbing gym twenty feet off the ground instead of three hundred, but the principles are the same.

Boone's expression of pure terror is priceless. He's a skilled climber, but he's afraid of heights. Go figure. I fire off another series of shots. If I can get one of my photos on the cover of just one climbing magazine, I can justify pursuing an art degree instead of the more practical Business Administration. I don't have the luxury of pursuing a 'fun' career unless I'm sure I can support myself with it.

"Sky, back off, now. This isn't safe."

"I'm fine."

"Well, I'm not."

"Okay. Sorry." I bend my knees and reach behind me so I can pull myself around with the rope. I realize it's the wrong move, even as I do it. But it's too late.

I slip on the loose gravel, lose my balance and tumble, headfirst, over the edge. My foot catches the side of Boone's helmet as the rope flips me right side up with a bone-jarring jerk. I watch in horror as he pops a nut then pendulums to the right. He screams when he slams into the cliff.

"Boone! Are you okay?"

"Fuck!"

"What hurts?"

"My ankle. I think it's broken."

"Anything else?" I don't see any blood, but he's pressed against the wall, so I can't really tell.

"No. Just my ankle. But it really hurts."

"You're okay. Try to stay calm." I love Boone like a brother, but he tends to be a little overly dramatic. At least that last cam held.

Someone below yells, "Hang on. Help's coming."

I check my watch every few seconds, so even though it feels like it takes forever, I know it's only been ten minutes when a sun-kissed, ruggedly handsome face peers over the ledge. It's been over four years since I've seen Rowdy Daletzki, but I'd recognize those ice-blue eyes even if it had been a hundred.

My stomach clenches as heat floods my cheeks. Damn. All I can see is his chiseled face and broad, muscular shoulders, but my imagination fills in the rest. His helmet hides his coal black waves but I'll bet his hair is just as silky as it ever was. My fingers tingle with the desire to find out. It's clear that Rowdy's even hotter at twenty-one than he was at seventeen. Much hotter.

"Are you injured?" Rowdy's voice is still smooth as velvet, but it's deeper than I remember.

I blink and lick my lips as heat floods my body. It takes a few seconds for his words to cut through the haze of lust clouding my brain. Jesus, what's wrong with me? What sort of a slut gets turned on during a rescue?

It's obvious Rowdy's checking me out, but it's purely clinical. He acts as if he doesn't recognize me. Sure, my hair's shorter now. It only reaches my shoulder blades instead of my waist. It's darker too, more of a mahogany brown instead of a sun-bleached, chestnut red. I spent the last three years indoors with my sick mother instead of surfing with my friends in San Deigo so the sun didn't have a chance to lighten my hair. I'm a size six instead of a size two. My boobs are a solid C instead of barely a B. But I haven't changed that much.

My eyes are still hazel and too big for my face. There's still a cleft in my chin. I still have the same full lips Rowdy could never get enough of. There's no way he doesn't know who I am.

"I'm fine. But Boone thinks he's hurt."

Rowdy's gaze unlocks from mine. His brow furrows. "Boone? Are you okay?"

"I've been better." His voice is soft, quiet. No longer frantic. And that scares me. Maybe he really is hurt.

I shouldn't have pushed Boone to let me lead. I shouldn't have gone off route. I should've tied Boone off into the anchor instead of keeping him on belay while I traversed back and forth trying to get the best shot. This is my fault.

Rowdy presses a button on the two-way radio attached to his shoulder harness. "Base, this is Rowdy Daletzki. We have one injured climber on the top third of the final pitch of The Bastille Crack. Male, twenty-one, conscious and responsive. We also have an uninjured female stranded near the summit."

Rowdy continues to talk into his radio as another helmeted face peers over the ledge. A gorgeous, feminine face. Crap. It's Rowdy's stepsister, Anna. She was always trying to get Rowdy to break up with me.

She appraises me with undisguised loathing then looks at Rowdy with more than just sisterly affection in her gold-flecked, dark brown eyes. I want to claw them out of her head.

Rowdy returns his gaze to me. He speaks with cool professionalism. "Okay, Skylar. Let's get you out of here so we can get to Boone."

I knew he recognized me. I want to say something to him, but my brain seems to have blown a fuse. All I can do is nod like an idiot as Anna slips over the edge to attach redundant gear to my harness. She glares at me the whole time. I'm tempted to ask, 'just what the hell is your problem,' but decide antagonizing the person who literally has my life in her hands is a bad idea.

Rowdy pulls me to safety then passes me off to a kid that looks way too young for the job. Anna double checks Rowdy's gear then belays him down to Boone.

The kid guides me into a rescue litter and holds the back of my head as he lays me down. It takes me a second to figure out what's going on. I try to sit up, but he puts a restraining hand on my shoulder.

"My name's Wade Summers. I'm with Boulder Mountain Rescue. Do you mind if I check you out real quick?"

"I'm fine."

"What's your name?"

"Skylar Layton."

"Well, Skylar, I'd feel a lot better if you'd let me do a quick exam."

"Whatever." I figure it'll be quicker to just let him do his thing than to argue with him.

"Can you tell me what happened?"

I repeat the story as he pokes at me from head to toe.

"How long were you suspended in your harness?" Wade wraps a blood-pressure cuff around my arm.

"Ten...fifteen minutes? I don't know." It felt like forever. "Why?"

"Suspension trauma."

I have no idea what that is.

The blood pressure cuff deflates. Wade grins at me. "Other than a couple of scrapes, you seem to be pretty healthy, but it wouldn't hurt to get you checked out at Avista while they're taking care of Boone."

I sit up and lean towards the edge, hoping to get a glimpse of Boone…and if I'm being totally honest…Rowdy.

Wade grabs my arms. "Where do you think you're going?"

"I just want to see how Boone's doing."

"The last thing Boone needs is for you to shower him with scree or fall on top of him. Stay put."

"What's taking so long?" My body trembles, but it's probably just from the adrenaline leaving my bloodstream. It has nothing to do with seeing Rowdy again. Yeah, right.

Wade tears open a foil packet then dabs at my bloody hands with an antiseptic wipe.

I yelp and jerk my hand out of his.

"Sorry. I'll try to be more gentle." He holds a gloved hand out to me, palm up, and waits for me to place my hand in his.

I talk to Wade to distract myself from the pain. "I'm not a wimp. I just have a more advanced nervous system than most people."

Wade arches his eyebrows.

"I'm joking."

He grins and shakes his head then gives my shredded knuckles another swipe.

I flinch. I really do have a low pain threshold but I refuse to let it get in my way.

"I'm almost done."

I recognize the Boulder Mountain Rescue insignia screen printed on his royal blue t-shirt, but not the WEMT acronym embroidered over his impressive left pectoral muscle. "What's WEMT?"

"Wilderness Emergency Medical Technician."

"Is that what Rowdy is?"

Wade's eyebrows disappear under the fringe of curls on his forehead. "You know Daletzki?"

"I used to." I can't help the sigh that escapes.

Wade's mouth quirks to the side. "Daletzki's actually a full paramedic with several specialist certs."

"Certs?"

"Certificates. He's an expert in just about every type of wilderness rescue. If you get into trouble, Rowdy Daletzki's the guy you want."

Rowdy's the only guy I want, whether I'm in trouble or not, but I keep that thought to myself. "From what I remember, Rowdy was pretty damn good at getting himself, and everyone else, into all sorts of trouble."

"Sounds like you have a few stories to tell. I'd love to hear 'em over a cup of coffee." Wade's grin widens.

I look away. Even though I'm getting nothing but friendly vibes from the guy, and he's extremely cute with a drool-worthy, athletic body, I don't want to encourage him. There's absolutely nothing wrong with Wade Summers. He isn't the problem—Rowdy Daletzki is.

The awkward moment stretches out between us as half a dozen rescuers slip over the side. Wade's radio squawks. Rowdy's voice crackles through the mild static. "Patient is secure. Belaying to bottom. What's the status of the female climber?"

"She's shaken up with minor lacerations. I'll escort her down Fowler Trail to the parking lot."

"Hey, I'm not shaken up."

Wade grins and shakes his head. "Correction. Female climber is *not* shaken up. I'm still escorting her to the parking lot."

When we get to the trailhead, I'm shocked to find Boone sitting sideways in the back seat of his beat-up old Jeep Wrangler with his leg in a vacuum cast. Rowdy, Anna and half a dozen other blue-shirted rescuers are standing around, talking.

"Boone? What's going on?"

"My ankle's definitely broken."

"Holy crap. Why aren't you on your way to the emergency room?"

"I'm not paying for an ambulance and I can't exactly drive myself."

I don't blame him. An ambulance is too expensive to be used as a taxi. "Rowdy wouldn't give you a ride?"

At the sound of his name, Rowdy snaps his head around and lasers me with ice-blue eyes. It simultaneously heats my blood and sends a chill up my spine.

I refuse to let him intimidate me. "Why's Boone still sitting in the parking lot?"

"He refused transport in an ambulance."

"And you couldn't drive him?"

"Liability issues."

"You're his friend. Or at least you were."

"Sky, it's okay." Boone shifts his weight and grimaces.

"No, it's not. You're in obvious pain and he's just standing around with his hands in his pockets."

"Can we go now?"

I jog around to the driver's side and slide behind the wheel.

Rowdy shuts Boone's door then leans in through the window. "I'll follow you to Avista."

"Why?" If he couldn't be bothered to drive him to the hospital, why does he want to follow us there?

Rowdy gives me another arctic glare. "Like you said, he's my friend."

I glance in the rearview mirror and see Wade slide into the passenger seat of Old Blue. It thaws a little of the ice around my heart to know that Rowdy still has the same old Chevy truck he had in high school. We had lots of deep conversations and intense make-out sessions in that thing.

I hope Wade is tagging along for Boone's sake and not mine. Boone didn't have many friends growing up. He tried so hard to fit in with the fringe groups in high school. The goths and stoners tolerated him without actually accepting him. Rowdy was his only real friend. As far as I know, Boone never even had a girlfriend. "So, is Wade a friend of yours?"

Boone's mouth curves up into a shy smile. "We met at CU last year. He's a great guy."

I pull into the ambulance unloading area at Avista but before I can get my door open, Rowdy's pulling Boone out of the back seat.

"Go ahead and park. I'll get Boone inside."

By the time I park the car and persuade the ER nurse to let me join Boone, Rowdy's gone.

Chapter Two

Rowdy

The Dark Horse Bar and Grill is surprisingly crowded for a Wednesday night. I don't come here often. Can't afford it on my salary. But until the fall semester starts at CU, it's the best place to pick up women. And after that run-in with Skylar, I definitely need a woman. What the hell is she doing back in town? And what was Boone thinking, letting her lead on The Bastille Crack? Skylar's always been reckless, but Boone knows better.

I need another drink.

An hour later, I've got a nice buzz going and a curvy little tourist on my lap. So why do I feel like my dog died? And why the fuck am I still thinking about Skylar?

The crowd cheers. I look up and notice the Rockies' game is playing on the big screen over the bar. That explains the mob.

The tourist's beer-scented breath warms my neck as she whispers seductively in my ear, "You ready to get outta here?"

I should be, but I'm just not feeling it. Hell, I can't even remember her name and she's reminded me at least three times. "I just got here."

I take a long pull on my Coors, hoping that'll get me in the mood. She's pretty enough for a bar whore. She's got that bleached-blonde, spray-tanned, tramp-stamped, easy-woman look. She could have her pick of just about any guy here. I should feel lucky. But all I feel is depressed.

I need something stronger than beer. I'd buy a shot of tequila if it didn't cost more than an entire bottle of the cheap shit I get at the liquor store.

The tourist pushes her lower lip out. I'm sure she thinks it's a sexy little pout, but it looks ridiculous. She's gotta be at least thirty. Grow the fuck up.

She walks her fingers up my chest then taps the end of my nose. "We could have more fun back at my hotel."

I pat the side of her hip and shift my weight. "Hop up. My legs are falling asleep."

Her eyes widen then narrow as she slides off my lap. She grips the handle of her souvenir beer mug so tightly her hand shakes. For a moment, I wonder if she's going to throw the designer brew in my face.

Whether she does or not, I'm done with this one. I can tell she's the clingy type. The type that'll get pissed off when I leave immediately after sex. If you want hugs and cuddles, don't go home with random guys you meet in bars.

She tosses her long, blonde hair over her shoulder, flips me off, then saunters away towards the pool tables.

Every man but me drools as she passes, hips swaying, boobs bouncing and practically popping out of her low-cut, two sizes too small tank top.

I lift my index finger to signal I'm ready to settle my tab then freeze when Skylar walks through the door. Boone hobbles in behind her. He's on crutches with a velcro boot on his left foot. I feel a twinge of guilt for not sticking around a little longer at the hospital. But it can't be too bad if he's out cruising bars already.

Derek nods at my half full bottle of Coors. "You ready for another?"

"No, I'm fine." I lower my hand, embarrassed that I've been sitting here pointing at the ceiling ever since Sky walked in.

Derek smirks at me. "Don't tell me some conniving female finally got her hooks in you."

"What are you talking about?"

He nods at Skylar. "You're staring at that chick as if she were the only woman on the planet. And I saw the way you shoved that slam-dunk hottie off your lap. You could've nailed that one in the bathroom."

Derek's eyes widen when he spots Boone. "Oh, wow. What happened to Boone Dog?" He gives me a suspicious look. "Please tell me you aren't the reason he's on crutches. You know the code."

"If you say bros before hoes, I'm going to punch you in the mouth." I drop a twenty on the bar. "Keep the change."

"Thanks, man." Derek scoops up the bill and grins at me. He thinks I'm joking about punching him.

I'm not usually a big tipper, especially not when it's one of my housemates behind the bar, but I want to get out of here before Skylar and Boone spot me.

Too late.

Boone pins a crutch against his ribs with his elbow and waves.

Skylar's gaze locks on mine. She lifts her chin and clears a path through the crowd for Boone. She doesn't inspire the same level of raw lust in the drunken horde as the hot little tramp I had in my lap, but more than one asshole adjusts his junk as Skylar weaves her way through their midst.

I'm trapped. If I leave without at least saying hello, I'll look like a pussy. "Shit."

Derek gives me a sympathetic smile then moves to a customer at the other end of the bar. I don't blame him for ditching me. There's so much tension in the air you can feel it. Like static electricity before lightning strikes. I'd run for cover too, if I could.

Boone flashes a grin at the girls sitting on either side of me. "Do you lovely ladies mind scooting down a bit so we can talk to our friend?"

One girl huffs in obvious annoyance, but they both do as he asks. Funny, I hadn't even noticed them. The one on my left immediately strikes up a conversation with Boone, leaving me to deal with Skylar on my own. My blood pressure climbs until I can hear my pulse behind my ears. I take another long pull on my beer, delaying the inevitable.

Skylar watches me from beneath her lashes. The tip of her tongue darts out and slicks the surface of both lips then disappears. It was too fast to be intentional. A nervous tic, not a conscious act of seduction, but the way her lips glisten, like ripe cherries after a rain, makes my mouth water. Doesn't matter. I'm not falling for that shit. I'm not a love-struck, horny teenager and I'm sure as hell not a frightened, battered kid, desperate for affection. Not anymore.

I'm a hard-hearted, mean son of a bitch that can get laid whenever he wants and I'm not letting Skylar Layton, or any other woman, anywhere near my heart ever again.

I keep my own lips pressed to the mouth of my beer bottle and damn near chug the rest of it. It's just beer, but I'm definitely feeling it. I should have splurged and ordered a quesadilla before I started drinking. "What are you doing here, Skylar?"

I know I'm being rude, but what I really want to ask her is, *Where the fuck have you been?*

"It's a long story." She licks her lips again.

Damn. I wish she'd quit doing that. I pick at the label on my now empty bottle of Coors. I don't give a rat's ass what her excuse is, but I am curious. Doesn't mean I care. "I've waited four years to hear it."

The right side of Skylar's mouth twitches before she smiles. Most people wouldn't notice it, but I do. She's nervous. She swallows then clears her throat. "You know what they say about people that peel labels off bottles?"

"That they're sexually frustrated?" A single, bitter laugh escapes my throat as I slam the bottle on the bar a little too forcefully. "I wouldn't know anything about that."

She flinches, but I'm not sure whether it's because of the sudden noise, my harsh tone of voice, or my sarcastic remark.

Instead of apologizing, I change the subject. "How long are you in town?"

"As of six forty-five this morning, I live here."

"You live here? In Boulder?" I grab the rounded edge of the bar. I'd assumed Skylar was just here for a short vacation. The thought of randomly bumping into her on a regular basis flips my panic switch.

Skylar shakes her head. "I'm living with Boone in Eldorado Springs."

His house is less than half a mile from mine. I am so fucked. "Why are you living with Boone?"

Identical red patches bloom across Sky's cheeks. She tucks a short, strawberry blonde curl behind her ear. "I can't afford to rent an apartment."

Bullshit. Her family's loaded. They could buy an entire apartment building if they wanted. And even if rent was a problem, it's pretty ballsy of her to come back after so many years of no contact and take advantage of Boone's generosity. "Where were you when Will and Lori died? We missed you at their funeral."

All the color drains from her face.

Shit. That was harsh, even for me. "I'm sorry."

"Really?" Her eyes sparkle with unshed tears. "Because of all the things you could've said to me, I can't think of anything that would've hurt me more."

Boone levers himself off the barstool with his crutches. His eyebrows draw together, tilting up in the center as he shakes his head at me. "Not cool, man. Not cool at all."

I stand up and grab his upper arms. For a skinny guy, his biceps are hard as rocks. "It's the beer talking. And the stress of..." I don't have to finish the sentence. Boone knows what I'm talking about.

His body sags into the crutches. "I know you went through hell when she disappeared. But you don't know the whole story. None of us did. You need to let her explain."

"I don't need anything from her."

Sky's voice trembles. "Please, Boone, let's just go home, okay?"

As a paramedic, I've seen a lot of pain and suffering on peoples' faces. I see it on Skylar's right now. I see it on Boone's, too. Yeah, I'm definitely an asshole. But assholes don't get their hearts ripped out of their chests and stomped on.

Boone and Skylar turn around and make their way through the crowd to the door.

I just stand here and watch them go.

~***~

I punch my pillow again and roll to the other side of my bed, but it doesn't help. Nothing does. I'm exhausted but every time I close my eyes, I see Skylar's filling with tears. "Fuck. I don't care. I don't care. I don't care. I'm over it."

Before Will and Lori died, I would have given my right nut to know what happened to Skylar. I would have given anything to see her again. But when she didn't show up for their funeral, I decided it was time to move on.

And now it's time to haul my sleep-deprived ass out of bed. The morning sun will crest my southeast windowsill any second now. Might as well get out of here before the heat gets unbearable. My bedroom, over the detached garage, is the largest by far, but it has its drawbacks. The main problem is no bathroom or running water. It's not so bad in the summer. I have an Eldorado Springs hot and cold water dispenser and a mini-fridge. But the ten-yard dash from my room, down a full flight of narrow stairs and across the yard to the house is brutal in the winter. I grab my shaving kit, robe and a towel then head to the house.

My stubborn, masochistic brain continues to dwell on Skylar as I shower. I crank the heat up, hoping the hot water will clear my head. It doesn't. Two questions seem to be stuck on auto-repeat. Why did she disappear without a trace? And why did she come back?

I'm not going to be able to let it go until I find out. I'm obsessive about puzzles. Derek buys Sudoku books and leaves them lying around all over the house. He'll work on a puzzle until it gets hard then move on to the next one. He's got entire books of partially solved puzzles. It drives me crazy. This thing with Skylar isn't any more significant than that. It's nothing more than an unsolved puzzle. I'll get Boone to tell me her story. Once the mystery is solved, I can stop obsessing over it.

I need someone to give me a ride back to The Dark Horse to get my car. It might as well be Boone. The sooner I learn why Skylar disappeared, the sooner I can move on.

Derek bangs on the bathroom door. "Dude, hurry up. I've got class in less than an hour."

I wrap my towel around my hips and open the door.

Derek fans the steam and glares at me. "If you used all the hot water, I'm gonna kick your ass."

"It's Thursday. You're supposed to shower at The Rec."

"I'm running late."

"Not my problem, buddy. And Wade's next." With four of us living in one tiny house, we have to manage our limited resources creatively.

"I gave Wade ten bucks to trade with me, so get out of my way." Derek grabs the door and tries to push past me.

I stand my ground. "You still owe me for your share of the cable bill."

"Come on, Rowdy. I'm in a hurry. I'll give you the money tonight."

I step into the narrow hall.

Derek squeezes past me and slams the bathroom door.

I should have gotten the money from him last night while his wallet was still full of cash. Most people consider tips part of their salary. Derek considers it 'free' money. He routinely blows through a night's haul the next day, buying lattes for cute girls at The Laughing Goat. I don't care what he does with his money, as long as he pays his bills.

I go back to my room, yank open my top drawer and notice I'm down to three pairs of boxer briefs. Shit. Yesterday was my laundry day, but I'd been so blindsided by Skylar, I'd forgotten all about it. Now I'll have to haul my shit down to the laundromat. I dig the pair of jeans I wore last night out of my hamper and the last clean t-shirt out of my drawer. It's the one Derek gave me for Christmas last year. It's so offensive, I never even tried it on, but it's either scrounge something out of the dirty clothes or wear the shirt with Ralphie the bison humping Cam the ram emblazoned on the front.

I enjoy sticking it to CSU as much as the next guy, but this shirt is downright crude. I can't wear it out in public, much less to class.

We have a strict 'if it's not yours don't touch it' rule in the house. I poke my head out of my bedroom window just in time to see Derek burst out the front door.

"Hey, Derek, can I borrow a shirt?"

"Sure." He slams the door hard behind him. Derek doesn't do anything gently. But he's generous to a fault, which is why we all put up with him. He'd wait and give me a ride if I asked, but a detour to The Dark Horse would make him more than a little late. Missing one class during summer session is like missing two during a regular semester. The poor guy's already struggling to keep up.

Derek's bedroom door only opens partway. I have to shove myself through the gap. "God, Derek. You are such a pig."

His closet and drawers are empty. Every article of clothing he owns is either on the floor, draped over his desk chair or… what the hell? I nearly gag at the sight of a used condom hanging over the edge of his trashcan. I back out of his room and yank the door shut. Damn. We're all in charge of our own rooms, but if he causes us to lose our damage deposit, I won't be the only one to kick his ass. Anna's small but she's wicked strong with a temper to match.

I turn the vulgar shirt wrong side out and pull it on over my head then grab my phone to call Boone and give him a heads up.

It goes straight to voice mail. Of course it does. What am I thinking? It's only eight forty-five.

I grab my backpack, jump on my mountain bike and head up the canyon. I'm ninety-nine percent certain that Skylar will be up. I don't want to see her, but I don't really have a choice. I'll have to play nice so she'll let me in to drag Boone's lazy ass out of bed. Derek won't be the only one late for class if I don't get a ride.

Chapter Three

Skylar

I don't know what I'm expecting to find when I open the front door, but it certainly isn't Rowdy Daletzki. My heart jumps into my throat. I swallow, trying to force the traitorous organ back into my chest where it belongs. "What are you doing here?"

His pale blue eyes widen just a fraction as his lips part.

I catch a glimpse of the old Rowdy and immediately regret hurting his feelings. But all sympathy disappears when he flashes me a panty-dropping, crooked grin. It's obviously fake and so not him. He even presses an open palm over his chest.

"Ouch."

"Don't pretend to be offended. That's the exact same thing you said to me last night."

He drops the wounded, bad boy act but the old Rowdy is already gone. The new, perpetually angry Rowdy grits his teeth. "I came to apologize."

"Apology accepted." I stand on the threshold and grip the edge of the door so hard my fingers ache. It's all I can do to keep from throwing my arms around his neck. I have to remember that the gorgeous man in front of me is not the same sweet boy I fell in love with so long ago. I refuse to believe Boone's claim that Rowdy is broken beyond repair, but I can't deny that he's damaged. The old Rowdy would never hurt me on purpose. *We missed you at their funeral.*

I'm not giving up on him, but I'm not going to let him walk all over me either. "You still haven't answered my question. Do you need something?"

I'm tempted to close the door in his face when he flashes me that sexy, crooked grin again. But then he rubs his forearms with his hands and I melt. He used to do that all the time when he was nervous. More proof that the old Rowdy is still in there, somewhere.

"I need a ride to The Dark Horse to pick up my car."

Figures. "Let me guess. You let some cheap piece of ass drive you to her place then woke up all alone this morning with no car."

Rowdy's smile slides off his face. "If it's any of your business, I had a little too much to drink last night so a friend drove me home. I need someone to take me to my car so I can get to class."

"What happened to your vow to never use drugs or alcohol?" He'd made that promise to me the summer before my junior year of high school then asked me to do the same. He claimed that his stepdad had been a decent guy before he became a raging alcoholic. Rowdy didn't want either of us to take a single step down that path. And I hadn't. It pisses me off that he did.

Rowdy's face darkens under his tan. He's more than a little scary, reminding me again that I don't know him.

He closes his eyes and takes a deep breath then opens them as he exhales. The anger is gone. A deep sadness is all that remains.

I have no right to remind him of broken promises. I open the door and wave him inside. "Have a seat while I go get Boone's keys. I'll give you a ride."

"Just go wake Boone's lazy ass up."

"He can't drive a stick with a broken ankle."

"Shit." Rowdy steps back out onto the porch and jams his helmet on his head. "I'll just ride my bike."

"What time does your class start?" What am I doing? I'm not usually so pathetic. If the old Rowdy hadn't slipped past his crusty veneer, I might have been able to slam the door in his handsome face instead of begging him to let me give him a ride.

He grimaces as he snaps the buckle under his chin. "My class starts in about an hour, but it's at the Westminster Campus."

"You'll never make it in time." I notice his shirt's on wrong side out. "Who dressed you this morning?"

He blinks twice then drops his gaze to the center of his shirt. "Oh. That."

"Don't you want to fix it?" I wouldn't mind getting a peek at the muscles straining the exposed seams of his black t-shirt, but I don't want him to know that. I turn my head and tuck a stray curl behind my ear, pretending the thought of him peeling his shirt off isn't making me drool.

"I neglected to do my laundry last night. This is my last clean shirt."

"That doesn't explain why you're wearing it wrong side out."

He smiles and I get another glimpse of the old Rowdy. Damn.

"It's *clean* as in not previously worn. The graphic on the front is pretty raunchy."

I squint and lean a little closer, trying to make out the design, and unintentionally get a whiff of pure Rowdy. Clean and untainted by artificial fragrances. My emotions are all over the place. This isn't your normal roller-coaster mood swing. This is a tilt-a-whirl, bolted onto a roller coaster, strapped to a rocket mood swing. Memories slam into me, one after the other…kissing, touching—

"Skylar?"

My eyes snap open, six inches from his chest. Crap. I jerk my head back, horrified that he caught me sniffing him. "I…uh…can't see the design. What is it?"

The wide grin on his face tells me he knows exactly what I was doing. "Believe me, you don't want to know."

What I really want is to die. Right here, right now. Just let the ground open up and swallow me whole.

The corners of his almond-shaped eyes crinkle. He's all but laughing out loud. "If you're sure you don't mind giving me a ride, I'd really appreciate it."

"No problem." I turn and jog up the stairs, grateful for the excuse to flee. I knock on Boone's bedroom door.

"Go. Away." Boone is not a morning person.

"I need to borrow your car. Where're your keys?"

He groans for five long seconds before I hear him fumbling around with his crutches. He cracks his door and squints at me. "Why do you want to borrow my car?"

"Rowdy left his at The Dark Horse last night. He needs a ride."

That wakes him up. "Rowdy's here?"

"Yeah. He forgot your car is a stick and came to bum a ride. I told him I'd do it. Is that okay?"

Boone yawns then drops his keys into my open palm. "Be careful, Sky."

"I'm giving him a ride, not my heart." *Liar.*

~***~

Rowdy plugs his iPhone into Boone's cassette adapter. He skips three songs before letting one play all the way through. I don't recognize it or the next two. Apparently, Rowdy is now a devoted fan of heavy metal. One more change I'm not fond of. When I pull into The Dark Horse's parking lot, he turns the volume down then twists sideways and leans against the car door. He crosses his arms over his chest and arches an eyebrow.

I swallow and clear my throat. "I suppose you'd like to know why I disappeared."

"It has crossed my mind."

Rowdy's deep, quiet voice does funny things to my stomach. I want to tell him everything, but it's hard. So much harder than telling Boone. I guess I should start with an apology for disappearing without a word. "Boone said you went through a rough patch after I—"

"A rough patch?" Rowdy's voice slams into me.

My shoulders jerk involuntarily. "I'm paraphrasing. Don't be mad at Boone."

"What did he say?"

Man, he's scary. I keep my voice steady and calm. "All he said was that you were upset when I disappeared but that it wasn't the only trauma you suffered that night."

"And?" Rowdy's pupils dilate.

"He said it wasn't his story to tell."

"It's not." Rowdy explodes out of the car.

I brace myself, expecting him to slam the door.

But he doesn't. He just stands in the parking lot, shoulders heaving with each breath. He finally slows down and sucks in a lungful of air, holding it forever before he exhales. He puts one hand on the roof of the car and shoves the other in his pocket. He sticks his head inside and says, "Thanks for the ride," then gently shuts the door.

"Rowdy, wait." I try to follow him, but my door's stuck. I jerk on the handle so hard it rocks the car, but it still refuses to open. Damn rusted out, piece of crap Jeep.

He peels out of the parking lot without so much as a backward glance, dragging a huge chunk of my heart behind him.

Chapter Four
Rowdy

I slow down to five miles over the speed limit when I merge onto Foothills Parkway. The last thing I need is a speeding ticket. I should have just taken the bus. I would have missed my first class but that would've been better than accepting a ride from Skylar.

I need to blow off some steam before I explode. There're only two things that help when I get like this—booze and sex.

I should've let that tourist take me to her hotel room last night, but I just couldn't get in the mood. Alcohol didn't work its magic either.

I got smashed after Skylar left, but it didn't help. I was up all fucking night. A chill runs down my spine. What if Skylar's return has somehow messed up the anesthetizing effect of sex and alcohol?

I'm five minutes late for class, but it's not like they're going to start without me. I apologize to my students then take the focus off myself by announcing a pop quiz. I'd planned to give it to them next week, but Skylar hijacked my brain this morning. She's all I can think about. I need to get my shit together. If I demonstrated CPR on the infant dummy right now, I'd probably crush it.

I sleepwalk through the rest of my classes. I don't like driving when I'm tired so I head to the combination bookstore coffee shop for a boost of caffeine.

There's a girl at the table across from mine, sneaking peeks at me every time she takes a sip of her latte. She catches me staring at her and folds her arms under her boobs, putting her cleavage on prominent display.

I give her a crooked smile and raise my eyebrows. One quick flick up then back down, signaling my interest without being overly creepy.

She licks her lips.

Gotcha. I give a little nod towards the door then stand up and walk out. I don't need to look back to see if she's following me. I can feel her gaze on my ass.

I lean against the wall and give her body a quick sweep from the top of her purple-streaked head to the hot pink tips of her toes. "What's your major?"

She smiles and gives me the once over as well. "General education. What's yours?"

"I'm an instructor. So if you have any interest in Emergency Medical Services, you're off limits."

"I suck at math and science, so no chance of any medical careers in my future. And I won't be a student here until fall semester."

That takes care of the last shred of decency telling me to leave this girl alone. I'm only subbing for the regular instructor while she's on maternity leave. No conflict of interest here.

"I know this is a dick thing to say, but I have a meeting I need to be at in a couple hours so if you want to hook up, we need to do it now." She needs to know up front that I'm not a nice guy.

Her smile flatlines for a moment but then she grabs my hand and says, "Oh, what the hell. You're hot and I'm horny. Might as well just admit it and get to it."

Wow. I was not expecting that.

She drags me off campus to her apartment. The cardboard boxes stacked haphazardly all over the place adds credibility to her claim that she isn't a student yet. I wrap my fingers around her waist and pull her hips against mine, surreptitiously looking for stains on her sheets. I don't see any so I turn my gaze to her face.

Her eyelids flutter as she tilts her head up, signaling her desire to kiss me. I ignore it and grab her thighs.

She wraps her legs around my waist.

I carry her to the bed then fall with her onto the mattress.

She rolls me onto my back then straddles me. Her hands dive under my shirt. I lift my shoulders so she can peel it off over my head.

"Ohmigod." Her sudden burst of laughter surprises me. "Where'd you get this?"

She drapes my shirt across her chest, proudly displaying Ralfie and Cam in their obscene act of interspecies copulation.

I roll my eyes. "My perverted housemate gave it to me. If you want one, I can give you his number."

She tosses the shirt onto the floor. "I'd rather have your number."

"I don't do the relationship thing, okay? So if that's what you're looking for, we better stop right now."

"You really are a dick." She skims her hand over the front of my jeans. "If you weren't so hot, I'd kick you out on your ass."

"So, you're okay with this?"

"That depends."

"On what?" I'm suddenly, and inexplicably, not sure that *I'm* okay with this.

She crosses her hands and grabs the hem of her shirt then lifts it off over her head. "On how fast and how hard you get me off."

"Do you do this a lot?"

Her fingers freeze on the front clasp of her bra. "Are you asking if I'm a slut?"

I guess I sort of am. I swipe a hand over my face. "How about we go out for a cup of coffee?"

She widens her eyes. "Seriously?"

"Yeah." I frown, not sure what the hell's going on with me but I'm sick of fucking nameless girls to chase Skylar out of my head. It doesn't work anyway. I'm just tired of it all. I'm not ready for a relationship, but I need a change. As long as we keep it casual, no strings attached, sex might be a little more satisfying if I take a girl out a couple of times before I fuck her. "Why not? I haven't been on a date in years."

"Well, if you want a date, you need to call and ask for one." The girl—I still don't know her name—grabs a sharpie off the nightstand, pops the cap off with her teeth, then writes her info on my palm.

Cherri Payne 303-555-1234.

She snaps the cap back on and grins at me. "That's Cherri like the fruit, not the wine."

"Okay." I grab my shirt and turn it wrong side out again then slip it on.

Cherri licks her lips as she watches me. I can't believe I'm walking away from this. I pause at her bedroom door and say something I haven't said to a girl in four years. "I'll call you tomorrow."

Chapter Five

Skylar

I swing by Target, Michaels, and Superior Pet Shop to grab some employment applications on my way back from dropping Rowdy off. Uncle Will's life insurance paid off the mortgage and Boone gets the same tuition break I do at CU, but the property taxes alone are more than most people pay for rent. I intend to pull my weight whether Boone wants me to or not.

The only one that's hiring right now is Superior Pet Shop so I go ahead and fill out the application while I'm there then grab some groceries at Whole Foods.

There's a brand new, black Mercedes-Benz SUV parked in front of Boone's house. It still has the dealer tag taped to the window.

When I go into the kitchen to put away the groceries, I hear voices coming from the backyard. I peek out the window over the sink and find Boone and Wade, sitting in reclining lawn chairs. They're both sipping on bottles of Coors.

The sliding screen door complains with a gritty screech as I open it. Both boys look over their shoulders.

"Hey, Sky, you're back." Boone grins at me. "You remember Wade, right?"

"Of course." I smile and nod as I step onto the flagstone patio. "Wade Summers, Wilderness EMT, knight in shining armor."

Wade jumps to his feet and offers me his chair. I wave him off and grab one of the metal chairs pushed under the glass patio table. "Thanks, this is fine."

"Grab a beer and join us." Boone nods at 'The Hole,' an eddy near the shore of South Boulder Creek. It's a natural cooler, protected on three sides by large rocks.

Aunt Lori always kept The Hole well stocked with soda and bottled water. There was an occasional bottle of beer in the mix, but that was for Uncle Will. We all knew better than to steal it.

My chest aches as I think about all we've lost. "It's barely eleven o'clock. Don't you think it's a little early to be drinking?"

"In this heat?" Boone gives me an 'are you crazy' glance then shakes his head. "It's only beer."

Wade is still standing. He sets his half empty bottle on the glass surface of the patio table. "Would you like a Coke?"

"Sit down. I'll get it." The creek is only a few steps away from the edge of the patio. It's running low, especially for this time of year, so I can still hear Boone's voice over the murmuring water. Something he obviously doesn't realize.

"Just ask her out for coffee or ice cream. As long as you don't make a big deal out of it, she's not going to shoot you down."

"I don't want to piss Rowdy off. He's not the easiest person to live with as it is."

Boone's laugh is derisive. "Rowdy lost whatever claim he might have had to Skylar when he decided to fuck his way across the county."

I plunge my hand into The Hole and grab a Coke. The freezing water makes my bones ache, but it's nothing compared to the ache in the middle of my chest.

I wipe the top of the can off with the hem of my t-shirt as I head back to the patio. The water in South Boulder Creek is crystal clear, but it's frequently infested with bacteria and parasites. I'm not taking any chances.

Wade's gaze travels to my slightly exposed midriff, but he blinks and looks away immediately. Good boy.

I smooth my shirt down over my stomach and pretend I didn't catch him checking me out. I need to have a chat with Boone about his misguided efforts to hook me up with his friends. And protect me from Rowdy.

I sit down then pop the top on my Coke.

Wade clears his throat. "The Boulder Mountain Rescue meeting tonight is open to the public. Would you like to go?"

I was expecting an invitation to go out for coffee or ice cream, which I would have politely declined. But there's a good chance Rowdy will be at the BMR meeting. "That might be interesting."

Boone groans and rolls his eyes.

"What?" Wade shifts his gaze to Boone, obviously confused by his reaction.

"Dude, that was dumb."

I jump in and change the subject. "Would it be appropriate for me to bring homemade chocolate cookies?"

A wide grin spreads across Wade's handsome face. "Are you kidding? When are cookies not appropriate?"

"It's the least we can do after the BMR rescued us. Right, Boone?" I emphasize *we* hoping Boone will agree to go with us.

He shakes his head. "I need to keep my foot propped up. I overdid it a little last night, but you two kids go have fun. Just be sure you're home before curfew."

"Very funny." I glare at Boone, the traitor. He's joking but he's also trying to turn this meeting into a date.

Wade hangs out with us until noon, never taking so much as another sip of beer. My stomach growls. "I'm going to make kale salad with lemon-strawberry dressing for lunch. Would you like to join us?"

"Thanks, but I need to head back to campus. I have a class at one. Maybe next time." His eyes twinkle as he smiles at me. "I'll pick you up at five thirty."

As soon as Wade leaves, I smack the back of Boone's head. "Why are you trying to set me up with him?"

I expect him to laugh, but he just sighs. "You could do a lot worse than Wade Summers. He's a great guy, pre-med student at CU and his folks are absolutely loaded."

I groan. "I'm not interested in dating."

"You're not fooling anyone but yourself."

I press the cold can of Coke against my temple and close my eyes. Boone's wrong. I'm not fooling myself either. I know exactly why I accepted Wade's invitation. I'm desperate to see Rowdy again. Even if he is an ass.

~***~

Wade picks me up at exactly five thirty. He's wearing a white button-down shirt with the top three buttons undone and the cuffs rolled up to his elbows. His black jeans fit him perfectly, showing off his narrow hips and muscular thighs. I imagine wrapping my legs around his waist and pressing my mouth to his, hoping to kindle a spark of attraction. Nothing.

If I hadn't already tried the 'fake it till you feel it' technique with Ethan, I'd be tempted to try it with Wade. But I learned my lesson. Just because a guy is hot, doesn't mean he can't be hurt. I can still see the tears streaming down Ethan's sweet face when I told him it was over. I can still hear him begging me for more time.

I hand the foil-covered platter of cookies I baked to Wade.

His whole face lights up. "For me?"

"For everyone." I need to make it clear there's no chance of anything romantic developing between us.

He opens the passenger side door of his Mercedes SUV then holds my elbow as I climb inside, balancing the cookies in his other hand.

I try to make a joke out of it. "Contrary to what you witnessed on The Bastille yesterday afternoon, I can climb into a car without assistance."

"I'm sure you can."

I look over my shoulder at him. He's still smiling but it's strained. I wait for him to slide behind the wheel then try to explain. "I appreciate the gesture, but I don't want to lead you on. I'm not interested in a relationship right now."

"Neither am I." The tightness around his mouth indicates otherwise. "Let's just spend some time together and see where it goes."

"Wade—"

"Boone's my best friend and you're living in his house so we're going to bump into each other a lot. It'll be easier if we're friends too. Besides, you can never have too many friends, right?"

"Just so you know, I don't do the 'friends with benefits' thing."

"I'm pretty sure Boone would kick my butt if I even suggested it." Wade's cheeks flush bright red. He braces his hand on the back of my seat then backs out of the driveway.

I'm surprised when he pulls into The Dark Horse parking lot. "The meeting's here?"

Wade's cheeks turn pink. "The meeting doesn't start until seven thirty. I thought we'd grab a bite to eat first."

I get a sinking feeling in the pit of my stomach.

Wade seems to sense my displeasure. "If this were a date, I'd take you someplace a little more romantic and a lot less rowdy."

Rowdy. I can't help but wonder if that was a Freudian slip.

~***~

My blue cheese veggie burger is delicious, but I'm so nervous about seeing Rowdy at the meeting that I can't eat more than a couple bites.

Wade leans forward and whispers as if he's afraid someone might hear him. "If you don't like it, I can order something else for you. We have plenty of time."

"That's okay. I'm not very hungry. I ate too much cookie dough this afternoon."

Wade's eyebrows pull together. "You ate raw cookie dough?"

"The eggs were fresh. I just bought them this morning."

"That doesn't mean they weren't contaminated. Do you have a fever?" He leans across the table and presses the back of his hand against my forehead. "It's a little early for salmonella symptoms to manifest. How's your stomach feel? Any nausea or diarrhea?"

"Wade!" I scoot back until my spine is pressed against the hard wooden booth.

"Sorry." His cheeks flush as he leans back. "Pre-med mindset."

I don't have food poisoning, but I do have asthma. And it picks the most inconvenient times to flare up.

"Skylar?" Wade's forehead creases with worry. "Are you okay?"

"I'll be right back." I grab my purse and head to the bathroom. I hate using my inhaler in public. I know it's not a sign of weakness, but it sure feels that way. I've got my head down, digging through my purse, so I push through the door of the ladies' room with my shoulder…and run into a couple of frat boys. "Oh!"

They both laugh. One of them says, "And another one bites the dust."

"What are you doing in the women's restroom?"

"The signs on the doors are reversed. This is the men's room."

I clutch my purse to my chest and back out. The sign on the door clearly reads *Ladies* but it's painted on a giant hand pointing at the men's room. Which also has a giant hand pointing back at the other door. I'm not amused. But I am starting to wheeze.

I dig my inhaler out and take a puff, wait a few seconds then take another. Relief is almost instantaneous.

"Next time, don't run off looking for privacy. Take your medicine when you need it."

I whirl around and find Wade standing next to me. "Why didn't you warn me about the bathrooms?"

"You didn't tell me where you were going. All you said was, *I'll be back,* then darted away like a bat out of hell. I tried to catch you but a crowd of people got up from the bar and blocked my way."

"Oh." It's not the most intelligent response but I really can't think of anything else to say. It's a good thing I'm not trying to impress the guy.

~***~

When we get to the Boulder Mountain Rescue meeting, I scan the parking lot for Rowdy's truck. I'm simultaneously relieved and disappointed when I don't see it.

So, when I walk inside and find Rowdy standing in front of a whiteboard and talking to Anna, it comes as a total shock. "How'd he get here without his truck?"

"Rowdy and Anna carpool all the time." Wade jumps to the correct conclusion immediately. He knows exactly who I'm talking about.

I was so focused on Rowdy and Anna that I forgot about Wade. I try to act nonchalant as if I'm just curious about an old friend instead of dying inside. "Are they dating?"

He sets the platter of cookies on a plastic folding table then turns so he's facing me head on. "Rowdy doesn't date."

"That's what Boone said."

"You still have a thing for him." He states it as a fact, not a question.

My first reaction is to deny it, but that's a blatant lie so I go with a half-truth instead. "Rowdy's changed so much, I feel as if I don't even know him at all."

Wade removes the foil from the cookies then wads it into a ball and tosses it into the trash. "I didn't know him before his mom died so I can't say whether or not he's changed."

"Rowdy's mom died?"

All conversation stops. The room is suddenly silent. Heat floods my cheeks. My gaze flies to Rowdy. He's staring at me. No. He's *glaring* at me. My blood turns to ice water.

I've only seen Rowdy's stepfather a few times but every time was terrifying. He was always so angry. He'd look at Rowdy as if he were solely responsible for every bad thing that had ever happened to him. I see that same look in Rowdy's eyes now. And as scary as he looks, I'm more afraid *for* him, than of him. I know how it feels to lose your mother. Rowdy's not just angry. He's in pain.

We were friends before we were a couple. No one knows Rowdy the way I do. And even if we can't be together again, I can still help him. I *will* help him. Just not tonight.

Chapter Six

Rowdy

I continue to stare at the door even after Wade and Skylar leave together. The words, *I'm going to kill him,* are on an endless loop in my brain. I know I have no claim to Skylar but seeing his hand on her arm makes me want to rip it off and shove it up his ass.

Anna snakes a hand up my back to my shoulder. "Are you okay?"

I shrug it off without answering. I don't mean to be rude. She's only looking out for me. Other than Boone and the shrink Lori dragged me to for a year, Anna's the only person I've ever been able to open up to.

She wasn't there the night her dad killed my mom, but she never blamed me. She knows about the guilt I still carry. She also knows how devastated I was when Skylar disappeared. I wouldn't have survived without Anna's help.

The meeting goes by in a blur. I have to give my report of the incident on The Bastille Crack. I refer to Boone and Skylar as the male and female climbers to protect their privacy, as well as my sanity, then ask Anna to take over the 'what can we learn from this incident' part of the discussion.

I can't be clinically detached from any part of the incident. What I learned from Skylar a long time ago is promises are made to be broken. You can't trust anyone. And the more you love someone, the more it hurts when they desert you.

I can't wait to get out of here, but I refuse to run away. Unlike that chicken shit, Wade. He had no right to tell Skylar about Mom.

We're supposed to hang around and talk to prospective members and benefactors, but I'm afraid I'll end up punching someone if they look at me the wrong way. I make my way over to the refreshment table and grab the last chocolate cookie.

A medley of flavors blooms on my tongue—bittersweet chocolate, butter, raisins, dates, walnuts and a pinch of cayenne pepper.

These aren't pre-packaged cookies from Costco. Nope. These are Skylar's homemade chocolate cookies. She used the recipe we invented, together. I should have recognized them by smell if not by sight. I blame my foggy state of mind for not warning me before I bit into it.

I used to crave these cookies, but it turns to ash in my mouth and lights a fire in my stomach.

I'd like to blame the sudden heartburn on the cayenne, but I know better. I hate the fact that Skylar baked *our* cookies for Wade.

I spit the cookie into a paper napkin and toss it in the trash. As I brush the crumbs from my hands, I notice Cherri's number on my palm. I said I'd call her tomorrow, but I can't wait that long. I also said I'd take her out on a date, but if I don't relieve this insane pressure, I'm going to explode. I'd get drunk but I don't think booze alone is going to do it.

When we get back to the house, I immediately head for my room. I don't like the way Anna's staring at me and I'm in no mood to listen to one of her lectures. Cherri answers on the third ring. Classic.

"Hello?"

"Hey, Cherri, it's Rowdy Daletzki. Are you busy?"

"Um...no. Not really."

"Do you wanna be?"

She giggles. *"What do you have in mind?"*

I tell her in sordid detail as I grab my keys off the hook by the door and head for Old Blue.

~***~

"It's okay. Don't worry about it." Cherri's voice is tight. I can tell she's trying not to cry. I wish she'd just let me get her off.

I sit on the edge of her bed with my head in my hands. "I honestly don't understand. I swear this has never happened to me before."

"You're a little young for ED. Maybe you should see a doctor."

Maybe I should. A fucking heart doctor. "This was supposed to be a date. Do you want to go get coffee or something?"

"Sure." She doesn't sound too excited about it but I don't blame her.

"I'll let you pick where we go, how's that?"

"Can we go to The Laughing Goat?" She grabs her bra off the floor then slides under the covers to put it on…as if I haven't already seen her boobs.

"I didn't know there was one in Westminster."

"There's not. But it was my favorite place to hang out before I dropped out at CU."

She obviously wants me to ask why she dropped out, but that might lead her to believe I actually give a shit. "We can go to The Laughing Goat if you follow me there. I don't want to make another trip back to Westminster."

Cherri smiles agreeably. "Sure, no problem."

During the solitary drive to Boulder, it dawns on me that Cherri will probably try to use the long drive back home as an excuse to spend the night with me. Not gonna happen. I never take girls to the house.

I swear the universe hates me. There have to be at least a hundred coffee shops in Boulder. What are the chances that Wade and Skylar would be tucked away in an intimate little corner of The Laughing Goat? "Shit."

"What's wrong?" Cherri follows my gaze before I can pry it off Skylar's face.

"Oh. Well. That explains a lot."

"What are you talking about?"

She tilts her head and arches her eyebrows, giving me an 'I'm not stupid look.' "You're still hung up on your ex. When did you break up?"

"Four years ago."

She blinks then leans in closer, lowering her voice. "You've gone four years without having sex?"

"No. Of course not." I don't want to discuss this with her. Or anyone. Ever. "She just got back into town yesterday."

"Did she bring the hottie with her or pick him up when she got here?"

Seriously? "He's one of my housemates."

Cherri's eyes flash. "That's just wrong."

"Let's get out of here." Preferably before Wade and Skylar see us.

"You can't run away from this kind of shit. Trust me." She stretches up on her toes and tries to pull my face down to hers. "Follow my lead."

I turn my head so her lips slide across my cheek. She doesn't let the near-miss dissuade her and presses every square inch of her body against mine. I'm knocked off balance in more ways than one and grab her hips to keep from falling over.

She moans. Right there in the middle of The Laughing Goat. "Oh baby. I just can't keep my hands off you."

My gaze is drawn to Skylar like a suicidal moth to a flame. Her open mouth forms a perfect circle.

I've never really experienced a 'deer in the headlights' moment—until now. I'm completely frozen. Cherri's practically dry humping me but all I can do is stand there with my fingers clutching her curvy ass.

Wade gives me a disgusted look then stands up and pulls Skylar to her feet. He wraps an arm around her shoulder.

Skylar leans into him, turning her face away from me. They have to walk past us to get out the door. Wade hunches over her, sheltering her with his body.

Her chest heaves as she takes several quick, wheezing breaths, snapping me out of my paralytic trance. That sounds like asthma.

I pry Cherri off my body and run out the door. "Skylar, wait."

Wade stops and steps in front of her. His stance is protective, as if he thinks I'd actually hurt her. "Leave her alone."

My hands clench into fists. It takes every bit of self-control I possess to not hit him. I shove him to the side.

Skylar sinks to the curb. She moves into the classic, tripod position with her hands on her knees, gasping for breath.

Wade grabs her purse and starts digging through it. "Where is it?"

Skylar didn't have asthma four years ago but she sure as hell has it now. I grab her purse out of Wade's hands, turn it upside down and shake. Her phone is the first thing to hit the ground, followed by the usual assortment of tampons, makeup, Tic Tacs and crumpled Kleenex. Her inhaler bounces onto the sidewalk with a *plink*. I grab it and shake it then hand it to her as I support her head and shoulders with my other arm. "Can you do it or do you need help?"

"Help." Her voice is barely a whisper.

"I'm going to give you a puff. Ready?"

She nods and inhales as I administer the first dose. I hear Wade talking to the emergency dispatcher on his phone, but it's just background noise to me. All I can hear is Skylar's labored breathing and my own blood rushing behind my ears.

She coughs, expelling most of the first dose, so I repeat the procedure. She sits up a little straighter and takes charge of her inhaler, pushing me away.

I don't want to add to her distress so I let her, even though it squeezes my own chest to do so.

Cherri kneels in front of Skylar and hands her a steaming paper cup with The Laughing Goat logo on the side. "It's hot tea."

She takes a sip then gives Cherri a weak, but sincere smile.

Cherri sits down on the curb next to Skylar and rubs her back as if they're best friends. I'll never understand women.

~***~

When the ambulance arrives, Skylar refuses treatment. I want to shake some sense into her, but I doubt she's gotten any less stubborn over the past four years. My best guess is she's worried about the cost.

"Your insurance should cover it."

"Don't have any."

"How can you have asthma and not have insurance?"

She takes a deep breath, demonstrating her improved pulmonary function. "I'm fine."

"No, you aren't. Do you have an asthma plan?"

She gathers the scattered contents of her purse and nods.

"And what does it tell you to do after an acute attack?"

She zips her purse with such force, I'm surprised she doesn't break it. "I can't afford a trip to the ER."

"God, Skylar. I'll pay for it, okay? You need a doctor."

She shifts her gaze to Wade. "Take me home?"

He shakes his head. "Rowdy's right. You at least need to be checked out at the ER. If you won't go by ambulance, let me drive you to the hospital."

Skylar glares at both of us then grabs her iPhone off the ground and pushes the home button. "Siri, I need a cab."

I snatch her phone and end the call. "I'll take you home."

She glares at me. "You're on a date."

I want to scream *it's not a date* but I'd already told Cherri it was. Even I'm not that big of an asshole.

Cherri flashes me a sad smile then gives Skylar a one-armed hug. "Medical emergencies trump dates, every time."

Wade shocks the hell out of me and says, "If you want to take care of Skylar, I can give Cherri a ride home."

She looks up and smiles at Wade then tucks a strand of purple hair behind her ear. "Thanks, but I drove my own car."

Skylar grabs Cherri's hand. "I'm so sorry I messed up your date."

God, here we go with the 'date thing again.

Cherri says, "It wasn't really a date. We're just out for coffee."

Thank you!

"I sort of threw myself at him and he was just too nice to flat out reject me." Cherri winks at me then stands up and tucks her hand into the crook of Wade's elbow. "Do you mind walking me to my car?"

Wade grins at Cherri then turns to Skylar. "Is that okay?"

"I don't mind, if Rowdy doesn't."

"It's fine." That came out a little louder and a whole lot harsher than necessary.

Skylar's eyes widen for a second then narrow into slits. "I'm sorry I ruined your evening."

"Stop apologizing. You didn't ruin my evening." *You ruined my fucking life.* I take a deep breath then lean over and extend a hand. "Can you walk to my truck, or should I carry you?"

She ignores my hand and stands up on her own. "I told you I'm fine."

When we get to Old Blue, the damn thing refuses to start. It's out of gas. I never run out of gas. What the fuck is wrong with me. I swallow my pride and call Wade to tell him that Skylar and I need a ride.

I follow Skylar to Wade's ridiculously expensive Mercedes SUV. Her shoulders are halfway to her ears. She keeps her hands fisted and close to her hips as she walks. What the hell is she so pissed off about?

My stomach drops when I realize she's probably mad because I ruined *her* date. I sent Wade off with a woman whose every move screams *do me*. No wonder she's pissed. But I'll be damned if I'm going to apologize for it.

When we get to Wade's car, Skylar reaches for the front passenger door. I put my hand on top of hers. "Get in the back."

"Quit bossing me around."

"I want to be able to help you if you have another attack in the car. There's more room in the back."

"That's ridiculous."

We're still arguing when Wade jogs up. He's got a shit-eating grin on his face but it disappears immediately. "What's going on?"

"Skylar's being stubborn and stupid."

Her mouth falls open.

Wade's no help at all. His gaze shifts back and forth between me and Sky.

I open the rear passenger door and glare at her. "Get in the car."

She glares right back, but slides in and scoots across the bench seat, all the way to the other side, behind Wade.

I climb in next to her and slam the door. She and Wade both flinch. I lean forward and stick my head between the bucket seats. "Take us to Avista."

Skylar unbuckles her seatbelt and paws at the door, looking for the handle.

"Stop." I grab her hand. Her fingers immediately weave through mine. The gesture is so natural and familiar. So is the pain that stabs the center of my chest. I jerk my hand back as if she burned it but I can still feel the imprint of her on my skin. I don't remember her hands being so small. "I'm serious about paying for the ER."

"No." She folds her arms over her stomach and hunches forward.

"You can pay me back later if it'll make you feel better."

"I can refuse treatment at the hospital just as easily as I can for an ambulance. You can't make me go."

She's being childish and unreasonable but the rapid movement of her upper thorax could be signaling another asthma attack.

I raise my hands in surrender. "Fine. You win. We'll take you to Boone's, okay?"

She arches her eyebrows. "Promise?"

God, I hate that word. And I really hate how easily it rolls off her tongue. "I don't make promises. But I don't lie, either."

"Everything okay back there?" Wade's watching us in the rearview mirror.

Skylar uncrosses her arms and leans her head against the back of her seat. "Let's go."

I scoot back over to my side of the car and buckle up. The tension builds during the ride to Eldorado Springs.

"So, Rowdy, where'd you meet Cherri?" Wade's voice is overly cheerful. "She seems a lot nicer than your usual mark."

If he weren't driving and if I weren't afraid of upsetting Skylar, I'd smack the back of his head. "She's just a student at Front Range."

"A student?" His wide eyes are full of censure in the rearview mirror.

"Not one of mine, asshole."

"You're a teacher?" Skylar's voice is about half an octave higher than normal. "Wow. I'm impressed."

"Don't be. It's just part-time and it's only for the summer semester. It's not like I'm a professor or anything. All you need to teach at Front Range is an associate degree." I've never been ashamed of my two-year degree...until now. All my housemates, except Wade, who'll go to med school when he graduates, are working on advanced degrees. Derek's in his final year of law school and Anna is working on her MBA.

"Don't disrespect Front Range." Skylar's tone of voice is pleasant, but there's an edge to it. "If I didn't have a scholarship to CU, that's where I'd go."

"You have a scholarship?" Wade segues into the change of topic easily. If I weren't so pissed at him for being with Skylar, I'd be grateful. The fact that Skylar seems proud of my two year degree gives me a strange sense of satisfaction. And that worries me.

Wade pulls into Boone's driveway just as Sky finishes her story about her great-grandfather donating his entire fortune to CU in exchange for a tuition waiver for all of his direct descendants. I've heard it before. Boone gets the same deal. Lucky bastard.

Wade cuts the engine. "Forever?"

"Yep."

"So if you and I got married, all our kids and grandkids could go to CU for free?"

"One date and you're already talking about marriage?" This time I give in to my urge to smack the back of his head. "Idiot."

Skylar laughs. "We weren't on a date."

"Can I at least walk you to the door?"

"That's not necessary." No way in hell am I letting him steal a kiss from her. "I'm spending the night. No point in both of us walking her to the door."

"What?" Sky and Wade speak at the same time.

The sane part of my brain agrees with their obvious shock and disapproval. But the stupid part argues that there's a valid reason for me to stay. "If you won't go to the hospital, at least you'll have a paramedic in the house."

Wade says, "I want to check on Boone," and follows us into the house.

I'm appalled by the amount of dust in the air. Boone's really let the place go since Will and Lori died.

He's sitting in Will's old recliner watching a movie. He fumbles with the remote then mutes the sound. "What's going on?"

I point at Skylar. "Your stubborn cousin had two asthma attacks tonight and refuses to go to the ER."

Boone frowns at her. "When did you get asthma?"

Her shoulders slump as she sighs. "After we moved to New Orleans."

"Why didn't you tell me?"

"You didn't ask?" She laughs then frowns when no one else thinks it's funny. "I didn't want you to get all weird about it. I have it under control—most of the time. And you never would have taken me climbing if you'd known."

"Damn straight." Boone's expression shifts from concern to anger. "I can't believe you did that to me. What if you'd had an attack on the wall?"

"I felt fine this morning."

"What changed?"

Skylar bites her lip then mumbles. "I'm out of Advair."

Advair is a daily medication. You're supposed to use it every day, whether you have symptoms or not. I struggle to keep the frustration out of my voice. "When was your last dose?"

"Can we discuss my medical irresponsibility later? I'm really tired."

"You didn't answer my question."

Wade says, "Give me your prescription. I'll go get it refilled for you."

I'd forgotten that he was here.

"I can't get it refilled yet."

"Why not?" Wade's never had to worry about money.

I lean in close and whisper, "I'll loan you the money, okay?"

She shakes her head.

"You could die, Skylar."

"I'm fine."

"Repeating that over and over won't make it true. Now either hand over your prescription or let me drive you to the ER."

"Fine." She pulls the scrip out of her purse and shoves it at me. "But I'm paying you back."

"I understand."

Wade grabs it out of my hand. "You stay here and keep an eye on her. I'll take care of this."

"Wade, no." Skylar tries to reclaim her prescription, but Wade keeps it out of reach.

"My money's just as good as his."

"I'm still paying you back."

"No need." Wade shrugs his shoulders. "You can buy me lunch or something if it makes you happy."

I know he's not trying to brag about his wealth. Wade's not like that. He just takes it for granted. But it still pisses me off.

Skylar's expression softens when she turns to me. "I hate to ask, but could you help me put my allergy-proof mattress pad on my bed? If I stir up the dust mites, it could trigger another attack."

"Sit down." I point at the couch. "I'll go take care of it."

Instead of following my advice to sit down and rest, Skylar follows me into her bedroom.

I avert my gaze from her open suitcase. But not before I catch a glimpse of her underwear. When we were teens, she always wore boy-shorts and sports bras. Not thongs and see-through bits of lace. I can't help but wonder what—or who—prompted the wardrobe change. I know it's none of my business and I have no right to feel jealous, but I can't help it. Damn. I need to stay focused on the task.

Skylar's body brushes against mine as she dashes past me.

My dick springs to life. Great. I adjust myself while she's not looking. Why couldn't it respond earlier at Cherri's when it would've done some good?

The back of Sky's neck turns red as she digs through her suitcase, rearranging things to hide the more interesting articles of clothing. She hands me the zippered mattress pad then closes her suitcase and shoves it in the closet. "I'm going to go take a shower. If that's okay?"

"Just not too hot. Steam can help, but it can also trigger another attack. And leave the bathroom door unlocked."

Her lips part as her eyes widen.

"I'm a paramedic, not a pervert." That would have been more convincing if she hadn't already caught me staring at her underwear. "I won't come in unless it's an emergency."

"Okay." She clutches a small bundle of clothes to her chest as she backs out of the room.

I try not to picture her in the shower, soaped up and slippery, water cascading down her back as I change the mattress pad and remake her bed with what I hope are clean sheets. I finish before she does and sit on her bed to wait.

The sound of gravel crunching under tires announces Wade's return. I get up and intercept him on the front porch. I reach for the sack in his hands. "Thanks. I've got it from here. See you tomorrow."

Wade lowers his voice. "Look, man. I didn't mean to intrude on your territory, but Boone said you and Skylar were over."

"We are." The Walgreens bag rustles in my clenched fist. What's wrong with me? I don't want Skylar. So why does the thought of her being with Wade twist my gut into knots? It must be some weird nostalgic reaction.

Wade's a nerd, but he's a good guy with a bright future and no baggage. He'd be perfect for Skylar. I need to back off.

"So..." Wade rubs the back of his neck. "What about Cherri?"

"What about her?"

"You care if I ask her out?"

"Hell no. Go for it." I slap him on the back. "You want her number?"

A sheepish grin spreads across Wade's face. "She already gave it to me."

Chapter Seven

Skylar

I slip into a t-shirt and a pair of yoga pants instead of my regular pajamas, which don't cover nearly enough skin. I'm tempted to put on a little mascara and lip gloss, but Rowdy's in full paramedic mode. He's not interested in anything other than my health.

My heart skips a beat when I find him sitting on my bed. He's rubbing his eyes so he doesn't see me. I take the opportunity to study him. He was always attractive, even during those awkward pre-teen years, but he's absolutely gorgeous now.

He looks up and smiles at me with the same boyish charm he's always possessed. It lights up the entire room. "Feeling better?"

I nod. "Much."

He stands up and hands me a white paper bag. "Here's your prescription."

"Where's the receipt?" I can tell by the two tiny tears near the top that it was stapled to the bag.

He shrugs.

"Did you take it or did Wade?"

"Does it matter?"

I fold my arms across my chest. "It's bad enough that I can't pay for my own meds. I need to know how much money I owe Wade."

"Believe me, he'll never miss it."

"I'm not taking a single dose until I have the receipt."

Rowdy sighs then pulls it out of his pocket.

I cringe when I see the amount. I knew it would be expensive without insurance but I had no idea it would be over a hundred dollars.

"Breathe, Skylar." Rowdy puts his hands on my shoulders and guides me to the bed.

"How am I going to afford this every month?"

"Don't worry about that right now." He kneels in front of me and gazes into my eyes. "There're lots of resources in Boulder County. I'll help you figure it out. Okay?"

"Okay." I hope he's right. I took a year off after high school to take care of Mom. I'd hate to postpone college for another year, but I will if I have to. If I work full time and save everything I make, after paying for food and rent, maybe I'll be able to start next spring.

Rowdy taps the bag with his forefinger. "Now take your meds."

"Yes, sir." I roll my eyes then follow his orders. I always hated inhaling the dry powder even before I knew how expensive it was. I suck it in and hold my breath as long as possible, then cough as I exhale. "I have to go rinse out my mouth."

When I return, Rowdy's sitting on my bed again. I wonder if he has any idea the sort of fantasies that inspires.

He stands up then pulls down the covers.

I can't help the nervous giggle that escapes. "Are you tucking me in?"

His cheeks flush. It's absolutely adorable.

"Get in bed, Skylar." He's back in full paramedic mode.

I try to cover my frustration with sarcasm. "Are you going to read me a story, too?"

"Do you want me to?" He flashes his panty-dropping, crooked grin.

"Don't do that."

The smile falls off his face. "Don't do what?"

"Use that fake, sexy smile on me."

His lips part in the familiar, natural smile that's always warmed my heart. Unfortunately, it's warming other parts of me, too.

"You think my smile's sexy."

Damn. "Not the one you've perfected by looking in the mirror. That might work on your bimbos, but it won't work on me."

His face slides into neutral.

This must be his professional face. The one he uses with regular patients. I don't like it. I prefer his angry face. The one he uses on 'stubborn and stupid' patients, like me.

"I didn't realize my smile was offensive. I'll work on it."

I sigh before I can stop myself. "It's not offensive. It's just not...you."

"Don't pretend you know who I am." His voice is quiet but it's hard and sharp. It cuts me to the bone.

I roll onto my side, towards the wall. I don't want him to see how easily, or deeply, he affects me.

"I'm sorry. I didn't mean to upset you." The mattress dips as he sits on the edge of my bed. He gives my shoulder a gentle squeeze then jerks his hand away as if touching me was painful. "I'll be in Boone's room if you need me."

"I won't."

Chapter Eight
Rowdy

Skylar knows damn well that I was referring to her physical health when I said I was here if she needed me. Her 'I won't' response is so full of spite it fills the room with hostility. The bed springs creak when I stand up.

"Rowdy, wait."

I freeze in her doorway, one hand braced against the frame. I should run and never look back. I've been with her for less than an hour and already she's eating through my ironclad defenses like acid. Skylar devastated me last time. I won't survive if she does it again. I need to leave but my feet are nailed to the floor.

"Do you remember the first time we kissed?"

What the fuck? Skylar's question blasts a hole through my chest, shattering the last of my defenses.

"Yeah." *As if it were yesterday.* I was fourteen, skinny, awkward and terrified. She was thirteen and sporting braces, a lopsided ponytail and a sunburned nose. I remember the feeling of vertigo as I tried to decide whether or not to risk six years of friendship for something more. We'd climbed The Naked Edge earlier that day and it wasn't nearly as scary as teetering on that precipice of indecision. "What about it?"

"I think about it a lot." Her voice is so quiet it's barely above a whisper, but her words are like a battering ram.

Why is she bringing up all this old shit? What kind of game is this? I need to get out of here but if I leave without answering her, I might as well hand her my balls. I turn around and face her like a man. "I remember bumping noses, knocking teeth and cutting my mouth on your braces."

Her shoulders slump. She drops her gaze to her hands.

Great. Only a dick would leave after a hateful remark like that.

"Was it the first time you'd ever kissed anyone?"

I try to make up for my chicken shit answer with pure truth. "I had all my firsts with you, Sky."

She looks up. Her eyes sparkle with unshed tears but she doesn't look quite as miserable now.

I tap the tips of my fingers on her wall. Once, twice, then fist my hand to make it stop. "I should leave and let you get some rest."

"Please don't go." Her voice trembles and it damn near breaks what's left of my heart.

"What's wrong, babe?" Shit. I didn't mean to call her babe.

"I miss my mom."

She's been here for less than a day and she's homesick already? She used to stay here for the whole summer. The only time she cried was when she had to leave me to go back home. "Why don't you give her a call?"

"I can't." A broken sob rushes out of her chest. "She died."

I cross the room in two strides and pull her into my arms. It's the first time I've felt whole since she left. It's going to hurt like a son of a bitch when she pushes me away. I know this, but I can't ignore her pain. It would be like driving by an accident and not stopping to help. "Try not to cry. It can trigger another attack."

"I know." Skylar's hands are trapped between our bodies. She spreads her fingers out over my chest then fists her hands in my shirt. "Just hold me for a second. I'll be okay."

The sane part of my brain screams, *What the fuck are you doing? Run!* The self-destructive rest of me ignores the warning and walks blindly into the fire. "Do you want to talk about it?"

"I want to explain why I disappeared."

"Okay." My voice cracks like a thirteen-year-old boy going through puberty.

She takes a shuddering breath. "Did you hear about the huge scandal at Pulman, Under and Klept a few years ago?"

"The biotech company?" I fight the urge to rest my chin on top of her head and release her instead. At least a sliver of self-preservation survived. "They went out of business, right?"

"The FDA shut them down after one of their miracle drugs was linked to an increase in patient mortality." Skylar sits on her bed and pats the mattress. "Dennis, my mom's boyfriend, worked for them."

I pretend I didn't see her invitation and lean against the wall instead. "Was he involved in the scandal?"

She nods. "He was part of the group that falsified data to keep the human trials open. He testified against everyone else to stay out of jail."

"Wow. When did this happen?"

"I found out about it the night that you and I... The night we..."

The night we promised to love each other forever? The night I gave myself to you completely, heart, mind, body and soul? The night I foolishly believed you did the same? That night? "The night we had sex?"

"Yeah." Skylar takes a trembling breath. "Mom called me right after I'd snuck back inside my bedroom window. She told me to take a taxi to Denver International Airport and come home. But she wouldn't tell me why."

"What are you saying? That you guys went into some sort of witness protection program or something?"

"That's exactly what I'm saying."

"Why didn't you tell me?" Every muscle in my body tightens. I can't believe she didn't trust me enough to tell me what happened. "I wouldn't have told anyone."

"I know that. But Mom said anyone I told would be in danger. She told me I couldn't even tell Uncle Will and Aunt Lori. I wanted to call you, Rowdy. More than anything. But I couldn't risk your life just to say good-bye."

The room spins as the world realigns itself with a new reality. Skylar didn't desert me. She was trying to protect me. All this time I believed she was hiding from me because I was accused of murdering my own mother.

Fuck. She doesn't know what happened. She didn't even know that Mom was dead until Wade blurted it out. "Did they catch all the bad guys?"

"They're all in prison. Well, everyone except for Dennis."

"But, you're safe now, right?"

"I was never in danger."

"Why did you come here?" Skylar spent every summer in Eldorado Springs with Boone's family, but she lived in San Diego.

"You know why." Hope flares in her eyes.

She looks so young, as if time stopped for her when she disappeared. It sure as hell didn't stop for me. I feel so fucking old.

"You shouldn't have come back."

Her chin trembles as tears leak out the corners of her eyes.

"Skylar…" I hate hurting her but I don't want her to hurt me either. "It's been four years. People change."

"God, that's exactly what Boone said." She leans forward, clutching her pillow even tighter. "What happened to you that night after you went home?"

"I don't want to talk about it." My voice trembles. I sound like a child. I feel like one, too. A frightened, needy, abused, vulnerable little kid. And I fucking hate it.

Chapter Nine
Skylar

Rowdy pushes off the wall and starts to pace. He keeps his gaze trained on the floor in front of his feet, for the most part. But every third or fourth step, he looks up and glances at me. I know he's trying to decide whether or not to tell me about the 'really bad thing' that Boone hinted at yesterday.

Rowdy slides both hands into his hair and tugs. I hate to see him get so worked up, but if I let him off the hook now, I might not get another chance to crack through that tough shell of his. So I wait in silence and let the tension build.

He stops in the middle of the room and drops his hands. He takes three deep breaths then turns to face me. "Why do you care about my past?"

"Because I care about you."

"I'm surprised you haven't looked it up online." He glances at my laptop, sitting open on the desk.

"I googled your name every day and never found anything online." Great. If that doesn't sound like an obsessive stalker, I don't know what does.

"I didn't turn eighteen until after it happened, so they kept my name out of the papers."

"Can't you just tell me about it?"

"No." His voice cracks. The color drains from his face. Whatever it was, it must have been huge. His shoulders slump as he exhales. "My mother's name was Blaire Jones. Not Daletzki."

"Oh." None of us wanted to risk running into Rowdy's stepdad so we always hung out in the canyon or here at Boone's house. When I thought of his mom at all, she was just 'Rowdy's mom.'

"You don't mind if I look up the article?"

Rowdy presses his lips together. "Good night, Skylar."

I don't want him to leave, but he obviously doesn't want to stay. And I want to read the article. "Goodnight, Rowdy."

Typing the correct information into the search engine makes all the difference. The link to the archived article pops up on the top of the first page.

Keith Jones, 39, was arrested early Saturday on charges he fatally shot his wife during an argument at the mobile home they shared in the unincorporated town of Marshall, near Eldorado Springs. He remained jailed after being arraigned on criminal homicide and other charges in the Saturday night shooting of 38-year-old Blaire Jones.

Mrs. Jones's 17-year-old son was also taken into custody in

connection with her death. The minor's name has not been released due to his age. Police say Mrs. Jones's son claims he came home from a date and found his intoxicated stepfather pointing a gun at his mother. He claims the gun accidentally discharged while he was trying to wrest it from Mr. Jones.

Jones claims his stepson was already armed with the weapon when he barged into the bedroom where he and his wife were having a heated discussion and threatened to use the gun on Mr. Jones. He attempted to disarm his stepson who then willfully and purposely fired the weapon.

Police waited to file the charges because there were no other witnesses and they needed to determine from autopsy and other evidence whether Mr. Jones or his stepson fired the weapon and whether or not it was accidental.

My vision blurs as tears fill my eyes. This is so much worse than anything I could have imagined. I close the page and erase the search history then shut off my laptop.

The pipes rattle as the shower starts. Boone was already in his pajamas when we got here so it must be Rowdy. I wait for him in my doorway.

Steam pours into the hall when he comes out of the bathroom. He's backlit, wearing nothing but a towel around his narrow hips.

I run to him without thinking and plaster myself against his damp chest. I bury my face in his shoulder before I have a chance to consider the consequences. "God, Rowdy. I'm so sorry."

He pries my arms off his neck. His voice is hoarse. "It's not your fault."

"I know. But I still hate that it happened. And I'm so sorry about your mom."

"Stop." He speaks through clenched teeth. His fingers dig into my wrists as he yanks my hands over my head and pins them to the wall behind me. His pupils dilate, swallowing his irises until they're nothing but an ice-blue rim.

A shiver runs from my head all the way down to my toes. My heart thumps against the base of my throat as he leans in. He's going to kiss me.

There are at least a hundred reasons for me to stop him, but I can't seem to think of a single one. I can't stop trembling either.

Rowdy presses his forehead against mine and whispers my name. His voice is rough, deep and seductive. "Skylar?"

"Yes?"

"Go to bed." He lets go of my hands and steps back.

I take a slow, shaky breath, pretending I don't want to scream. Or cry. Or punch him in the mouth. Or crush my lips against his. Or rip that towel off his body.

Rowdy turns and strides down the hall to Boone's room. Every muscle in his back is hard and sharply defined, as if cut from marble.

Chapter Ten

Rowdy

I steal a pair of sweats out of Boone's bottom drawer then sink onto the spare twin bed. I prop my elbows on my knees and stare at my shaking hands. I can't believe I almost kissed Skylar. Or how badly I wanted to. I don't kiss girls. Not anymore. She ruined me in more ways than one.

There's a quiet knock at the door. I squint my eyes closed. I don't want to deal with this right now. Or ever. I don't want Skylar to see me like this.

"I hope you're decent because I'm coming in whether you are or not." The doorknob turns.

"Please, don't." I stand up, but Skylar's already through the door before I can take a step.

She crosses the room and wraps her arms around my waist. Every muscle in my body tenses as she presses her face against my shoulder. Her tears fall on my collarbone then slide down my bare chest.

"Did you read it?"

She nods.

"The part about how I was...involved?"

"It was an accident." She slides her hands up to my shoulder blades and leans back to study my face. "It wasn't your fault."

I close my eyes and try to block it out, but it's too late. Blood roars behind my ears as the darkness descends...

The blast of the Colt Python stabs my ears. Pain explodes in my wrist and elbow. The hot metal scent of gunpowder stings my nose. A rusty iron taste coats my tongue and invades the back of my throat. A fine, pink mist hangs in the air.

Keith screams at me. But I can't hear him over the ringing in my ears. Mom is lying on the dirty, grey carpet. There's blood everywhere. It's leaking out of a quarter-sized hole between her blank, staring eyes. Pouring out of the back of her head. Fanning out across the floor. Dripping down the wall.

The ringing in my ears fades. I hear sirens, getting closer, louder. Keith wraps my fingers around the gun. He jams the barrel under my chin. He's going to kill me. He pulls the trigger.

Click.

Keith swears and opens the cylinder. It's empty. Red and blue lights flash through the window. I should be relieved, but all I am is numb.

Chapter Eleven

Skylar

"Rowdy?"

He's trembling. And as much as I'd like to believe it's because the only thing between my breasts and his naked chest is a thin layer of cotton, but I don't think he even knows I'm here.

I pat his cheek.

His gaze shifts, as if he's searching for me, but can't see me.

"What's wrong? Rowdy. Please, look at me."

"Skylar?" He's dazed and confused, but at least he recognizes me.

"What happened?"

"Nothing."

"It didn't look like *nothing* to me. Where'd you go?"

He blinks then rubs his eyes. "I just zoned out for a second."

"It was more like ninety seconds and you were completely out of it. What's going on?"

At first, I don't think he's going to answer me. When he does, it's with a flat, emotionless tone of voice. "Involuntary recurrent memory."

"That sounds serious. What is it?"

"Flashback." He blinks again and shakes his head quickly, as if trying to fling water out of his hair. He seems more in control now. "And it's potentially career ending so don't mention it to anyone."

"You're okay, though, right?"

"Did I do anything weird?"

"Like what?"

"If you have to ask, that means I didn't." He smiles, but it looks more like a grimace.

"What triggered it?"

"Stress."

"I shouldn't have pressured you."

He sighs. "I didn't want you to know."

"Why? Did you think I wouldn't understand? That I would judge you?"

He shrugs. "I thought it was the reason you disappeared."

His admission stabs me through the heart. I can't believe he didn't have more faith in me.

"When you didn't return any of my calls, I got worried. At first, I thought Will and Lori were keeping us apart, but they were just as baffled about your sudden disappearance as I was."

My chest aches as I imagine their concern. "What did they say?"

Rowdy's lips twitch into a slight smile. "They quizzed me pretty hard about what happened between us that night."

Blood rushes to my face. "What do you mean?"

"They thought you might have left because we had a big fight or something."

"What did you tell them?"

"The truth."

It's hard to force the words past the lump in my throat. "You told them we had sex?"

Rowdy takes my hands and holds them next to his chest. "I didn't want to. But you'd been gone for three days. No one could get in touch with you or your parents. I didn't want to withhold any information that might help find you."

I see his point, even if I don't see how that particular detail could help anyone find me.

"I didn't lose faith right away." He weaves his fingers between mine. "In fact, I clung to every excuse I could think of no matter how ridiculous or far-fetched. When your Facebook and Twitter accounts were deleted, I assumed that your mom heard about what happened and didn't want you anywhere near me. I hung on to the hope that it wasn't your choice. I thought that once school started in the fall, you'd borrow a phone and call me. When that didn't happen, I told myself that as soon as you were eighteen, you'd reach out to me."

I lift his hands to my face and press his knuckles against my cheek.

He turns my hands over and kisses both palms. "I was upset when you didn't call, but I rationalized my way past it. I told myself that even though you were eighteen, you were still in high school. Still living under your mom's roof and her rules. I took a bus to San Diego and went to your old high school to try to find you. You weren't there and none of your old friends knew where you'd gone."

"You talked to my old friends?" The thought simultaneously warms my heart and intensifies the ache.

Rowdy smiles and nods. "I was surprised by how many of them recognized me. You never told me that you plastered the inside of your locker with my photos or kept a laminated picture of me in your purse and another one stuck in the sun visor of your car. I was practically a celebrity."

My face is on fire. But hearing Rowdy's deep, quiet chuckle is worth the embarrassment. "How many of my friends hit on you?"

"All of the girls and two of the guys." He smiles, but it's a sad, barely there, smile. "I turned them all down. I didn't break any of my promises until after the funeral."

My heart stops. I take a step back to give myself some breathing room. "Why then?"

"I ran out of excuses." He shrugs. "You were nineteen. I couldn't blame your absence on your mom anymore."

"Is that when you started to hate me?"

"I never hated you." Rowdy lifts my chin with his forefinger and ducks his head to capture my gaze. "I tried. Every day since the funeral, I tried to hate you. But it never worked. I could be angry with you, furious even, but hate you? Never."

I'm melting into a puddle of Rowdy-adoring goo. I need to reestablish a few boundaries, before I forget how. I rock back on my heels.

Rowdy slides his palms down my arms, guiding my hands to his shoulders. He digs his fingers into my hips and pulls me against his body. Holy crap, he's hard.

I instinctively lean into him. We're both trembling.

I sway on my feet. "Can we sit down? I'm feeling a little lightheaded."

He pulls back and searches my face. "Do you need your inhaler?"

"No. I'm just nervous."

He chuckles. "Me too."

"You're nervous?"

"I haven't done this in a long time."

"That's not what I heard." I push away from him.

He catches my wrists, completely encircling them with his fingers. His voice deepens to a growl. "What have you heard?"

"That you're with a different girl every night." I stare into his eyes, daring him to lie to me.

"That's a gross exaggeration." He lets go of my hands and sits on the edge of the bed.

I sit beside him and put a hand on his knee. "I get that you felt betrayed. And I understand why you broke your promise to never make love to anyone but me. But I don't understand—"

"I didn't break that promise."

"Don't lie to me, Rowdy." My heart aches. I hate that he sleeps around, but I can forgive him as long as he stops doing it and doesn't lie about it. If he lies, we don't have a chance.

"I've fucked more women than I can count, but you're the only one I've ever made love to."

I really shouldn't find that obscene remark the least bit endearing. I bite my lip to keep from smiling. I can't let him think for one second that I'm okay with his promiscuity. Because I most certainly am not.

"I've never kissed anyone but you, either." His cheeks flush. I definitely find that endearing.

"You're joking, right?"

"I don't like kissing, so I don't do it." He cups my cheek. "If anyone has a problem with it, they can walk away."

"Has anyone ever walked away?"

He quirks one side of his mouth up into a lopsided grin then caresses my lower lip with his thumb. "Never."

"That cocky attitude of yours is not the least bit sexy." My shallow, rapid breathing and racing heart indicate otherwise. *Who's the liar now?*

He brushes his lips across mine, barely touching them, softer than the stroke of a butterfly's wing. He kisses my neck, right below my ear. "Did you seriously just use cocky and sexy in the same sentence?"

"I thought you didn't like kissing." I tilt my head, giving him better access to my throat.

"I lied." He kisses a trail across my collarbone. "I don't like kissing anyone but you."

My eyelids flutter shut.

He brushes his lips across mine again. Once, twice, and then his mouth captures mine. His tongue sweeps across the seam of my lips.

I can't refuse him. He tastes so good. A hint of cinnamon layered over something that is pure Rowdy. I search for an analogy so I can always remember it. His taste, his smell. God, I missed it. But how do you describe the taste of pure bliss?

He moves slowly, gently. So tenderly. His kiss is just as I remembered. It awakens something deep inside me. Something that has lain dormant for the past four years. A whole-body yearning that's so intense it's painful.

I love that he's being careful with me, but I need more. I keep one hand over his heart and tangle the other in his hair. I pull his face closer and suck his lower lip into my mouth.

A primitive, animalistic sound rumbles deep inside his chest, vibrating against my palm. He thrusts his tongue into my mouth. No longer gentle, he's claiming more than just my lips. I follow his lead as he establishes a seductive rhythm that promises so much more.

"God, Rowdy. What the fuck?"

We break apart, gasping. Anna is standing in the hall, just outside Boone's bedroom door. *What the fuck, indeed?*

"Anna. What are you doing here?" Rowdy's not nearly as upset about the interruption as he should be.

"Wade said you were spending the night here."

"I am."

Anna jams one fist on her hip and points at me. "With her?"

Blood rushes to my face, but I'm not embarrassed. I'm pissed. I've been waiting for this kiss for four years. "What we do is none of your business."

Her nostrils flare as she shifts her attention to me. She lowers her voice but cranks up the intensity. "Rowdy Daletzki works with me. We make life and death decisions on a daily basis. If he's doing something that jeopardizes his mental health, then yes, it *is* my business."

"Calm down, Anna." Rowdy sounds and looks exhausted. Why isn't he putting this bitch in her place?

I stand up and fold my arms over my chest. "You need to leave."

She ignores me and extends a hand towards Rowdy. "Come on, Cowboy. Let's go home."

"Cowboy?" She's got a pet name for Rowdy? Might as well stab a hot poker through my chest.

He rolls his eyes. "A few years ago we got a call out for a mountain biker cornered by a bull. I was the first one on the scene. The 'bull' turned out to be a lost calf looking for his next meal. I slipped a prusik cord over his head and led him off the trail so the biker could continue his ride. And now *everyone* calls me Cowboy."

I'm glad he emphasized *everyone,* making it clear that Cowboy is not Anna's exclusive little term of endearment.

The bitch wiggles her fingers, impatiently. "Some of us have to work tomorrow. Let's go."

"What are you? His mother?" I regret the words as soon as they leave my mouth, but the damage has already been done.

Rowdy's fingers tighten around my hand. I squeeze back to keep him from crushing my bones.

"I'm sorry." My voice is breathy. Barely audible.

"It's okay." Rowdy's voice is just as hushed as mine. He clears his throat. "Go home, Anna."

"After everything she's put you through, you're just going to forgive her?"

"I already have."

My heart melts. I know we have a lot of issues to work through but those three little words just made everything a whole lot easier. How can I hold anything against Rowdy when he's already forgiven me?

"So. You're just going to pretend none of it matters?"

"I'm not pretending. The past doesn't matter. And like Skylar's already said, this is none of your business." The slight edge in Rowdy's voice is a clear warning.

A warning Anna ignores. "Where was she when you needed her the most? Gone. Who picked up the pieces after she disappeared? Me."

I can hold my own in a cat fight, verbal as well as physical, but I know how much Rowdy hates confrontations. I'll keep the claws in and let Anna prove what a bitch she is.

Her eyes soften as she gives Rowdy her full attention. They even sparkle with unshed tears. She's obviously changing tactics. Her voice is soft with a slight tremble. "You haven't had a meltdown in nine months. I don't want to see you slide back into that dark place."

"I told you. I'm fine." Rowdy's speaking through clenched teeth now. If I were Anna, I'd back the hell off.

"Please, Rowdy. Come home."

She's trying to make it sound as if they're living together and not just housemates. I'm not buying it. Boone, Wade and Rowdy have all said there's nothing going on between the two of them.

Rowdy shakes his head. "Skylar's got some health issues that I'm monitoring tonight."

"Asthma? Oh, please." Anna rolls her eyes. "She's just manipulating you."

I'd like to manipulate her right out the window.

Rowdy narrows his eyes. "Are you questioning my diagnostic skills?"

"If you're honestly worried about it, call Wade. He can babysit her."

Rowdy crosses the room and puts his hands on her shoulders. He gently pushes her back into the hall. "Good night, Anna. Go home."

She does a great imitation of a trout as Rowdy shuts the door in her face.

~***~

I wait until I hear the front door close before I speak. "Do you want to go back to my room?"

"Do you want me to?"

"I'm not asking you to have sex with me."

"Oh-kaay." Rowdy drags the word out, sounding confused.

"I don't want to mislead you. We have a lot of unfinished business to discuss and I'd rather not be disturbed when Boone comes to bed. That kiss was amazing and I'd like to do it again, but you aren't getting laid tonight."

Rowdy frowns then grabs a light blue t-shirt out of one of Boone's drawers and tugs it on over his head. The fabric strains across his chest, shoulders and biceps.

I hate that he covered up all that glorious skin and sculpted muscle, but it's a good thing. I don't trust myself to stick with my self-imposed rule of no sex until I'm sure I can trust him. If there was some way to know that he'd be able to stop whoring around and be faithful to one woman—to me—I'd jump his gorgeous bones right now.

He tugs on the hem of the t-shirt, but a good two inches of his stomach is still exposed between it and the waistband of his sweatpants. "Maybe we should wait until tomorrow to continue this conversation."

I don't want to wait. I want to get it all out in the open and deal with it. "I'm not going to be able to sleep."

"Me neither." He bites his lip then grins at me. "Let's go to the tree house."

I'm not sure that's any safer than a bedroom. It's where we made love for the first, and only, time. I feel as if I'm sixteen again. Blissfully naive and desperately in love. "Okay."

I grab the blankets off my bed and head for the patio door. It's much cooler outside. The crickets' song is drowned out by the sound of rushing water. Uncle Will was a structural engineer and he used every bit of his skill to build the tree house. I never really appreciated the architectural beauty of our alpine retreat until now. It doesn't look like much from the ground, which is sort of the point, I guess. It looks like part of the landscape. Instead of just one tree, it's hung from several blue spruce evergreens, nestled in a grove of aspens right next to South Boulder Creek. With a little maintenance, and barring any catastrophic natural disasters, it should last for generations. The rope ladder, however, should probably be replaced sooner rather than later. I pick up a splinter as I crawl inside. The floor needs to be sanded and refinished. All the wood surfaces need to be sealed. Seeing it in such disrepair saddens me. As soon as I get a little extra money, I'll fix it up.

It probably shouldn't be my first priority. Boone's obviously having a hard time maintaining the house and yard. But the tree house is my all-time favorite place on the planet. It's private, cozy and safe but sways with the movement of the trees. Especially when someone jumps on the rope bridges connecting the separate platforms. I smile as I remember how freaked out Boone got whenever Rowdy and I would team up to shake the trees.

Some of my best memories revolve around this place. But all of them combined don't equal the single, mind-blowing, life-changing memory that marked the end of my childhood.

I move over to give Rowdy room to hoist his large frame inside.

"So... Rowdy..." My cheeks are on fire. I'm not shy by nature, but Rowdy's always been able to stir up feelings hidden deep inside me that no one else can touch.

He leans against the opposite wall and stretches his legs out in front of him, crossing his ankles. His bare feet are level with my knees. He laces his fingers behind his head and grins at me. "So... Skylar?"

He's enjoying my discomfort a little too much. "Why do you sleep with so many different women?"

He presses his lips together for a few seconds then purses them as he exhales. "Don't get pissed off, but why do you think that's any of your business?"

All of a sudden, it's hard to breathe again. Damn asthma. Damn Rowdy.

He glances at his watch then squats in front of me. "Are you okay?"

"Are you late for an appointment or something?"

He shakes his head but takes another peek at his watch.

He's counting my breaths. I shove my arm at him. "Want to take my pulse while you're at it?"

He puts his middle two fingers over my wrist.

I jerk my hand out of his. "Cut it out."

He blinks, obviously surprised that I'm pissed off. "What's wrong?"

"I hate being fussed over."

"And I hate watching you struggle to breathe because you're too damn proud to use your inhaler."

Vanity is part of it, but mostly I'm trying to conserve my medication. I shake the canister as I push all the air out of my lungs then inhale and administer a dose. I count to eight then exhale. "Satisfied?"

"That was textbook perfect. Are you feeling better?"

I nod my head. "Glad you approve of my technique."

Rowdy ignores my sarcasm. "You'd be surprised how many people can't coordinate the act of depressing a canister with inhaling."

"Can we talk about something besides asthma?"

"What do you want to talk about?"

"You."

"Me?"

"Okay, us."

"What about us?" He moves back to his spot against the far wall and folds his arms over his chest, tucking the tips of his fingers under his armpits. "I didn't know there was an *us* anymore."

Wow. That hurts. "I don't want to play games with you. We used to be so open and honest with each other. It was one of the things I loved about *us*."

"I don't want to play games with you, either. But it's been four years. I've done a lot of things you aren't going to like."

"I'm not going to hold anything you've done in the past against you. All I'm concerned about is what you do from this night forward."

"You've already told me you don't want to have sex with me."

"No. I said we weren't having sex tonight."

He smiles as he stretches, expanding his chest. "I might be able to hold out until tomorrow."

"God, Rowdy." I kick the side of his thigh. "I'm trying to be serious."

"I am serious." He's not smiling now. "I need to have sex on a regular basis to blow off steam."

I'm trying to keep from losing it, but man, he's pushing all my buttons. "You use women to blow off steam?"

"I don't use anyone. The women I have sex with get just as much out of it as I do." He bends his knees, pulling his feet back until they're flat on the floor. "I suppose you've been completely celibate for the past four years."

"Not exactly."

"And what does that mean...*exactly*?"

No games, right? If I expect him to be honest with me, I have to be honest with him. "It means that I messed around with a guy but I haven't had sex with anyone but you."

"No shit?" Rowdy's eyes widen.

"No shit."

"You must be fucking horny."

I glare at him. He's right, but there's no way I'm admitting it.

"Wait. Just one guy?"

"We can't all be sluts like you."

"How long were you together?" Rowdy clenches his jaw.

What is his problem? "Eight months."

"Did you kiss him?"

"Yes, I kissed him. We did a lot of other stuff, too. Do you want all the details?"

"Do you love him?"
"No."
"Did you ever love him?"
"No."
"Does he love you?"
"What difference does it make?"
"Are you still together?"
"Would I have kissed you if we were?"
"Answer the question, Skylar."
"No, Rowdy. We aren't together."
"When did you break up?"
"Three weeks ago." I'm suddenly so tired I can no longer hold my head up. I hug my shins and rest my forehead on my knees. "The day after Mom's funeral."

Chapter Twelve

Rowdy

Skylar's mother hasn't been dead a month yet and I'm cross-examining her about an ex-boyfriend. An ex-boyfriend she didn't even have sex with. What the fuck's wrong with me? I crawl across the floor on my hands and knees. "Hey."

A tear slips out of the corner of her eye.

I wipe it away with my thumb. "Do you miss him?"

She shrugs. "We were pretty good friends before we got together."

"That's how we began." My voice is as rough as the gravel road in front of Boone's house. I hate the idea of her being with another guy...as evidenced by my reaction to seeing her with Wade. But it's the thought that someone else might have owned even a part of her heart that's shredding mine.

"Ethan and I were nothing like you and me."

"How's that?"

"I only went out with him because my mom wanted me to."

"Why did she want you to go out with someone you weren't into?"

"I think she wanted me to have someone that could comfort me after she died."

Skylar brushes another tear off her cheek, triggering a need to protect her that's so strong it hurts.

This is exactly why I don't want to get involved with her again. She has entirely too much power over me. But I can't help myself. I scoot in next to her and sling an arm over her shoulder. I pull her closer and kiss the top of her head. "I'm so sorry."

"Do you believe in an afterlife? In Heaven?"

"I don't know." Mostly, I just believe in Hell.

"Rowdy?"

"Hmm?" I rock her gently back and forth in my arms. If I keep this shit up, I'm going to grow a damn vagina.

She takes a deep breath, holds it for a few seconds then shivers when she exhales. "I know we can't pick up where we left off, but maybe we can start over."

I freeze. "What do you mean?"

Her heart's pounding so hard I can see the pulse in her neck.

"What we had was amazing and rare and beautiful. It was a once in a lifetime, fairytale kind of love."

"Fairytales aren't real."

She lifts my arm off her shoulder and leans away from me, but keeps her gaze locked on my face. "Don't you dare try to pretend that what we had wasn't real. You promised to love me forever, right here." She slams the side of her fist against the wood floor.

"We were kids, Skylar." I rub my forehead, trying to alleviate the pounding behind my eyes.

"Are you saying you didn't mean it?"

"I meant every word, but I didn't know anything about life...or love. And I'm still pretty damn clueless." I'd been beaten, burned, ridiculed and humiliated beyond belief. But Mom's death is the only thing that's ever hurt me as much as losing Skylar. The two events are so closely entwined that I have a hard time separating them. I know it wasn't her fault. But the fact remains that I know how it feels to lose her and I don't ever want to go through anything like that again.

"I'm not asking you to marry me." The moon peeks out from behind a cloud, illuminating her eyes. "All I'm asking is for you to give us a chance. Can you do that?"

What am I supposed to say? My heart's already agreed without waiting for any input from my brain.

I lift my hand, extending my pinkie finger, just like I did when we were kids. "Friends?"

Skylar grins and hooks it with hers. "Friends."

I tug her closer. "With benefits?"

She licks her lips. "With *limited* benefits."

"How limited?"

"I think we need to take it slow."

"I think we need to get naked."

"Rowdy!" She lightly slaps my chest.

"I have needs, woman." I mean it as a joke, sort of. But Skylar doesn't laugh.

"If we're going to have any chance at all, you can't sleep with anyone else."

"I figured as much." I make a mental note to stock up on tequila. "Can you give me an estimate on when you might be ready for full benefits?"

She smiles and shakes her head. "Let's just take it one day at a time, okay?"

"Do you have any idea what a sacrifice this is for me?"

"It's going to be hard for me, too."

"That's what she said." I give her my patented 'sexy' grin that she hates and wiggle my eyebrows.

Skylar tries not to laugh and snorts like a pig. And even that's cute.

"Hey, you left yourself wide open for that one. Don't blame me."

An eerie, whistling sound rises above the noise of the creek. My mouth goes dry. Eldorado Canyon turns into a wind tunnel when storms roll out of the Rockies. The lightning is legendary. "Storm's coming."

Skylar's eyes widen. So does her smile. "Awesome!"

I stand up and offer her my hand. "We need to get back to the house."

"Are you kidding me?" She ignores my outstretched hand and heads towards the cargo net linking the main part of the tree house to the observation deck above. "Come on!"

The girl has no sense of self-preservation. Never did. "Skylar, it's not safe."

"What happened to your sense of adventure? You used to love watching storms."

That was before I started hearing the blast of a pistol with every clap of thunder and seeing a muzzle flash with every bolt of lightning. "I grew up. Don't make me carry you out of here."

She eyes me warily then returns her gaze to the open door. She shifts her weight, hunching down ever so slightly.

"Skylar." I draw out her name. "Don't."

She glances over her shoulder and grins at me.

Shit. I lunge for her but she's too fast. She leaps through the open door. Lightning flashes, imprinting the image of her hanging in midair on the back of my eyelids. Thunder booms and echoes off the canyon walls. "Damn it, Sky!"

The tree house lurches then sways with the aftershocks of her slight weight hitting the ropes.

"Come on, Rowdy. The lightning rod on the house will protect us."

A feeling of vertigo washes over me as I realize there's more than one way to lose Skylar. "Get back here right now or the deal's off."

She's halfway to the observation platform. She pauses and looks over her shoulder again, this time with a frown on her face. "What deal?"

"We can't be friends if you're going to act like an idiot."

She cocks her head. "Are you kidding me?"

"I couldn't be more serious. Get your ass on the ground or we're done."

"Okay, okay. Jesus." She climbs back towards me, feet first.

I hold onto the door frame then lean out and grab the waistband of her pants as soon as she's within reach. All I'm trying to do is to get her inside as fast as possible so we can get out of here before we're fried by lightning. But that's not what happens. I had no idea fabric could stretch that much.

Chapter Thirteen

Skylar

Cold air rushes over my ass as Rowdy practically jerks my pants off. I squeal and scramble for purchase, arms and legs flailing. My elbow impacts something hard and sharp.

Rowdy swears and grabs my upper arm. He hauls me inside with one hand.

My pants are around my knees. I'm wearing a tiny, see-through, black lace thong. The bottom half of me is practically naked and on full display. I reach around and grab the hem of my shirt, yanking it down past my bare ass. But Rowdy's not even looking at me.

He's holding a cupped hand in front of his bleeding mouth.

"Oh, crap."

Rowdy glares at me and points at the trapdoor.

I nod then climb down without a word. As soon as Rowdy's feet hit the ground, he grabs my hand and drags me into the kitchen.

My elbow's throbbing. I can only imagine what his mouth feels like. "I'm so sorry."

He pulls his phone out of his pants, scrolls through his contacts then hands it to me.

"You've reached the after-hours office line for Dr. Clint Maxwell. If you have a true dental emergency that cannot wait for regular office hours, press one."

My hand shakes as I follow the automated instructions. Finally, a human answers. "This is Dr. Maxwell."

"Hi, my name's Skylar Layton and I accidentally hit my boyfriend, Rowdy Daletzki, in the mouth with my elbow." Oh crap. Did I really just call him my boyfriend?

"Were any teeth knocked out?"

I repeat the question to Rowdy. He lowers his hand and opens his mouth.

I cringe when I see the damage. "No, but one of his front teeth is really crooked. And it wasn't like that before."

I run to the family room to tell Boone what happened and once again borrow his car. I try to apologize to Rowdy during the drive to Boulder but he just holds a hand up and shakes his head. I guess he doesn't want to hear it.

The storm catches up with us just as I turn onto Broadway. I love thunderstorms, but I can't enjoy this one. I'm a walking disaster zone. First Boone, now Rowdy. I wonder who's next?

Dr. Maxwell meets us at the front door of his office building. I hold my breath as he examines Rowdy's mouth.

"Is he okay? He's not going to lose the tooth, right?"

"Not if I can help it." Dr. Maxwell explains each step of the process as he examines and then splints Rowdy's tooth. Basically, all he does is straighten it out then glue it to the adjoining, undamaged teeth on either side with little globs of resin. He shines a bright, blue light on it for a few seconds then leans back and removes his latex gloves, tossing them into a biohazard bin. He claps Rowdy on the shoulder. "Call my office tomorrow and set up an appointment for two weeks from today. Nothing but soft food for the first week."

"Soft food?" It sounds more like 'thof foo.' Rowdy closes his eyes and groans.

Dr. Maxwell chuckles. "You let me poke and prod a lateral luxation without complaint, but the thought of a restricted diet makes you whine?"

Rowdy rolls his eyes then points at my chest. "Smoothies. Lots and lots of smoothies."

It takes a second for my brain to decipher his impaired speech. But when it does, I know exactly what he wants.

"Chocolate, banana and peanut butter?" Aunt Lori used to make smoothies for all of us when we were kids. Rowdy was the only one that liked peanut butter in his.

He grins and nods. "Lots of peanut butter."

"You got it." The lump in my throat swells. Not only is it obvious that Rowdy's forgiven me for practically knocking his tooth out, he's going to let me take care of him.

Since we're already in Boulder, Rowdy insists I drop him off to get his car.

The storm blows itself out before we get back to the house. Rowdy parks behind me then jogs to Boone's car and opens my door. The clean scent of rain and pine is a welcome change to the usual dust.

When we get inside, I notice that Boone is no longer in the recliner. I follow Rowdy upstairs, admiring the view of his muscular butt. He walks past Boone's closed door and leans against the wall next to my room, feet spread a few inches more than shoulder width apart.

I hope he doesn't think he's going to be spending the night in my bed. I'd love to fall asleep wrapped up in his arms, but I don't trust myself.

He hooks his thumbs in the waistband of his sweats, tugging them dangerously low. His fingers fan out over his hip bones. "Do I get a goodnight kiss?"

"Are you sure you want one?" Not only did I mess up his tooth, I also split his lip.

"I want a lot more, but I'll settle for a kiss." He takes my wrists and leads me into the space between his legs, placing my hands on his chest. His heart thumps against my palm. It's beating almost as fast as mine. He grabs my ass and pulls me closer. The evidence of just how much more he wants presses against my stomach, causing every muscle below my waist to clench. His gaze drops to my breasts. I'm sure he's getting an eyeful. I can feel my nipples straining against the thin fabric of my t-shirt.

My knees turn to jello. I slide down his body. Not far, just a couple of inches, but that slight amount of friction triggers a needy whimper.

Rowdy growls in response. His abs contract as he sucks in a breath through his teeth.

I try to pull back, but he holds my hips in place, digging his fingers into my ass. He slips one hand under my shirt and skims the surface of my ribs with his fingertips. The heel of his palm brushes against the side of my breast.

I want him to touch me. Desperately. It's all I can do to keep from turning into him. Both of us are trembling, now.

I'm not a virgin. We've made love before. He wants me. I want him. This shouldn't be such a big deal. But it is.

I stare into Rowdy's eyes and remember how I used to see love and adoration reflected there. A mirror of my own feelings. Now, all I see is lust. His and mine. It's a raw, animal hunger, demanding and reckless.

This is not what I want. My body disagrees. But if I let Rowdy use me, the way he's used all those other girls, I'm afraid I'll lose him forever. I'd rather free solo every route on The Redgarden Wall than risk that. "Rowdy, stop."

He freezes then slowly slides his hand out of my shirt, tracing the same path as before, only in reverse.

"I'm sorry."

He gently pushes my hips away from his then drops his hands. "Me too."

I can tell from his tone of voice that he's not apologizing. He's just sorry I stopped him.

In all the time we were together, he never once made me feel guilty for slowing things down. The night we made love, he kept stopping to ask me if I was sure. I was then. I'm not now.

Rowdy wraps his fingers around my upper arms and moves me to the side so he can step away from the wall. He leans in.

My pulse throbs in my neck as I lift my chin and close my eyes. His warm breath caresses my face. I lick my lips and silently remind myself to be gentle.

He presses his cheek against mine and whispers, "Goodnight, Skylar," then disappears into Boone's room.

Chapter Fourteen

Rowdy

I feel like a dick for not kissing Sky goodnight, but she's the one that wants to take things slow. If I withhold what she wants, it might motivate her to speed things up a bit. Yep, I'm definitely a dick.

Skylar's always looked at the world through rainbow-colored glasses. She needs to see me as I really am. Not as the kid I used to be. That boy died when my mother did.

I head to the bathroom for another shower. This will be the third one today, but if I don't rub one out, I'll wake up with a bad case of blue balls in the morning. Or end up having a wet dream in Boone's spare bed. I doubt he'd appreciate that.

My earlier shower dissipated the light scent of Skylar's organic body wash. It reminds me of apples, but that's not quite it. There's also a hint of something earthy and green. Whatever it is, my dick sure as fuck likes it. I check the label. It's chamomile. I should have taken care of business the first time I was in here, but I didn't want to act like a perv, jerking off with her in the next room. Nothing's changed, except the intensity of my desperation.

I put Boone's bloodstained t-shirt in the sink to soak then step into the tub and pull the shower curtain closed. Skylar's shampoo, conditioner and body wash are tucked into the back corner. I pop open the cap of her body wash and take a whiff. My eyes roll into the back of my head. *Fuuuck.*

I'm tempted to squirt a tiny amount into my palm, but that's crossing a line too pervy even for me. I grab the bar of goat milk soap off the wire rack hanging from the shower head and lather up. I take my throbbing dick with my right hand and press my left fist against my mouth to stifle the groans, but change my mind when my mouth explodes in pain.

I'll just have to try to control myself and hope Skylar and Boone can't hear me over the rush of water. I force my eyes open so I can stay aware of my surroundings and remember to be quiet. But even with my eyes open, I still see Skylar's face…the flush on her skin…the lust in her eyes. I still feel the way her body trembles against mine. I still hear her desperate whimpers. I still smell the delicious scent of her dark brown hair.

My body shudders as I spasm, coming harder than I have in a long time.

A quiet knock on the door startles me. I cut off the shower.

"Rowdy?" Skylar sounds worried. "Are you okay?"

Guess I wasn't as quiet as I thought. "I'm fine."

"It sounds like you're in a lot of pain. Do you need some Tylonal or Advil for your tooth?"

"I'm just a little sore." I brace one hand against the tile wall and cringe. Could I sound any more pathetic?

"Are you sure there's nothing I can do for you?"

I grab the same damp towel I used earlier today and rub it over my body. "Go to bed. I'll see you in the morning."

I wait until I hear her door creak shut before heading back to Boone's room. He's in bed, but not asleep.

"So. What's going on with you and Skylar?"

"We're taking things slow."

"Anna didn't seem to think so."

"You heard that, huh?" Boone was in the family room with the TV on when Anna arrived. His ears must be better than mine.

"Dude. I'm pretty sure the entire town heard. That girl's a whack job."

"Hey."

"Just saying."

"You don't know her like I do. She had a really rough childhood."

"So did you, but I don't see you blowing up and attacking people for no reason."

"I almost punched Wade Summers in the jaw tonight."

"What!" Boone rolls onto his side and props his head up with his elbow. "Why?"

"He was trying to keep me away from Skylar." I can't believe I'm spilling my guts to Boone. We used to be as close as brothers, but that changed when I started fucking around with girls and drinking. Boone's no boy scout. He's had his share of one-night stands and if the recycle bin in the kitchen is any indicator, he's going through at least a six-pack a day of Coors.

But he doesn't think I'm good enough for his cousin. I'm not, but it still pisses me off.

Boone's voice drops. "I told Wade to ask Skylar out."

I take a deep, calming breath before I open my mouth and say something I'll regret. "Why?"

"Skylar's stuck in the past. She still believes the two of you have a shot at making it work."

"And you don't?" Anger simmers under my skin, itching and burning like poison ivy.

Boone sits up and tucks a pillow under his broken foot. "Wade is more like you were four years ago than you are. He and Skylar make more sense than the two of you. If you're ready to settle down and try to have a real relationship with one girl, you should consider Anna."

"God, Boone. She's my sister." I'll never settle down with just one girl. Unless it's Skylar. That realization sucker punches me in the gut.

"Anna's just your step-sister. There's no reason you two can't hook up."

"Anna and I have no interest in hooking up with each other."

"Are you blind? Anna's been drooling over you for years."

"You're delusional."

"Anna wants you and she'll do whatever it takes to get rid of the competition."

"Anna knows how hard it was for me to get over Skylar. She doesn't want to see me get hurt again. That's all."

"Are you?"

"Am I what?"

"Over Skylar?"

I want to say *hell yeah,* but Boone's got some sort of internal bullshit detector. He can always tell when someone is lying. "I thought I was."

"You remember what I said about hurting her?"

"Yeah, I remember."

"I meant every word."

Chapter Fifteen

Skylar

After tossing and turning most of the night, I wake up a little after six. My skin feels too tight for my body and it has nothing to do with the dry climate.

I'm a little irritated with Rowdy for not kissing me goodnight. Okay, that's a lie. I'm not irritated. I'm flat-out pissed. What was that all about anyway? Is he punishing me because I won't have sex with him? Does he think I'm enjoying this?

If people could die from sexual frustration, I'd be dead. I'm twenty years old and have never had an orgasm. Something I never should have confessed to Ethan. I was trying to make him feel better about not 'meeting my needs,' but instead he became obsessed with the idea of being my 'first.'

I think I've been close a couple of times. When Rowdy and I used to make out, I'd get this intense feeling deep inside my lower belly. But Rowdy always stopped and asked if I was okay.

Ugh. Just thinking about it is making me horny. I'm tempted to try to take care of it myself, but that's never worked either. All it does is frustrate me. I need to get out of this house. A long run up the canyon might help.

I take my morning dose of Advair then head for the bathroom. Boone's door creaks open. I know it's not Boone. It's too early.

"Morning." Rowdy's voice is deeper, huskier and sexier than it was last night. He's wearing the same sweats he had on yesterday, but no shirt. The V cut of his sculpted abs draws my gaze lower.

"Sorry." I lick my lips and swallow, trying not to drool. "I was trying to be quiet."

"You didn't wake me up." He yawns and stretches, expanding his already broad chest. "I'm still an early riser."

I can't keep from grinning. It may seem insignificant, but it's one more thing I can add to my small list of things about Rowdy that haven't changed.

"Do you want to go out for breakfast?" Rowdy runs a hand over his tousled hair, creating even more disarray.

"Actually, I was thinking about going for a run."

"Do you want some company?"

Running with Rowdy won't do much for my sexual frustration situation. Just the thought of his bare chest, gleaming with sweat, makes me squeeze my thighs together. But I'm a glutton for punishment. "Sure."

After hitting the bathroom, I duck back into my room and throw on a pair of sweatpants, a sports bra and a tank top. If I were going by myself, I'd wear my skimpy, little running shorts, but I don't want to make things harder for Rowdy. I snicker at the unintentional innuendo and decide to go with the shorts anyway. He deserves a little torture for teasing me last night.

I grab my rescue inhaler and my running shoes. Rowdy's already outside, leaning against Boone's car. His eyes darken as his gaze roams over my body.

I fold my arms across my chest to hide my puckered nipples.

Rowdy smirks as if he believes he won this round. "Do you mind if we jog down to my house so I can grab a pair of shorts?"

"Whatever." Game on, buster.

He pushes off the car. "In fact, go grab a swimsuit. We can cool off in the pool after our run."

I roll my one-piece racing suit up in a towel and stuff it inside my day pack, along with my wallet, a bottle of sunscreen and a tube of Burt's Bees lip balm.

Rowdy's house is less than a mile from Boone's and it's downhill all the way, but I'm sweating like a pig and wheezing before we're halfway there. I'm also praying that Anna's already left for work.

Rowdy—who doesn't have so much as a drop of sweat on his honey-hued skin—stops and insists I use my inhaler before we go any further. At this rate, I'm going to run out of Albuterol before the month is up. It's not as expensive as Advair, but it's not cheap.

Rowdy's house is tiny. I'm surprised that four people can live together in such a small space without killing each other.

Instead of going to the front door, Rowdy stops next to the detached garage. "Do you want to come in or wait out here?"

"You live in the garage?"

He shakes his head and grins. "Above it. It's actually the best room in the whole house. Except for the sun in summer and no running water. But it's nice and cozy in the winter. And it's private."

My great mood burns away like morning dew as I picture a giant bed, red lights and a mirrored ceiling. "I'll come up."

I follow him around to the back of the garage and up a steep flight of stairs. Rowdy opens the door without unlocking it. Trusting soul. Or maybe he just has so many sluts coming and going that a locked door is too big of a hassle.

He holds the door open for me. "It's not much, but it suits my needs."

I mumble, "I bet it does," under my breath. All he needs is a horizontal surface and a box of condoms.

Rowdy frowns. "What's that supposed to mean?"

"Nothing."

My mouth falls open when I step inside. His twin-sized bed is small, but neatly made with a navy blue comforter and a single white pillow. A huge flat screen television takes up most of the wall over a small, uncluttered desk. A mountain bike, a snowboard and three pairs of skis are mounted on the wall next to the stairs. An acoustic guitar sits in the corner next to his bed.

Boys and their toys. "This is nice."

Rowdy's frown softens, but his expression remains guarded.

My eyes are drawn back to the bed. "That looks like it might be a little crowded when you have company."

"You're the first girl that's ever been up here. Except for Anna."

My face burns. I turn around and drag a finger across the strings on his guitar. I'd rather he have a dozen different girls in his bed than *her*.

Cherri had her hands all over Rowdy, and she's absolutely gorgeous with big, perky boobs and long shapely legs, but she's nice. I can see us becoming friends. As long as she keeps her hands off Rowdy in the future.

But Anna? No way. That girl gives me the creeps. "It wasn't too crowded for Anna?"

"God, Skylar. Anna's my sister."

"Stepsister."

"She's never been in my bed and I've never been in hers." Rowdy scrunches his nose and shudders. "We aren't blood relatives, but we might as well be. Okay?"

Rowdy's only kidding himself if he thinks Anna doesn't have a thing for him. But the idea obviously creeps him out as much as it does me, so I drop it.

He holds up the bike shorts. "If you don't want a show, close your eyes."

"We're going for a run, not a bike ride."

"These are tri-shorts. They work for biking, swimming and running." Rowdy tosses them on the bed then drops his hands to the drawstring on the sweats he borrowed from Boone.

I turn my back and squeeze my eyes shut as an extra precaution to be sure I don't give in to temptation and sneak a peek. "You're a triathlete?"

"Nah. I just do 'em for fun."

"Fun?" What have I gotten myself into? "Keep in mind that I'm not used to the high altitude."

"You can turn around now."

Holy hell. Those shorts should be illegal. They look as if they're painted on, leaving very little to the imagination.

"See something you like?"

Busted. I jerk my eyes up to his.

The corners of his mouth twitch, but at least he isn't blatantly smirking at me. Not yet.

I pick up the guitar and sit on the bed. "Do you actually play this thing, or is it just part of your decor?"

He frowns and takes it out of my hands. "I'm a man. I don't do 'decor.'"

"When did you start playing guitar?"

Rowdy's Adam's apple bobs as he swallows. "About a month after you left."

He sits beside me on the bed and strums the guitar with the edge of his thumb. It sounds fine to me. But he tilts his head to the side, bringing his ear closer to the instrument. He alternates between twisting the little tuning pegs at the top and plucking the strings. And then the magic happens.

His fingers dance over the strings, filling the room with music. I don't recognize the melody, but it's so poignant and haunting it brings tears to my eyes.

Rowdy's lips move silently as he plays. I wait for him to finish then ask him to sing the words for me.

He smiles and shakes his head.

"Why not? You have a great voice." The stereo in Old Blue was broken when Rowdy bought it so he and I would sing every song we knew when we were driving around. He always had perfect pitch and an amazing range. Me, not so much. "Please?"

"Maybe some other time." He puts the guitar back on the stand then turns sideways to look at me. "I'm still working on it. It needs another verse."

"Wait. You wrote that?"

He shrugs, like it's no big deal. "It's therapeutic."

"Music therapy, huh?"

Another shrug. "When the Harris's took me in, Lori insisted I take up a creative hobby to help me deal with shit. I suck at glass work. Oil paint fumes make me puke. I didn't have much luck with pottery either. But when I found this old guitar at a garage sale, it was love at first sight."

"You lived with Aunt Lori and Uncle Will?"

"I had my eighteenth birthday in jail so I wasn't eligible for foster care. I wasn't ready to deal with the real world either. Will and Lori insisted I stay with them until I got my shit together. It took about a year. Boone didn't tell you?"

I've only been back for a few days. Boone and I still have a lot of catching up to do, but not telling me that Rowdy lived with his family is a huge omission. "Why did you move out?"

Rowdy stands up then takes my hands and pulls me to my feet. "If we don't get started, it's going to be too hot to go for a run."

Chapter Sixteen

Rowdy

I can't believe I played that song for Skylar. I can't read music so I just started messing around, creating my own. At first it was all angry music while I worked through my desire for Keith to die a horrible, bloody death. I still hate that motherfucker but I take solace in the fact that he'll be getting fucked in prison for the rest of life.

After a few months, I started writing sappy love songs. And then sad love songs. When I finally realized that Skylar was gone for good, I came full circle and started writing angry songs again. I wrote *The Naked Edge* right after Lori and Will's funeral. It's a jumbled up, bi-polar mess of sad and angry. I'd hoped it was a sign that I was finally moving on. But here she is, again. Sitting in my bed. Gazing at me with those expressive hazel eyes of hers.

"Please?" She clasps her hands under her chin and blinks.

I know that look. She's not going to give up until I give in. I guess I can play one of the sappy love songs. "If I sing you a song, you have to make me a batch of chocolate chili cookies."

Her smile lights up the room. "Deal."

"I wrote this a long time ago so it's pretty simple."

"I'm sure it's wonderful."

I close my eyes and let the music take me back to the time before I gave up on Skylar. "It's called *Where You Are*."

I open my eyes when the last note fades.

Skylar's voice cracks. "You wrote that because of me, didn't you?"

"Whatever gave you that idea?" I try to lighten the mood by making a joke out of it, but there's nothing funny about the way Skylar's eyes are filling with tears.

I set my guitar back in the stand then take her hands. "It was a long time ago and..."

She stares at our interlocked fingers and nods. "And you don't feel that way anymore."

"I've been doing everything in my power to not feel anything at all for so long, I have no idea what I feel now." Other than terrified.

"Thanks for singing it for me." She pulls one hand free then swipes at her cheeks with her fingertips. "It's a beautiful song."

I want to get us both back to a happier place so I do the only thing I can think of. I tug her hand, pulling her in closer to kiss her, but she turns her head so my mouth lands on her cheek.

The 'kiss dodge' is one of my tricks, but I can't believe how much her rejection hurts. I let go of her hand and stand up. "We've screwed around here too long. I say we skip the run and head straight to the pool. Okay?"

"Sure." She smiles, but it doesn't get anywhere near her eyes.

~***~

I flash my pass and pay for Skylar's admission into the pool before she can dig her money out of her backpack.

She frowns at me and shoves a fistful of dollars at my chest. I hold my hands up, palms out. "How many times did you grab the tab at Red Robin's or pay for our movie tickets and popcorn when we were kids?"

"That was different. I was using my mom's credit card."

"Yeah, well, now it's my turn."

"Rowdy." She draws my name out and narrows her eyes at me.

I press my lips together to keep from grinning. She's about as ferocious as a wet kitten. "Go get changed. I'll meet you out on deck."

I rinse off in the historic bathhouse then wait by the exit for Skylar. Someone below shouts my name. I shade my eyes and squint. Anna waves at me.

I lean over the rail. "I thought you had to work the morning shift."

"I couldn't sleep last night so I took a personal day." She motions for me to join her on the sun deck next to the slide. "I need help getting sunscreen on my back."

Ordinarily, I wouldn't think twice about it. But after Boone's comments last night, and Skylar's today, I feel a little weird about smearing lotion over Anna's bare back. I nod towards the dressing rooms. "I'm waiting for Skylar."

Anna lifts her shoulders then lets them fall dramatically. I swear I can hear her sigh over the noise of the crowd. "Fine. Come join me when she's done primping."

I chuckle and shake my head. Skylar doesn't primp. Her idea of makeup is Chapstick and eyelash goop. At least, it used to be. I have no idea what her makeup routine is anymore. For all I know, she could be in there for another half hour. My smile fades. What am I doing? This is going to be so much harder than dating a stranger. We both need to scrape away the veneer of what we think we know about each other before we can start over.

"What are you frowning about?" Skylar's cold, damp hand snakes around my waist.

I shiver and grab her wrist. "Damn, woman. Your hands are cold."

"So is the shower. I hope the pool's warmer."

"You know better than that." I can't help grinning as I notice the only makeup she's wearing is a faint, grey smudge under her right eye. I swipe at it with my thumb. "You look like a one-eyed raccoon."

Skylar grins at me as she bats my hand away. "I didn't know we were going swimming so I didn't use waterproof mascara."

"They make that stuff waterproof?"

"It looks fake and it's hard to remove so I don't use it unless I plan to get wet or think I might cry." She rubs her middle finger under her eye then examines it. "Did I get it all?"

"You look great." I grab her hand and lead her towards the stairs. "Anna saved us a couple of spots on the sun deck."

Skylar puts on the brakes and gives my hand a hard tug. "I thought she had to work today."

"She decided to take a personal day."

"Did you tell her we were coming here?"

"I didn't even know we were coming here until this morning. Is it a problem?"

"She's already made it crystal clear that she doesn't like me." Sky's eyebrows draw together, puckering the skin above her nose. She rubs her thumb over the back of my hand. "Besides, I want to spend the day with just the two of us."

"She's already seen me. We can't leave without hurting her feelings."

"Fine. But if she acts bitchy, I'm putting her in her place."

"If you would just tell her why you disappeared—"

"It's none of her damn business."

"Why are you being this way?"

"I'm not exactly proud of the fact that I had to go into WITSEC because my mom's boyfriend is a criminal."

"Did you forget how Anna and I are related? Her father is serving a life sentence for murdering my mother."

Skylar gasps. Her eyes widen. "I'm sorry. I wasn't thinking—"

"No. It's okay." I shouldn't have brought that shit up. "I'm not trying to force you to tell Anna anything. But if you want her to forgive you, you need to tell her why you disappeared."

"I don't care if she forgives me or not. I just don't want her to come between us."

"She helped me get through the shittiest time of my entire life." She's still helping me, but something tells me confessing that to Skylar isn't a good idea. "She watched me go through it all—the grief, the disbelief, the insane hope that you'd come back, and finally the devastating acceptance that you were gone forever."

Skylar wraps her arms around my waist and lays her head against my chest. "I'm so sorry."

I pull her closer and kiss the top of her head. It's an ingrained reflex. If someone throws a ball at my head, I catch it. If they throw a fist at my face, I dodge it. If Skylar needs comfort, I give it.

"Hey! Keep it PG up there." Anna's shout is like a bucket of cold water straight from the spring. "This is a family place."

I kiss Skylar's forehead then take her hand and lead her to the sun deck below.

Anna's got two beach towels spread out. There's room for all three of us, if we squeeze in, but she's lying in the middle.

I nudge her shoulder with my foot. "Hey, scoot over."

She peers at me from over the top of her sunglasses. "I've already got this spot warmed up. There's room on either side."

"It's ninety-eight degrees and you've got sweat pooling in the middle of your back."

Skylar snorts then covers her mouth with the hand that's not clinging to mine.

Anna presses her sparkly, pink mouth into a fine line. Her nostrils flare as she sucks in a quick breath. She pastes a huge, fake smile on her face as she unties the back of her bikini top. "I don't want to risk flashing anyone."

Skylar squeezes my hand. "It's too hot to lay out in the sun. Let's go get wet."

I don't know if Skylar's trying to turn me on, but her choice of words sends my mind to places it shouldn't go, especially when I'm wearing form-fitting tri-shorts.

Anna's smile fades then turns predatory. She holds her top against her chest with one arm and reaches for her sunscreen with the other. "Do my back before you go, please?"

Skylar lets go of me, leans over, and snatches the bottle out of Anna's hand, quicker than an eagle grabbing a trout out of South Boulder Creek. "Sure. No problem."

Anna's mouth falls open.

Skylar kneels beside her and squirts a line of thick, white cream from the base of Anna's neck to the top of her ass, using at least half the bottle. She smears the goop around with one hand then wipes the remainder on Anna's towel next to her face. "There ya go, sweetie. That should last the rest of the day."

I know I shouldn't laugh. Hell, I shouldn't even smile, but I can't help it.

Anna's face is bright red. Her eyes look like golf balls. And her back looks like someone greased it with an entire can of Crisco. I cough into my fist to cover the grin I can't suppress.

Anna lasers me with a death glare, but all that does is trigger a full on belly laugh. My shoulders shake with the effort of holding it back. Finally, I give up and let it out.

Skylar tugs on my hand. I back away from Anna, shaking my head and laughing. I manage to choke out a feeble, "sorry," but know I'll pay for it later. Anna's going to kill me.

I follow Skylar up the ladder to the slide. Her swimsuit covers ten times as much skin as Anna's but damn, Sky's ass looks fine. We hang out in the pool until I notice Skylar's nose is turning pink. I'm pretty dark, naturally, but even I get burned at this altitude if I'm not careful. I press my finger against the tip of her nose. She cringes and jerks her head back.

"Did you put sunscreen on?"

"That's what took me so long in the dressing room. That, plus waiting in line for a bathroom stall to change in."

"Why do you change in a stall?"

"I don't do public nudity. Not even in a dressing room."

"What SPF is your sunscreen?"

"Thirty. And it's supposed to be waterproof."

"There's no such thing as waterproof sunscreen. Water resistant, but not waterproof." I gently lift the shoulder strap of her swimsuit. Now it's my turn to cringe. "We need to get you out of the sun."

"But we just got here."

I glance at the clock over the bathhouse. "We've been in the water for over two hours."

"Oh, crap."

"Come on. I think Wade's got some lavender and aloe back at the house."

~***~

There's a strange, yet slightly familiar car in the driveway. My stomach sinks when I recognize it. Goddamnit. What's Cherri doing here? I didn't give her my phone number, much less my address. How the fuck did she find me? Skylar's going to throw a shit fit. I just told her I never brought girls home. She's going to think I'm lying.

"Hey, isn't that Wade's car?"

Cherri's car is parked right behind Wade's SUV. I heave a huge, totally obvious, slightly suspicious, sigh of relief. "Yeah. And it looks like Cherri followed him home."

"Oh, I hope so. She was so sweet last night and I really need a girlfriend."

"Are you sure about that?" I wink at Skylar. "I hear they're a lot of work."

The tip of her tongue flicks over her bottom lip. "Really? I heard they come in handy when you're horny."

I choke on my own spit. "Are you trying to tell me something?"

"Like what?"

"Are you into girls?"

"No, I'm into you."

My heart kicks into high gear. "Are you saying that if you were my girlfriend, you'd come in handy?"

"I've been thinking about it all day. All last night, too."

"God, Skylar. You're killing me."

"I'm not ready to have sex, but I don't want to set you up for failure either."

"My imagination's running wild over here. Can you be a little more specific?"

Skylar's gaze drops to the bulge in my shorts. "I think we need to continue this conversation in your room."

I'm ready to toss her over my shoulder and haul her upstairs, caveman style, but she's sunburned. "We need to get the aloe and lavender oil from Wade first."

"As much as I'd like to see Cherri again, I don't want her to see you." Skylar nods at my very hard dick. "At least not like that. Why don't we go upstairs? I can call Wade from your room and ask him to bring it to us."

"Why do you have Wade's number?" I suck in a quick breath and hold up a hand. That came out a lot louder and harsher than it should have. "Sorry. I didn't mean to sound so…"

"Jealous?"

I nod.

"Rude?"

I frown.

"Obnoxious?"

"Hey. At least I didn't smear so much sunscreen on him that he looks like a greased pig."

Skylar's eyes light up as she laughs. "Greased pig?"

"If you tell Anna I said that, I'll deny it."

Sky pulls her phone out of her backpack and aims it at me. "Say it again."

I roll my eyes and open my door. "I'm not as stupid as I look."

Just the thought of Anna finding out I called her a greased pig deflates my stiffy. "Let's go see what Cherri and Wade are up to and take care of your sunburn."

Cherri, Wade and Derek are sitting around the kitchen table playing Hearts. Cherri tosses the Queen of Spades onto the pile. Derek groans and reaches for the cards. "Damn it, Cherri. That's twice you've stuck me with the bitch."

Cherri laughs then looks up and notices us. "Hey, Rowdy, Skylar. How're you feeling, hon?"

"I'm fine." Skylar smiles, but her voice is strained. "Nice to see you again, Cherri."

Cherri bites her lip. "I didn't sleep with him."

"What?"

Cherri nods at Wade, whose face is a dark shade of crimson. "We fell asleep on the couch, but we didn't have sex."

"Okay..." Skylar arches her eyebrows.

"I'm not the kind of girl that goes after another woman's man, even if she's got more than one."

"Wade's not my man."

"So...you don't care if we hook up?"

"Pff." Skylar flicks her wrist. "Have at it."

Cherri grins and stands up. Her chair scrapes against the cracked linoleum.

By now, Wade's face is almost purple. He scoops all the cards together and shuffles the deck. "We aren't finished with the game yet."

Derek laughs out loud and punches him in the shoulder. "Dude. What's wrong with you?"

Wade doesn't talk about religion. He drinks beer occasionally, but I've never seen him get drunk. He dates lots of different girls, but this is the first time he's ever brought one home. He hasn't gone to church since I've known him, but he wears a gold cross around his neck, keeps a Bible on his nightstand and a picture of Jesus hanging on the wall over his bed. I'm pretty sure it'd be hard for anyone, even me, to get laid with the Son of God watching.

I narrow my eyes at Derek then shift my attention back to Wade. "Skylar got sunburned this morning at the pool. Can we use some of that lavender and aloe stuff you mixed up for burns?"

"Sure." Wade jumps up then bolts down the hall to his room. Cherri's flip flops slap the bottom of her feet as she follows him.

Derek laughs again. "You'd think he'd be ready to punch that V card by now."

"Leave him alone." I keep my voice down, so Wade and Cherri can't hear me, but I make sure Derek understands I'm not going to stand by while he ridicules Wade for his beliefs. No matter how strange they are.

~***~

I wait outside my room, on the landing at the top of the stairs while Skylar changes clothes. She opens the door dressed in her running shorts and tank top but no bra. Her nipples harden under my gaze. Holy fuck.

She crosses her arms over her chest. "The worst of it's on my face."

"That makes sense." I squirt a little of the cloudy mixture in my palm then dab it on her nose with a fingertip. "We were in the water most of the time."

She closes her eyes and inhales deeply. Tears leak out of the corners of her eyes.

"I'm sorry. Maybe you better do it." I hold out the bottle of aloe and lavender.

"You're not hurting me. In fact, it feels wonderful. It's just the lavender smell. It reminds me of Aunt Lori. She used lavender oil straight out of the bottle whenever she burned herself."

"Which was pretty much every day." I breathe in and the sharp, sweet aroma takes me back, too.

Sky smiles and nods. "Did Boone keep her glass studio?"

"Boone kept everything." He locked off the master bedroom as well as the basement where Lori made intricate glass beads and tiny little dragon figurines she sold online.

"Aunt Lori was teaching me how to make beads before I had to leave. I wonder if Boone would mind if I used her studio."

"Boone's pretty touchy about his parents' stuff. Besides, I saw the beads you made." Lori gave them to me after Skylar disappeared. I still have them. They're in an old cigar box in my top drawer, along with Mom's wedding rings, half a dozen friendship bracelets Skylar made and every letter she ever sent me. "You should stick to photography."

"There's nothing wrong with those beads."

"They're lopsided with sharp, pointy ends that cut through even the toughest hemp."

She squints and cocks her head to the side. "How do you know?"

Shit. I tried to string three of them on a cord so I could wear them around my neck, but I don't want Skylar to know that.

"Answer me. How do you know my beads cut through hemp?"

I get up and fetch the frayed necklace out of my drawer then drop it into her open palm.

She presses the fingers of her other hand against her lips.

I want to tell her the stupid necklace doesn't mean anything to me. I want to say that I just never got around to throwing it away. The vulnerability in her eyes stops me. This...whatever this is between us...is hard for her, too. But she's not hiding her feelings from me. Skylar's already admitted she wants to revive what we once had. It'd be easier to resuscitate a five hundred pound heart attack victim, but damn it, I want to find what we lost, too. I want it so bad it hurts. I'm already in pain, there's no point trying to run away from it. Besides, only a coward would try to protect his heart by hurting someone else. Especially someone as honest, sensitive and trusting as Skylar.

"Can I have it?"

My mouth is suddenly so dry I can't swallow. It feels like I'm giving away a part of myself, but I just smile and nod.

She closes her fist over the misshapen beads and frayed string then presses it against her chest, over her heart. She sits perfectly still, clutching the simple necklace while I slick the tops of her shoulders with aloe and lavender. I recap the bottle then toss it onto my bed.

"What did you mean when you said that you didn't want to set me up for failure?" My face heats up. What the fuck? Am I actually blushing?

Skylar rolls one of the beads between her thumb and forefinger, studying it intently. "Do you remember some of the stuff we used to do?"

"Hiking, rock climbing, swimming, biking—"

"I mean the physical stuff. Making out."

"Yeah, I remember." We started out with closed-mouthed, dry kisses at the beginning of the summer but progressed to tonsil hockey and dry humping by the middle of July.

"We could do some of that."

"I'm afraid that would only frustrate us."

"You didn't always go home frustrated."

My damn ears are on fire. I used to come in my jeans when we were making out, but I always thought I'd managed to hide it from her. I even wore tighty whiteys under my boxers after it happened the first time. "You knew?"

"Boone told me."

"He what?" I'm going to fucking kill him.

"I thought I sucked at making out. We'd be going hot and heavy but then you'd stop and mumble some lame excuse about needing to go home and ditch me. I asked Boone for advice and once he was done laughing at me, he told me what was really going on."

"I have no idea how to respond to that."

"Don't be embarrassed. I was actually flattered that I could do that to you."

"I don't want to come in my pants."

"You could wear a condom."

"It's not about the mess. It's just lame."

"Oh." She ducks her head.

I grip her chin between my thumb and finger and make her look at me. "I think you misunderstood what I meant. I appreciate the offer, but what you're suggesting is a conditioning program for premature ejaculation."

She puckers her brow then chews on her lower lip for a second. "Is it better if I just...touch you?"

My dick twitches. It loves the idea of Skylar giving me a hand job. "Will you let me touch you, too?"

She shakes her head. "I'm not ready for that."

"Then neither am I."

Her eyebrows shoot up.

"This is a journey we need to take together. I'll wait until you're ready to come with me." *Literally.*

She angles her face towards me. I didn't shave this morning and I don't want to scratch her sunburned cheeks so I gently press my mouth against hers. The cut on my upper lip stings, but I barely feel it.

Chapter Seventeen

Skylar

Rowdy and I spend every free moment together, but it's not enough to satisfy me. I don't suppose anything less than twenty-four seven would be. But between teaching at Front Range, working part-time as a paramedic in the ER at Avista and his volunteer work with Boulder Mountain Rescue, Rowdy doesn't have much free time.

I'd join BMR but the sight of blood makes me sick and just the thought of a compound fracture makes me lightheaded so I'd only be helpful during the *search* part of any search and rescue mission. Plus, I don't think BMR would be too impressed with my reason for application essay. I doubt 'so I can spend more time with my boyfriend' is what they're looking for in potential recruits.

Old Blue's tires crunch on the driveway. I grab my purse and dart out the door. Rowdy doesn't have to work today, but I do.

My minimum wage job at Superior Pet Shop sucks. The uniforms are ugly. My boss is a dick. And I'm not allowed to work more than thirty-nine hours a week so I don't qualify for insurance. At least it's a job. And they claimed they'd work around my class schedule when classes start.

"Good morning, Sunshine." Rowdy hops out of his truck. He smiles at me, but it's strained.

Someone else is sitting in Old Blue. The sun glares off the windshield so I can't tell who it is until she scoots across the bench seat and adjusts the rearview mirror. Anna.

"What's she doing here?" I don't even try to keep my voice down.

"She needs a ride to work."

"We're supposed to go out for breakfast."

"Her car wouldn't start. What was I supposed to do? Leave her stranded?"

Yes. "Why couldn't Wade or Derek give her a ride?"

"Wade was already gone, and Derek has company."

"Fine." It's out of the way so we won't have time to go to the Walnut Cafe like we'd planned. "I guess we can grab something at Panera after you drop her off."

"I thought we could eat at The Garden Terrace Cafe."

"At the hospital? Why?"

"So Anna could join us."

I close my eyes and take a deep breath. I know damn well whose idea that was but if I throw a fit, I'll look like a jealous bitch. I clench my jaw so tight my molars ache. "If that's what you want."

"Sky, I know you don't like Anna, but she's trying really hard."

She's trying really hard to come between me and Rowdy. Every time we make plans, she finds a way to butt in.

"Please, just give her a chance. She doesn't have many friends. In fact, I'm her only friend."

"Do you ever ask yourself why?" The snarky retort slips out before I can engage the filter between my mouth and brain.

Rowdy pinches the bridge of his nose. "I know Anna's a little rough around the edges, but she's my sister."

"Stepsister." And she's not just rough around the edges. She's a raging bitch.

"I'm all she has."

"I'm sorry." Rowdy's compassion for stray animals and strange kids, like Boone, was one of the first things that drew me to him. Boone claimed he wouldn't have survived high school if Rowdy hadn't defended him against bullies. Anna's father was convicted of murder. That had to leave scars. That vile man left scars on Rowdy, too. Visible scars. But he only became more compassionate. I don't know what something like that would have done to me. I wish I could say that I'd have turned out like Rowdy, more determined to defend the oppressed, but there's a good chance I would have turned out just as warped and bitter as Anna. I slip a hand behind Rowdy's neck and pull him down for a kiss. "I'll try to be nice. For you."

He grabs my hips and pulls me closer.

Anna leans on the horn.

We jump apart like startled rabbits. I swear, I'm gonna kill that bitch.

Rowdy laughs. But makes up for it by smashing his mouth against mine in a kiss that turns my joints to jelly.

Anna lays on the horn again, but this time, we're both expecting it.

Rowdy whispers, "Let's give her something to honk about," then grabs my butt and lifts me off my feet.

I wrap my legs around his waist. We're just putting on a show to piss Anna off, but my body doesn't know that. Apparently, neither does Rowdy's. I feel every inch of him pressing against me. He kisses the tip of my nose then slides me down his body as he lowers me to the ground. I start to take a step back, but he grabs my hips and holds me in place. "Hang on a sec."

"Using me for a boner shield?" I can't resist teasing him.

"That was…" He closes his eyes then presses his forehead against mine.

"Freaking hot?"

He grins. "I was going to say unexpected, but yeah, definitely hot."

"Why was it unexpected?" I can't help but be a little hurt by his comment.

"I took pre-emptive measures in the shower this morning." He gives me a quick peck on the lips then releases me. "It didn't work."

"You good to go?" I glance at the front of his jeans.

"Yeah, but I won't be for long if you don't stop checking me out."

I jerk my eyes from the still obvious bulge in his pants to his face. "Sorry."

Rowdy laces his fingers through mine and leads me to his truck. He opens the driver's side door and frowns. "Scoot over, Anna."

She's still sitting in the middle of the bench seat. She narrows her eyes at me, but only for a second, then slides over to the passenger side. Did she honestly think I was going to let her sit in the middle next to Rowdy?

He wraps his fingers around my waist and lifts me into Old Blue. I scoot over just enough to allow him room to slide behind the wheel with the gear shift between my knees.

Anna plasters herself against the passenger door. "There's plenty of space. No need to crowd the driver."

Rowdy rests his hand on my leg and squeezes my knee. "I learned to drive with Skylar sitting right here."

The memory sends a rush of grief as well as nostalgia through my heart. Rowdy bought Old Blue the summer I turned fifteen before he got his license. Aunt Lori took us out to the back roads of Weld County and taught Rowdy how to drive. She also took us to Boulder and spent the day at the DMV so he could get his license.

"You stay right where you are." Rowdy lifts his hand to start the truck and get it in gear, but once we're on the highway, he puts it back on my leg, wrapping his fingers to the inside of my thigh.

A shiver of pleasure runs up my body as he traces the inseam of my jeans. He's closer to my knee than my crotch, but his touch, no matter how innocent, curls my toes. I told him I wanted to take things slow, and he's respected that, but I don't know how much longer I can hold out. I'm finding it harder and harder to obey my own rules. I think it might be time to remove a few boundaries. Maybe even tonight.

~***~

Breakfast was weird. Anna kept trying to dominate the conversation, talking about people and subjects I didn't know. But every time she did, Rowdy would interrupt her monologue with an explanation, obviously trying to include me. Hopefully he'll be a little less blind to her blatant manipulation in the future.

I watch the clock all day at work, even though I know it only makes time pass slower. I spot Old Blue in the parking lot as soon as I exit the store. Rowdy hops out then jogs across the parking lot to meet me. I grab his neck and pull his face down to mine. He smiles against my mouth then gives me a quick peck on the lips. "Missed me, huh?"

"As soon as I'm sure I won't get fired for asking, I'm going to try to get my schedule lined up with yours."

"We've got the rest of the day. What do you want to do?"

I want to go somewhere private and rip Rowdy's clothes off, but then he'd want to do the same to me. No getting naked until after dark. "Let's rent a movie and hang out at your place."

"It's a gorgeous day, cloudy and cool but no rain. Are you sure you want to waste it watching a movie?"

"I didn't say we had to watch it."

Rowdy tilts his head back and closes his eyes. "God, Skylar. Do you have any idea what you do to me?"

"We don't have to make out if you don't want to."

"I love making out with you." He slides his hand around my back and guides me to Old Blue. "Kissing you." He pins me against the passenger side door and brushes his lips against mine. "Touching you." He strokes my cheek with the back of his fingers. "Imagining all the secret things I want to do to you." He presses his body against mine and takes my mouth.

I don't just melt against him. I dissolve into him. Become a part of him. "Take me home. Now."

Rowdy keeps his hand on my thigh as he drives, only lifting it to shift. Neither of us speak. I'm fascinated by the rise and fall of his chest. His breathing is just as fast and ragged as mine. My heart falls when we turn the final corner and I see Anna's car parked in front of the house. "Crap."

"What's wrong?" Rowdy cuts the engine and frowns at me.

I nod at Anna's beat up Ford Mustang. "She'll figure out some way to interrupt us."

"She's not here. Remember? We gave her a ride to work because that piece of shit isn't running."

"Oh yeah." I wonder who's going to give her a ride home. I don't really care as long as it's not Rowdy.

He slides out of the truck then grabs behind my knees and pulls me to him. "Besides, I'm not going to let anyone interrupt us."

I wrap my legs around his waist, just like I did this morning, but instead of kissing me, Rowdy carries me up the stairs, two at a time. My heart bangs against the base of my throat as he lowers us both onto his bed. He tugs my hands off his neck then loosens my legs from around his waist. "Don't move."

I prop myself up on my elbows and watch as he strides across the room.

He locks the door then turns around and grins at me. "Like I said, no interruptions."

The bed creaks as he crawls on top of me, straddling my hips with his knees. He braces his hands on either side of my head, holding his weight off my body. "Same rules as before?"

We'd progressed to anything goes as long as it stayed above the waist and on top of clothes. "Not quite."

He arches an eyebrow.

"I'm not ready to have sex yet, but I want to take care of you."

"What do you mean?"

"You know how you said you took 'pre-emptive measures' in the shower this morning?"

"Yeah?" His cheeks flush. It's so freaking adorable.

"I want to do that for you."

"You want to give me a hand job?"

"Way to kill the mood, Romeo."

"This is too important to risk a major misunderstanding because you're too embarrassed to say what you mean." He straightens his arms, lifting his body into a pushup position. "Is that what you meant?"

I nod.

Rowdy's nostrils flare. "Ladies first."

"It won't work." Crap. I didn't want to get into this.

"What won't work?"

"I can't...you know." I roll my eyes.

"You don't think I can get you off?"

"I've never been able to reach that 'mystical' plateau."

"It's a cliff, not a plateau and I can definitely get you there. Whether or not you choose to jump is up to you."

"Whether or not you get me off has nothing to do with your sexual skills. If you turn this into a personal challenge, it'll just frustrate both of us."

"Is that what it was like with your ex? With Evan?"

"His name is Ethan, and it was an obsession for him."

"What an ass."

Ethan is actually a very sweet guy, but I'm pretty sure Rowdy doesn't need to hear that.

"Have you ever been able to get yourself off?"

My face blazes hotter than Redgarden Wall on an August afternoon. "No."

Rowdy kisses my forehead. "Let's not worry about reaching any destinations and just enjoy the ride." He lowers his body onto mine, but keeps the pressure light.

My hips rock forward instinctively. I know it's against the 'no dry humping' rule but I can't help myself.

Rowdy groans then slides lower, keeping the part of him I most desperately want out of reach. He kisses the swell of my breasts, through my shirt and bra, then sits back onto his knees. He reaches behind his head and grabs his shirt then pauses. "Is this okay?"

I slide my hands under his t-shirt and trace the dips and ridges of his sculpted abs. "Yes."

He pulls his shirt off in one fluid movement.

I run my hands over his chest, marveling at the smooth, silky feel of his caramel skin.

He tugs at the hem of my white blouse, pulling it out of the ugly black pants I have to wear to work.

"Wait."

Rowdy freezes. "I thought we agreed. Same rules for both of us."

"Just until dark, okay?"

"Why?"

My face burns. "No one's ever seen me naked before."

"Correct me if I'm wrong…but didn't we make love in the tree house four years ago?"

"Yes, but it was dark."

Rowdy climbs off my body then sits beside me on the bed.

I sit up and lace my fingers through his. "Please don't be mad at me."

He rubs circles on the back of my hand with his thumb. "I'm confused, not angry. Are you scarred or something?"

I nod. "Something."

"You've seen my back."

"I know." I saw the little round scars all over his back when we were kids, but he didn't tell me how he'd gotten them until our last summer together. I remember how hard it was for him to tell me. I also remember how much closer we became after his confession.

My hands tremble as I fumble with the top button of my blouse.

Rowdy slides his fingers under mine. He pauses halfway down and traces the top edge of my lacy, pink bra. "I like this color on you."

"Thanks." My voice is so breathy it's barely audible.

He finishes unbuttoning my shirt, but it only falls open a few inches. "God, Sky. You're so fucking beautiful."

"It's a birthmark."

"What?" He blinks.

"The thing I'm hiding." If the level of heat spreading across my face is any indication, I'm sure it's every bit as red as the stain on my back. "It's a birthmark."

His gaze shifts to my right temple where the tip of my eyebrow points to a tiny brown spot.

"No. Not like that. It's huge and dark red and—"

"And it doesn't fucking matter."

"I've had laser treatments, but nothing ever gets rid of it completely and it always comes back."

"I've seen port wine birthmarks before. It's nothing to be ashamed of, Skylar. But if you don't want me to see it, I won't look, okay? Where is it?"

"On my back."

The corners of his mouth lift in a gentle smile. He runs his fingers along the edges of my blouse, opening it wider. "I promise not to look at your back."

I shiver under the intensity of his gaze. My birthmark isn't my only insecurity. I have no idea how I compare with all the other girls Rowdy's been with. If Cherri's body is any indication of what Rowdy likes, I definitely don't stack up. And I know I don't have anywhere near the experience she does.

Rowdy cradles my shoulders with one arm and places his other hand in the middle of my chest. "Lie down."

I let him guide my head to his pillow.

He lies down beside me then slides one knee between my legs and peppers my face with kisses.

I whimper like a helpless kitten when he moves lower, blazing a trail of sparks down my throat.

He palms my breast then sucks my other lace-covered nipple into his mouth.

My back arches as I cry out.

He kisses the peak then lifts his head and gazes into my eyes. He slips a finger behind the front clasp of my bra. "May I?"

Blood rushes behind my ears. I nod.

Rowdy narrows his eyes. "Say it."

"Say what?"

"Tell me what you want, Skylar."

This is so different from the way he used to be. "I want you to unfasten my bra."

He pinches the clasp between his thumb and forefinger. "And then what?"

"Are you going to make me spell it out?"

"It's the only way I'll know for sure what you want."

I squeeze my eyes shut.

"Open your eyes, Sky, and tell me what you want."

My eyes fly open. "I want you to take off my bra and suck my nipples."

Rowdy's pupils dilate, swallowing his pale blue irises. He drops his gaze to the center of my chest and pops the clasp. My bra falls open, but still covers me. Rowdy lowers his head and pushes it out of the way with his nose, nuzzling and licking his way across my breast. I lift my shoulder, urging him to take my nipple in his mouth.

He smiles against my skin. "Patience, Sky. Enjoy the ride, remember?"

I fall back against the pillow.

Rowdy kisses the tip then makes his way across my chest to my other breast.

I'm a whimpering, writhing mess. "Please, Rowdy."

He swirls his tongue around my nipple before pulling it into his mouth. He continues to lick and flick the hardened bud as he sucks.

Every muscle in my body tenses as a pleasurable ache builds deep inside me.

Rowdy palms my other breast, teasing the nipple with his thumb.

I weave my fingers through his hair, holding him against me.

He slides his hand down my side, slowly, as if he's counting each rib, then dips his fingers into the waistband of my pants.

My abs contract, giving him more space, inviting him, begging him to touch me.

He pauses and lifts his head again. "Is this okay?"

I get a glimpse of the old Rowdy. "Yes."

He narrows his eyes. "Are you sure?"

"Please, Rowdy." This time I don't wait for his demand for me to tell him exactly what I want. "Touch me."

He groans, so low and deep his chest vibrates against my stomach. The sound is primitive and possessive. He turns his hand so the backs of his fingers graze my skin then slides to the front of my pants. He unfastens the button with his thumb then teases the zipper open.

I tremble with the effort of holding still.

Rowdy turns his hand over again. His calloused palm rough on my skin. "If you want me to stop, tell me now."

"No. Don't stop. Please, don't stop."

He claims my mouth with his then slides his hand lower. Inch by agonizing inch. The anticipation is killing me. My thighs tremble. His fingers trace the waistband of my panties. This is much further than we've gone since I came back.

"Please, Rowdy."

He slides his hand lower. There's nothing but a gauzy patch of lace separating us. He interrupts the kiss. "Fuck. You're so wet."

I close my eyes, embarrassed by my overeager body. "I'm sorry."

"Oh, Sky." Rowdy actually laughs at me. But then he slides his hand under the lace to my bare skin. "That's a good thing. A very good thing."

I grab his hair and tug, bringing his face to mine.

He gives me a peck on the lips. "Last chance. Tell me to stop."

I shake my head.

Rowdy watches my eyes as he slips a finger inside me. "God, Skylar. You're so fucking tight. If I hadn't already popped your cherry, I'd swear you were a virgin."

I move my hands to his shoulders and cling to him as my back arches off the bed. He's done this to me before, when we were teenagers. It felt good then but nothing like this.

Something indescribable is building inside me, coiling tighter, like an overwound spring.

I'm not a virgin, so what the hell am I waiting for? We both want this. *Need* this. "I want you, Rowdy."

"I'm right here, babe."

"Inside me."

He curls his finger and presses down with his palm.

I cry out his name and buck against his hand.

"Open your eyes, Skylar. Look at me." His voice is rough, deep, commanding.

I obey. I couldn't refuse even if I wanted to.

I'm so focused on his beautiful face and the sensations he's creating that I'm barely aware of his other hand on my breast. Until he pinches my nipple.

The spring inside me explodes. I lose control of my mind as well as my body. I keep my gaze locked on his ice-blue eyes as I fly apart. All I see, all I feel, all I know…is Rowdy.

Chapter Eighteen

Rowdy

I've gotten girls off with nothing but my hand before. I've heard them scream my name as I pound into them. I've even had a few simultaneous orgasms, but nothing I've ever experienced in my entire life can compare with watching Skylar come for the first time.

I feel a little guilty for being so demanding with her, but I knew she was close. And I wanted her to see my face as she came. I want her to remember this moment for the rest of her life. And I want to be there every time she comes.

She looks at me with such wonder it steals my breath. "Oh my god. So that's what all the fuss is about."

I kiss her forehead then slide my hand to her stomach.

Her eyes sparkle. "That was…just…wow."

I smile at her. "I'm glad you enjoyed it."

She rolls onto her side and drapes a leg over me. Her thigh rubs against my throbbing cock.

I bite back a groan and grab her knee. "Easy, there."

She runs her hand over my abs, back and forth, drifting lower each time.

My dick gets even harder. I can tell that Skylar feels it by the way her eyes widen.

She slides her leg out of the way and places her hand over my zipper.

It takes every bit of self-control I have to keep from thrusting against her palm. I grab her wrist. "Don't."

She blinks then frowns at me.

I weave my fingers through hers then press her hand over my heart. "You're still on a post-orgasmic high. I don't want you to do anything you'll regret once you come down."

"Like you already pointed out, I'm not a virgin."

"That's not a recent development. You weren't ready for sex an hour ago."

"I didn't know what I was missing an hour ago." She sits up and straddles my thighs. Her shirt and bra hang open and loose from her shoulders, but still cover her breasts.

I lace my fingers behind my head to keep my hands off her.

"At least let me do for you what you just did for me." She unbuttons my jeans.

I lift my shoulders off the bed and reach for her wayward hands. "You don't owe me anything."

"I let you touch me, so you have to let me touch you. It's only fair."

My heart's trying to jump out of my fucking chest. "I don't want to be unfair."

Her nostrils flare as she bites her lip. She drops her gaze to my fly and unzips my jeans.

I lie back on the pillow, but keep my head lifted so I can watch her face.

She slips her fingers under the waistband of my boxer briefs then lifts them away from my body and peeks inside. Her lips part as her eyes widen. "Oh, my."

My abs contract as I try to keep from laughing. "Bigger than you remember?"

"This is the first time I've seen a real penis."

There's no way I can keep from laughing out loud at that. "As opposed to what? A fake one?"

"It was always dark when we made out."

"What about Evan?"

She sits back and folds her arms over her chest. "His name's Ethan."

I want to kick my own ass for bringing up her ex, but it's too late to take it back.

"I never saw his either." Her gaze drops back to my cock. The tip is poking out of my waistband. "I didn't want to."

"Are you sure you want to do this?"

She bites her lip again and nods.

I lift my hips and slide my jeans and boxer briefs down past my ass.

Skylar tugs the front down and gasps when my cock springs free. "Was it that big last time?"

"I wasn't quite eighteen, so probably not."

She scoots off the bed and pulls my pants the rest of the way down my legs. She frowns when they get caught around the tops of my running shoes. I don't exactly need to take my shoes off for a hand job, but if Skylar wants me naked, then by god I'm getting naked. I use my toes to push my shoes off my heels then kick out of my jeans.

Skylar crawls back onto the bed and straddles my thighs.

I twist to the side and pull a condom out of my bedside drawer.

Her eyes widen again.

"It's just to contain the mess."

Her chest rises and falls as she sighs with obvious relief. But then she frowns.

"I don't want to."

I smile, refusing to let her see my disappointment. "Okay."

"I want to watch."

"Holy fuck, Sky." I could come just listening to her talk.

"Please?"

"Have you ever given anyone a hand job before?" *Please say no.*

She shakes her head.

"When I come, it's going to be like a goddamn geyser. You'll probably get jizz all over you."

She scoots off the bed.

I sit up and reach for my jeans on the floor.

"No." Skylar steps on them. A pink stain spreads across her cheeks, mottling her neck and upper chest as she shrugs out of her shirt and bra. She moves her hands to the sides of her pants and slides them slowly down her legs, leaving her in nothing but a tiny triangle of black lace.

"What are you doing?" My voice cracks.

"I don't want to get your…stuff on my clothes."

"You aren't worried about STDs?"

Her eyes widen. "Should I be?"

"Always. But I'm clean. I get tested all the time because of my job and I'm very careful."

She climbs back onto my thighs then strokes me with a fingertip.

"Holy fuck."

"Am I doing it right?"

"Here." I take her hand and wrap her fingers around my shaft then guide her in a slow rhythm. "Like this."

She's a fast learner. I let go and let her take over.

She sucks her lower lip into her mouth and stares at my cock like it's the most amazing thing she's ever seen.

Watching her watch me takes me to the edge, but I can't take my eyes off her face. I use every other trick I know to make it last. But when my balls tighten, I grab her shoulders and push her back, out of the line of fire.

~***~

Sky watches as I clean my chest off with a handful of tissues. It's awkward but telling her not to look would be even more embarrassing. For both of us. I toss the mess in the trash next to my bed then pull her down to lie beside me, tucking her head into the hollow of my shoulder. "So, what do you want to do now?"

"Can we do it again?"

"I'm not a teenager anymore. I need a little time to recover."

"How much time?"

I can't keep from grinning at her eagerness. "Maybe an hour or two."

"Do you think I'm weird?"

"For what? Enjoying the show?"

She nods.

"I nearly blew my load watching you come. So no, I don't think you're weird." I tuck a curl behind her ear.

She spreads her fingers out and presses her palm against my heart. "I feel really close to you right now."

"Sex intensifies everything." God. I sound like a fucking girl.

She traces a circle around my nipple. I'm nowhere near ready for another go, but my dick still twitches.

"Do you feel closer to everyone that gets you off?"

"Honestly? I usually can't stand to even look at a girl afterwards."

Her body stiffens.

"You're different, Skylar. This is different." I pick up her hand and kiss her palm. "You were right when you accused me of using women to blow off steam. I always made it clear I didn't want anything but sex. I can't respect anyone that's okay with that."

She lifts her head up off my shoulder and frowns at me. "That seems a tad bit hypocritical."

"I was just as disgusted with myself as I was with them." I press her head back down onto my chest. "But this...this makes me feel as if I've been redeemed."

She relaxes and snuggles closer, nuzzling my neck with her nose. "In an hour or two. Whenever you're ready. I want to make love."

I'll be damned if my dick isn't already at half mast. "Are you sure?"

She props herself up on an elbow and gazes into my eyes. "I've never been more sure about anything."

I grab her ass and pull her closer, pressing my growing erection against her leg.

Her eyes widen. "You said you couldn't do it again right away."

"I was wrong." This is actually perfect. I'll be able to last a lot longer. I ordinarily have great control, but there's nothing ordinary about my response to Skylar. I grab the condom we didn't use before and tear it open. Skylar tilts her head and watches me put it on. She's definitely getting an education today. Knowing that she's never seen this before makes me harder. But if I've had enough time to recover from my orgasm, she's had more than enough time to come down from hers. I've never done a double session before. The only time I ever wanted to was the first time, with Sky, but she was too sore. I wonder if I can get her off again? Should I even try? If I can't, will she get frustrated? I don't want to tarnish the experience of her first orgasm with a failed attempt for another.

Skylar palms my cheeks and turns my face towards hers. "Stop over thinking everything and just kiss me."

I chuckle quietly. "How is it possible that you still know me so well?"

"Because what's in there," she taps my forehead then presses a hand over my heart, "can't change what's in here. You're still the same sweet boy I fell in love with."

If only that were true. I roll her onto her back then kiss her so she can't see the pain in my eyes.

She hooks a heel behind my knee and squirms her way beneath me.

"Slow down, babe. We've got all night."

"I've waited so long for this."

I feel like I've waited my whole damn life for this. But I'm not going to let her rush it. I kiss a trail down her throat, across the swell of her breast.

She arches her back and tangles her fingers in my hair, trying to guide my mouth to her nipple.

I'd like to tease her a little longer, work her up a bit, but when she whimpers and whispers, "please," I can't do anything but obey.

I could suck on her breasts all afternoon, but her scent is calling to me, urging me lower. I've had more blow jobs than I can count, but I've never gone down on anyone. I've never wanted to. I want to now. Desperately. I release her nipple and kiss a trail down the center of her body, pausing to dip my tongue into her belly button.

She trembles.

I move lower. My heart pounds so wildly I'm afraid it's going to burst.

"What are you doing?" Skylar's body tenses as she tries to sit up.

I gently push her back down onto the bed then kiss her through the lace of her panties.

She bucks her hips, smashing into my face.

I pin her legs to the mattress with the weight of my body and do it again.

"Oh, god, Rowdy!"

I hook my thumbs in the bands of lace holding her panties in place and lift my chest. "Can I take these off?"

She nods and lifts her hips.

I slide them down her long, tanned legs then drop them on the floor beside the bed. She's bare except for a neatly trimmed landing strip of mahogany curls. I glance up and find her watching me with hooded eyes. Her chest rises and falls with each shallow, rapid breath. I maintain eye contact as I taste her for the first time.

Skylar's getting close again. I don't want this to end, but I want her satisfied even more. My 'red alert' ringtone blares out of my phone. Skylar jumps, but I don't even pause. She goes limp under me.

"You better get that." She recognizes the BMR ringtone.

I groan, making her twitch. I don't have to go on every call. There're over sixty volunteers in our organization but I'll feel like a douche if I don't at least find out what the emergency is. I grab my phone and read the text. My frown turns into a grin. "It's just a pick off."

"You're not going?"

I shake my head. "Most of the group is off work by now. There'll be plenty of responders and the caller was very specific about the climber's location. It's just a grab and go. Besides, I'm sort of busy."

Skylar returns my smile then sinks back into the pillow.

Bang, bang, bang. Sky and I both flinch.

"Rowdy, open up!" It's Anna. She sounds frantic.

"What's wrong?"

"Didn't you get the call?"

"I'm not going."

Bang. Anna pounds the door again. "You have to!"

"Goddammit, Anna. It's just a pick off. You and Wade could do it your sleep."

"I need a ride."

What the fuck? "Then ask Wade."

"He left already."

Skylar sits up. "It's okay. I'll go with you. And when you're done, we can come back and finish this."

"You wanna spend the night?"

Skylar grins. "It'll be just like when we were kids."

"No, it won't." I grab her and pull her against me. "It'll be so much better."

Anna continues to bang on the door as we get dressed.

"Knock it off, Anna. We're coming." *I wish.* I glance over my shoulder to be sure Skylar is ready before opening the door.

Anna pushes past me and glares at Skylar. "What's *she* doing here?"

"What the fuck is your problem?"

"It's bad enough you don't have time for your real friends anymore, but now you're letting her interfere with your duty."

A twinge of guilt needles me. The only thing that normally keeps me from responding to a call is alcohol. Or exhaustion. I take Skylar's hand. "Do you need to grab anything from Boone's house?"

"She can't go with us on a call." Anna wrinkles her nose, as if the idea itself smells bad.

"Knock it off, Anna."

"She's not a member of the team."

"She's a trainee."

"I am?" Skylar arches her eyebrows.

I grin at her and grab my keys. "You are tonight."

Anna's face darkens. "Has she filled out the paperwork? Passed her physical?"

I'm usually extremely patient with Anna, more so than anyone else, but she's seriously starting to piss me off. "She's only observing tonight."

"Doesn't matter. No one is allowed to go on missions until they're authorized."

"I'm not going without her."

"But..." Anna's mouth falls open. "You have to."

"No. I don't." I slide my arm around Skylar's back, cupping the dip of her waist. Her body is rigid. Every muscle tense. I pull her against me and smile when she relaxes.

Anna presses her lips into a thin, hard line. She huffs and rolls her eyes. "Fine. I guess she can come."

I kiss Skylar's neck, just below her ear and whisper, "Over and over again."

She grins and blushes.

There's no way Anna heard me, but she glares at me as if she did.

Chapter Nineteen

Skylar

I dig my phone out before getting into Old Blue. The protective silicone case makes it stick to everything. Pulling it out and putting it back in is a real chore. I have to cock my hip and straighten my leg to pry it loose. Something I can't do sitting down. I wait for Anna to get in and shut the door, then call Boone. He answers on the first ring.

"Hey, Skylar. What's up?"

"I just wanted to let you know I'm spending the night with Rowdy so don't wait up for me."

He sighs into the phone. *"Seems like things are moving sort of fast. Are you sure you're ready for this?"*

"We have a lot of history together so, no, we aren't moving too fast. And yes, I'm definitely ready for this."

"Why are you repeating everything I say? Is Anna there?"

"Anna, Rowdy and I are on our way to Eldo to pick off a stranded climber. I'll talk to you later."

"Be careful about antagonizing Anna. She fights dirty."

"Sounds like you have experience with that. Care to fill me in?"

"Just be careful, okay?"

"Me? Careful? You know I'm an adrenaline junkie."

Anna doesn't even wait for me to end the call before she leans across me and starts yelling at Rowdy. "Did you hear her? She's got no business going with us. She's a hazard to herself and everyone else."

Rowdy slams on the brakes then pulls off the road. "Goddammit, Anna, Skylar isn't going to hurt me again. She left because her mom's boyfriend went into witness protection. She didn't have a choice. We're together again and nothing's going to change that so you better get used to it."

If I weren't so thrilled about Rowdy's declaration, I'd be pissed off at him for telling Anna about WITSEC. But nothing can dim the joy I feel from hearing him say we're together and we're going to stay that way.

"But..." Anna's face goes from crimson to chalky white. Her chin trembles. She sounds like a little girl. "I don't like her."

"You don't have to like her, but if you want to stay friends with me, you have to be nice. I won't tolerate anyone abusing my girl."

Anna turns her face to the window. She swipes at her cheeks every few seconds. I actually feel sorry for her. Maybe once she gets used to the idea that Rowdy and I are a package deal, we can be friends. I glance at her reflection in the glass. She glares at me with pure hatred.

Rowdy starts humming some tune I don't recognize.

"Is that a song you wrote?"

"Yeah." He slides his hand a little higher up my leg. Nothing indecent, but it's enough to elicit a snort of disgust from Anna.

I want to ask Rowdy if the song is one he wrote for me, but I don't want to rub salt in Anna's wounds. I feel bad for calling Boone instead of texting him, now. I'd like to believe my only motivation was to get Anna to accept the fact that Rowdy and I are together. But I'd be lying. I wanted to hurt her. I don't like what that says about me. We'll never be friends, but I don't have to be a vindictive bitch.

~***~

We're among the first to arrive at the parking lot where everyone is meeting. Rowdy introduces me to an older guy, Mike Haskell, and tells him I'm thinking about joining BMR.

Mike frowns as he shakes my hand. "You can't participate in the rescue, understand?"

"Yes, sir."

"And stay out of the way."

Anna smirks at me. I refuse to let her bait me. Her grin fades when Mike assigns her to group four and puts Wade in charge.

She pushes her lower lip out in a pout. "I want to be in group one."

No surprise there. Rowdy's in charge of that one.

The wrinkles around Mike's eyes deepen. "Maybe you should sit this one out."

Anna's lips part into an 'O' but she recovers quickly. "Fine. I'll go with Wade."

I hang out near the BMR van so I can eavesdrop on the radio chatter. Everyone expects this rescue to be quick and easy. Someone mentions heading to The Dark Horse afterwards. I recognize Rowdy's voice through the static.

"Base, this is Rowdy. We're unable to acquire a visual of the victim."

Mike scowls. "What's your location?"

"Kloof Alcove. No one is on Half and Half."

"Check nearby routes."

"We did. We also interviewed several climbers. No one is aware of anyone requiring assistance."

Mike sighs. "Check out West Redgarden Wall."

The excited chatter dies out. Mike recalls everyone to base. Wade's group is one of the first to return.

Mike rubs the back of his neck as he talks to Wade. "I'm ninety-nine percent certain this is a prank call."

"What makes you think that?"

"Several things. The woman that called in the report hung up immediately after relaying the information. Emergency services location technology put her in the town of Eldorado Springs, not inside the park when she made the call. She didn't answer when dispatch called back. There's no voice mail and no name or address associated with the number."

Wade says, "Sounds like she used a burner phone."

Anna continues to glare at me as she leans against the van, arms crossed over her chest. But at least she's quiet.

"I hate wasting resources on a false alarm, but we need to keep searching until we're sure." Mike shifts his gaze from Wade to me. "Do you want to help with the ground search?"

"She's not a member!" Anna's outburst draws everyone's attention.

You don't have to be a member to participate in a ground search and she knows it. "I'd love to help."

"She's a liability." Anna continues to talk about me as if I'm not standing right in front of her. "She had to be rescued off The Bastille last month."

"I'm well aware of Skylar's mountaineering abilities as well as her tendency to push the envelope."

My cheeks heat up as I realize Rowdy must have been talking about me to Mike.

"She has asthma."

I take a slow, deep breath to calm my temper as well as demonstrate my breathing ability. "It's under control and I have an inhaler. And I promise I'll follow Wade's instructions to the letter."

"See that you do."

Anna mutters to herself as we follow Wade up the West Ridge Trail. I'm starting to feel less pity for her.

We search for hours, talking to everyone we meet. No one's seen or heard about a stranded climber. It's getting dark.

Anna jogs up to Wade then taps his shoulder. "Hey, I need to make a pit stop."

Wade nods. "Take Skylar."

I have to pee so bad my kidneys hurt but I didn't say anything because Anna and I are the only women in the group and BMR is a stickler for rules. The 'no one goes alone' rule means there's no getting out of it. I wait for the main group to disappear around a corner then step off the trail.

Anna grabs my arm. "Where do you think you're going?"

"To find a bush?"

"The ranger's station is less than half a mile from here."

"That's a huge waste of time."

"I need to do more than just pee so I'm going to the ranger station where there's toilet paper."

"TMI."

She rolls her eyes. "I suppose you never shit."

My bathroom habits are none of her business. I grit my teeth. "Fine, we can go to the ranger's station."

The tension builds as we hike. After about five minutes, Anna breaks the angry silence. "We need to talk."

"About what?"

"About how you're ruining Rowdy's life."

Aw crap, here we go again. "I'm not ruining his life. He's happy."

"His drinking's out of control, he's neglecting his duties and all he wants to do is spend time with you. You're an addiction."

"He doesn't drink any more than the rest of the guys. He's not neglecting his duties and I'm just as addicted to him as he is to me. It's not a problem."

"If you care about him at all, you'll leave him alone."

A couple of hikers pause on the trail.

"Can we talk about this later?"

Anna ignores me and talks louder. "You didn't see him after you left. He was devastated. If I hadn't been there to pick up the pieces, he would have killed himself."

The hikers don't even try to hide the fact that they're listening.

"He'd never do that."

Anna's shouting now. "You took his virginity the night his mother died then disappeared without a trace."

Naked Edge

Oh my god. Really? I can't believe Rowdy told her about our first time. I glare at the hikers, two women. "Do you mind? This is a private conversation."

They turn their backs and continue down the trail. One of them looks over her shoulder. "I'm pretty sure the entire canyon can hear your private conversation."

I rub my temples, but it doesn't alleviate the building pressure.

Anna's chest heaves with every breath. Her eyes are wild and wide. "I've invested too much into my relationship with Rowdy to just let you steal him away from me."

"Anna, listen to me. Rowdy cares about you. He might even love you, but as a sister, not romantically."

She moves closer, invading my personal space. "If you hadn't come back, we'd be together by now."

I take a step back, putting me closer to the edge of the narrow trail.

"He's mine!" Anna shoves me. Hard.

I windmill my arms, trying to regain my balance. It doesn't work. Pain explodes across my ribs as I bounce off a boulder. I try to relax as I tumble down the talus field like a rag doll. It's supposed to hurt less if you don't tense up. I don't think it's working. At least I'm wearing a helmet. I grab at anything I can as I roll down the rocky slope, tearing my nails, shredding my palms, but nothing I do slows my deadly descent.

I finally stop when I slam against a tree but the world continues to spin. A red tail hawk circles above me. I try to inventory my injuries without actually looking at them but everything hurts.

Loose rocks, some of them as big as my fist, continue to rain down on me. It should have stopped by now.

The scrape of boots on gravel fills me with relief. Someone's coming. But they should know better than to descend right on top of me. Are they trying to trigger a landslide? Whoever it is nudges my helmet with their foot. What the hell? "Don't."

"So, you're alive. Too bad."

Anna.

"Barely, no thanks to you."

She kicks me again. Every last shred of sympathy I had for her disappears.

She squats down beside me and cocks her head to the side. "Hmm...what to do, what to do?"

"Call for help, you crazy bitch. I can't walk out of here on my own."

"I don't think so." She unclips her multitool knife.

Fear replaces anger. "What are you doing?"

She flicks the blade open then waves it back and forth in front of my face. "I told you to leave Rowdy alone, but you wouldn't listen."

I don't swear very often but this is definitely an 'oh fuck' situation. "Rowdy will hate you if you kill me."

"Perhaps."

I try to claw my way into a sitting position, but I'm too weak. My vision turns grey around the edges. I try to remain conscious. And fail.

When the fog clears, the rough bark of the lodgepole pine is pressing against my back. I'm sitting up. Someone's holding my hand. I open my eyes. It's Anna. Thank god she came to her senses.

She squeezes my hand tighter. She's helping me hold something. I look down. My fingers are wrapped around her knife. Is she trying to stage a suicide? "No one will believe I killed myself."

"Maybe not. But they *will* believe you tried to kill me." She slowly draws the serrated blade across her forehead then lets go of my hand.

I drop the knife. "Oh my god! You really are crazy."

She leans over me and lets her blood pour onto the front of my shirt. "When Rowdy sees what you've done to me, he'll comfort me. Just like I comforted him. It'll be just like it was before you came back." Spit flies out of her mouth as she yells at me. "You ruined everything!"

I hope someone hears her ranting before she changes her mind and decides to just kill me. "You're right. Go find Rowdy and tell him what happened."

"You don't think he'll believe me." Anna narrows her eyes then jumps to her feet. She points at me. "You brainwashed him."

She paces back and forth, rubbing her hands as if she's washing them. "I need more time. I have to get him out from under your spell. Once I do, he'll see what a monster you are. He'll be glad I saved him."

"That's right." My vision is swimming again. "Go find Rowdy. Save him from me."

Anna pokes a stick through the carabiner attached to her knife and drops it into her pack without touching it. She removes my helmet. A breeze ruffles my hair. It feels good.

"Thanks." I must be going into shock. Why else would I thank her for anything?

Anna grins as she picks a rock up off the ground and holds it over my head. "Any time."

Chapter Twenty

Rowdy

The easy pickoff turns into an all out search.

We scour all the trails and interview climbers at the base of every cliff in the park, but no one knows anything about a stranded climber. Eldo is a popular place and any sort of rescue drama always draws a crowd. The fact that not a single person knows anything is highly suspicious.

Mike calls off the search when the last trail is crossed off the map. It's too dangerous to search off-trail in the dark when we don't even know if there's anyone out there. Everyone knows the park closes at dusk. Usually, if a climber is more than a few hours late and can't be reached, someone calls it in. But not every dickwad with a rope is smart enough to tell someone they're going climbing or when to expect them back.

It only takes half an hour for most of the volunteers to meet up in the parking lot. Skylar isn't one of them. I grab Wade. "Skylar was assigned to your group. Where is she?"

"She isn't here?"

"If she was, would I be asking?"

"She and Anna fell back to take a bathroom break."

My stomach drops. "When was that?"

"About two and a half hours ago."

"Shit." Sweat beads on my forehead. I feel a little guilty for not noticing that Anna's not back either. "And you weren't worried when they didn't show up?"

"Of course I was. I called Anna. She told me they decided to go to the ranger's station so they could use the facilities there. By then, we'd reached the fork where Eldo branches off from West Ridge. It was getting dark so I told her to just go back to base."

I pull my cell out and call Skylar. It goes straight to voice mail. The same thing happens when I call Anna. I run over to Mike. "Did Skylar or Anna check in yet."

"No."

"Did Anna call after splitting off from Wade's group?" My voice cracks.

Mike presses his lips together and shakes his head. "Wade. Get over here."

Wade explains the situation to the few members of the group still on site while I pace.

Mike authorizes us to search the trail between base and the girls' last known position. "Follow protocol. Stay on the trail. If you find something, mark it and call it in."

I don't care if it breaks the rules. I don't even care whether or not it's safe. I'm not leaving without Skylar and Anna.

Wade, Derek and I gear up again and head back into the canyon. The girls have to be somewhere between here and the fork in the trail. It's only about a quarter mile, but it's still a lot of ground to cover, especially in the dark. Even more so if they left the trail. My anxiety rises with every step I take. If we don't find them before we reach the fork...

I can't afford to think about that. We call their names every few seconds. But no one answers.

Chapter Twenty-One

Skylar

I wake up with the worst headache I've ever had. It's getting worse by the second. The acrid stench of vomit burns my nose. I gag. Pain explodes across my left side. I clutch it instinctively. *Shit.* That hurts. Everything hurts. My crotch and thighs are cold and damp. Did I piss myself? I try to open my eyes but it feels as if they're glued shut. I rub them with the base of my thumbs. The left half of my face is caked with dried mud. What happened? I'm on my side, wrapped around something hard and rough. It's a tree. God, my head hurts. I pry my eyelids apart, but I can barely see. It's dark. Where am I? The last thing I remember was lying in Rowdy's bed. We were about to make love when we were interrupted by a phone call. I try to sit up, but change my mind when a wave of nausea crashes over me. Bits and pieces of the past few hours float through my mind. Anna pounding on Rowdy's door... Sitting in Rowdy's truck... The ranger at the entrance gate of Eldorado State Park waving us through. That's it. I'm in Eldo Canyon. But it's dark. The park closes at sunset. I'm alone. And hurt. Where's Rowdy? I lick my parched lips and call his name. It's barely a whisper.

"Sky-lar." Someone calls my name, dragging it out.

It's hard to judge distances in the canyon, but it sounds as if they're a long way away.

"Ann-uh."

"Here." I try to answer. But it comes out as a barely audible croak. Every breath I take hurts. I can't suck in enough air to speak above a whisper. I'm so thirsty. How long have I been out here? The air is chilly, but the rocks are still warm.

They keep calling and I keep trying to answer. It sounds like they're getting further away. Half a dozen beams of light flicker in and out of my line of vision. They're so far above me. And they're definitely moving in the wrong direction.

"Sky-lar." That's Rowdy's voice.

"Over here." No way did he hear that. I know it's going to hurt, but I'm desperate. I pant three times then suck in a giant breath of air and scream.

"Skylar! Where are you?"

"Here." I'm whispering again. I'm in so much pain. I don't know if I can do it again.

"Sky! Keep talking so I can find you."

I whimper. Knowing exactly how much it's going to hurt makes it so much harder. I think of Rowdy out there, searching for me and fill my lungs again. This time I'm prepared and yell his name instead of just screaming like a wounded animal.

The lights are right above me. I must have passed out. They sweep over me then one by one converge on my face. I slam my eyes shut, but the beams are so bright it doesn't help very much.

"Hang on, babe. I'm coming." Rowdy calls out. "On belay?"

Someone answers, "Belay on."

"I'm coming, Sky. Do *not* move." One light continues to shine on my chest while half a dozen spotlight Rowdy's boots.

Oh. He's rappelling down to me. That can't be good. Did I deck off a wall? I don't have a helmet on and I never climb without one. I feel around my waist and thighs. No harness.

It only takes Rowdy a few minutes to reach me. I want to hug him so bad it hurts, but I can't sit up.

"Don't move." He pauses. "I need a litter, collar and beanbag."

It takes a second for me to realize he's talking over his radio.

"I need you to stay still while I check you out."

"You can't check me out." I gesture at the lights shining on my body. "People are watching."

Rowdy gives me a fleeting, closed lip smile. "I'm going to shine a light in your eyes. Try not to squint."

"What happened?"

"You fell." Rowdy runs his fingers over my skull. He's being extremely gentle, but it still hurts.

"Were we climbing?" We'd been planning to climb The Naked Edge together for awhile.

"No. What's your name?"

"You don't know my name?"

"Yes, babe, I know your name. I just need to know if *you* do."

"Do I have a concussion?"

"That's what I'm trying to find out."

"My name is Skylar."

"Good girl." I can't see him with that damn light in my eyes but I can hear the smile in his voice. I'm glad I made him happy.

"I know your name, too, Cowboy."

"Try again."

I was hoping for a laugh. I love it when he laughs. Maybe he doesn't want me to use his nickname. "Rowdy Daletzki."

"How old are you, Skylar?"

"Twenty."

"What day is it?"

"Crap." My voice trembles. "I can't remember."

"That's okay. I don't know what day it is half the time either. Do you remember what you had for breakfast?"

"Cheerios?" Boone and I only have one kind of cereal, so if I ate breakfast, that's what it would be.

"You don't remember going out for breakfast?"

"Oh, wait." I do remember. "We were supposed to go to The Walnut Cafe, but Anna needed a ride to work."

"That's right." Rowdy's hands move lower. His headlamp follows, giving my throbbing eyes a break. He traces my collar bones then moves to my ribs.

I yelp, which only makes the pain worse.

"Sorry." Rowdy holds his gloved hands above my stomach. "I need to palpate your abdomen."

"Palpate's such a weird word."

"It's a medical term that means—"

"Poke and prod everything that hurts."

"Pretty much." Rowdy smiles, but it's fleeting. "Tell me if you feel any discomfort."

"I hurt all over but my head and my ribs are killing me."

He lifts the hem of my shirt and peeks under it. "I'm going to unbutton your shirt."

"Why?"

"There's a lot of dried blood. I need to know where it came from."

His headlamp sweeps over my chest without pausing on my boobs. I'm impressed.

"You're bruised, but I can't find a single cut except for the one on the side of your head. And that flowed over your shoulder onto your back." Rowdy sounds confused. "Where'd all that blood on your chest come from?"

A chill runs down my spine as it all comes rushing back to me. "Anna."

"That's Anna's blood?"

I nod.

Rowdy presses his fingers against my cheeks. "Do. Not. Move. Your. Head."

"Sorry."

He picks his flashlight up off the ground and sweeps it around in a full circle, calling out Anna's name. He speaks into his radio. "We need a team to search the surrounding area for the second victim. She's injured and possibly disoriented."

What she is, is crazy.

When Wade arrives a few seconds later, Rowdy clicks off the radio. He rubs a finger over the back of my hand. "Wade's going to hold your head while I put a cervical collar on you."

"Okay."

He shifts his focus to Wade. "Keep pressure off the left parietal side of her head. There're signs of blunt force trauma."

No shit.

Wade's face is upside-down over mine but his frown does not look like a smile. "I told you there's a reason we wear helmets, even on the trails."

"I *was* wearing a helmet. Anna took it off."

"Can you tell us what happened?" Rowdy straps a foam collar around my neck. "Why was Anna bleeding? Did she fall when you did?"

They aren't going to believe me. It sounds crazy, even to me. They'll probably chalk it up to my head injury. "No, Anna didn't fall."

"Was she injured before or after she began assessing you?" Rowdy continues to examine, and cross-examine, me while Wade cleans and bandages the side of my head.

Anna's only injury is a self-inflicted knife wound. "She wasn't trying to help me."

Rowdy moves a stethoscope over my bare chest. I'm surprised he hasn't gone all caveman and covered me up so Wade can't see my bra.

"Can you take a couple of deep breaths for me?"

"You're kidding, right?"

"Just as much as you can handle."

Without the motivation to call for help, I can't convince my lungs to cooperate. All I manage are a few painful gasps.

Rowdy takes my blood pressure then calls in the report over the radio, including the good news that 'the patient is stable,' then focuses on my face. His movements are slower, more relaxed. "If Anna wasn't trying to help you, why'd she remove your helmet?"

"I think I better start at the beginning."

"Okay." Rowdy pokes at my hip bones. "Does this hurt?"

"No. Anna and I got into an argument. She blamed me for stealing you from her."

Rowdy sighs. "I don't know what's gotten into that girl. She's been acting strange ever since you came back."

"She's always acted strange." Wade pulls more medical stuff out of the pack. "You were just blind to it for some reason. But she's definitely gotten worse."

"She's my sister. I guess I just wanted to protect her."

I'm not letting that slide anymore. "She made it very clear that you two are not related by blood."

Rowdy moves his hands to my waistband. "I'm going to unzip your pants."

"No!" I try to grab his wrists but the sudden movement sends a hot knife through my side.

Rowdy lifts his hands then leans over and whispers, "This is just part of the exam. I'd do the same thing to any other patient in your condition."

"It's not that." My eyes sting as blood rushes to my face. "I think I wet my pants."

Rowdy brushes the tears off my cheeks. "It happens. Especially when you're knocked unconscious."

"Hey, Skylar?" The beam from Wade's headlamp is shining on what's left of my iPhone. "Did Siri piss you off or something?"

"She tumbled forty feet down a talus field. I'd be surprised if her phone wasn't broken." Rowdy shines his light on my right hip. "Your pocket's wrong side out. Do you remember pulling your phone out?"

"No." I'm ninety-nine percent sure that Anna is responsible for destroying my phone. She must have taken it while I was unconscious.

"I'm surprised you don't have pieces of it embedded in your hip." Rowdy's fingertips slide over my exposed skin.

Wade squats on the ground next to my shattered phone. "I'm no CSI expert, but it looks like someone intentionally smashed this phone."

He picks up a fist sized rock, revealing more shards of glass and electronic bits beneath it.

Rowdy's brow furrows, pulling his eyebrows together. He searches my face. "Did Anna hurt you?"

I don't want to cry. If I do, it'll make my ribs hurt even more. But the fact that Rowdy's already suspicious of Anna before I even tell him what she did touches my heart. Crying hurts even worse than I thought it would. I try to nod, but the neck brace won't let me.

"Shh...babe, don't cry. Breathe with me." He holds my hand and takes slow, shallow breaths.

"She pushed me off the trail."

Rowdy clenches his jaw so hard it shifts the straps of his helmet.

"Um...guys?" Wade's closer now. Both his headlamp and flashlight are focused on a rock about ten feet from my left shoulder. There's a bloody handprint on it. "Look at this."

"Don't touch it!" Rowdy yells at him. "Don't touch anything. This is a crime scene and that's evidence."

The mention of evidence ties my stomach in knots.

Rowdy reaches for the radio strapped to his shoulder. He's going to report this.

"No! Anna has a knife with my fingerprints on it."

His mouth drops open as his eyes widen. He takes his hand away from the radio without keying it then grabs a pair of shears and slices my left pant leg open from ankle to hip.

"Wait." My pants are already ruined but I don't want any more of my body exposed to Wade than it already is.

"Wade! Get over here." Rowdy obviously doesn't have the same concern. He's working fast again. His movements are even more frantic than before. "We're going to roll you on your side so we can get a look at your back then we'll slip a vacu-splint under you."

"Do you have to?" Just the thought of it tenses every muscle in my body.

Rowdy looks at Wade. "On the count of three. One, Two, Three."

I cry out when they tilt me onto my side. It's not the one with the broken ribs, but it still hurts like hell. I bite my lip to keep from screaming and taste blood.

"I'm sorry, babe. I know it hurts."

Cold air washes over my back when one of them lifts my shirt, exposing my birthmark. Hot tears stream down my face. I don't even care when they expose my butt. Gentle fingers slide over my skin, pressing gently as they go.

"No sign of stab wounds." Rowdy sounds much calmer.

They count to three again then roll me onto the vacu-splint.

"The worst is over now." Rowdy brushes the tears off my face, again. He obviously thinks I'm crying because of the pain, and that's part of it, but it's the humiliation of having my birthmark exposed that's causing this episode of emotional overload.

"We're going to pump the air out of the beanbag so it'll conform to your body."

It takes a few seconds for the pain to recede enough for me to speak. "Anna didn't cut me. She wrapped my fingers around her knife then sliced her forehead with it."

Wade and Rowdy both freeze. I count off the seconds in my head, waiting for someone to say something…anything.

"I don't fucking believe this!" Rowdy's voice echoes off the canyon.

I squeeze my eyes shut. Tears stream down the sides of my face, into my ears. I want to brush them away, but I'm completely immobilized by the vacu-splint.

"I'm going to kill that crazy bitch."

My eyes fly open.

Rowdy's trembling.

He's mad at Anna. Not me. Relief floods my veins. I can handle anything as long as Rowdy believes me.

Wade says, "We need to get Skylar packaged in the litter and get her out of here. Then we need to call the police."

Rowdy's phone trills. It's the ringtone he uses for all his close friends. He and Wade exchange a look. Rowdy pulls it out of his pocket and frowns. "It's Anna. She's Facetiming me."

He presses his thumb over the camera lens on his phone then angles it so Wade and I can see the screen.

"Oh my god, Rowdy." Anna's face is covered in dried blood. She's sobbing, but they're no tears. *"Skylar tried to kill me."*

"Where are you?" Rowdy's voice is calm but his hands are shaking.

"Did you hear me? Your crazy slut tried to kill me!"

"Then why are you calling me? Why haven't you called the police?"

"I... I..." Her eyes dart back and forth. *"You're the first person I thought of when I regained consciousness. I need help."*

Rowdy sighs. "How badly are you hurt?"

"She cut my face." Anna lifts her hair off her forehead to show him the wound right below her hairline. She did a good job of making sure she can easily hide the scar.

"Is that your only injury?"

"Isn't that enough?" Anna's screaming now. *"I was attacked. I barely escaped with my life."*

"Oh, really?" Rowdy's voice is still calm, but his eyes have narrowed to slits. "I've got a patient in a beanbag with a concussion, broken ribs and no fucking weapon."

"She's alive?"

A chill runs down my spine. Anna didn't want to knock me out. She was trying to kill me.

"You're with her?" Her eyes widen. *"Whatever she told you, it's a lie."*

Rowdy's face is a mask of rage. "There's a team out risking their lives trying to find you. Now where the fuck are you?"

Anna screams again. *"I have the knife she used to attack me."*

Rowdy removes his thumb from the lens. "And we have the rock you used to crack her skull with your bloody fingerprints all over it."

"Fingerprints?" Anna laughs. It's a shrill, frightening sound. *"Or just finger-shaped smears from a gloved hand?"*

"Fuck." Rowdy's shoulders slump. He takes two deep breaths then glares at his phone. "What do you hope to gain, Anna?"

"I won't go to the cops if you promise to give me a chance."

"A chance for what?" He sounds defeated. And that scares me more than Anna's craziness.

"I want you to spend time with me."

"Well, I don't want to spend time with you. Not anymore. I warned you not to make me choose."

"You have another choice to make, my love."

"I'm not your love."

"If you don't do what I say, I'm going straight to the cops."

"Why are you doing this?"

"You let that stupid whore brainwash you. All I need is a little time to undo the damage."

"How much time do you want?"

"As much as it takes."

"You need to call in your location so Mike can direct the team to you." Rowdy's phone goes blank. He shoves it back in his pocket. His face is grim.

Wade arches his eyebrows. "Did you record that?"

Rowdy's face falls. He sits down on the ground next to me and drops his head in his hands.

"I guess that means, no."

He groans as if in extreme pain. "I didn't even know I could do that."

"I think we should call the police. Right now." Wade stuffs the medical equipment back into his pack. "All three of us witnessed that conversation. It's our word against hers."

"She has hard evidence." Rowdy pulls out his phone and starts snapping pictures. He moves out of my limited field of vision. I track his movements by the flash from his camera.

"What are you doing?"

"We need to gather our own evidence." He comes back to the medical packs and takes out a new pair of gloves. "I hate to disturb the crime scene, but I'm afraid Anna will come back and destroy it."

"That makes sense."

Wade stays by side and tells me what's going on while Rowdy gathers everything into a biohazard bag then stuffs it into his pack.

He nods at Wade. They lift me onto the litter without a countdown.

Wade crisscrosses velcro straps over my body, tying me into the litter. "Anna's not critically wounded. The most they could charge Skylar with is assault."

Rowdy tightens and adjusts the straps. "It would be assault with a deadly weapon. They could also charge her with attempted murder."

"Damn it."

That's the first time I've ever heard Wade swear. I lick my lips. "I still think we should call the cops. The first one to report a crime has more credibility, right?"

"It doesn't matter." Rowdy brushes a wisp of hair off my cheek. "They'll haul both of you off to county lockup while they try to sort it out. It could take weeks."

"As long as I'm not convicted—"

"No way." Rowdy clips his climbing harness into the side of the litter. "I refuse to let you spend even one night in jail."

I can't help but wonder what horrors he endured four years ago when he was 'detained' after his mother's death.

"I don't see the advantage in waiting." Wade clips in on the other side. "Sooner or later, Anna's going to take her evidence to the cops."

"I don't think so. As soon as she does, she loses all her power over me. She needs that knife to keep me in line." Rowdy keys his radio. "Patient secure. Down slow."

He and Wade lift the litter. Due to the steep angle of the incline, they have to walk backwards, leaning against their harnesses. I know they've done everything possible to insure our safety—there are at least two people working the ropes above us using state of the art equipment—but it still freaks me out.

I'd rather free climb any wall in the park than be so helplessly dependent on others to get me down safely. I'm completely immobilized. I can't even brush the tears off my face. If the rope breaks, if they drop me, I'll log roll to the bottom of the canyon. But what really terrifies me is Rowdy's decision to do whatever Anna wants.

"You know she's going to demand that you break up with me." My voice trembles. "I'd rather go to jail."

"I'll only pretend to go along with her terms while I figure out a way to get her to incriminate herself." The litter shifts as we begin the long descent to the bottom. The beanbag does its job and keeps me stable. But it still hurts to breathe and I have to breathe more when I talk, so I decide to just be quiet and listen—even though it goes against my nature.

Rowdy says, "This isn't the first time she's blackmailed someone to get to me."

"Who else has she blackmailed?" Wade stumbles, jarring the litter.

"Watch it." Rowdy's voice is unnecessarily harsh. He clears his throat then continues with a much softer tone. "Anna found out some personal shit about Boone and used the information to make him kick me out of his house."

So that's why Rowdy moved out.

"She'd been trying to talk me into moving in with you guys for months. It worked exactly the way she wanted it to. When Boone kicked me out, I went straight to Anna."

"What reason did Boone give you when he evicted you?"

"He told me the truth, but I didn't believe him. I got pissed off at him for using Anna as an excuse. I knew he didn't approve of some of the choices I was making." Rowdy glances at me.

"You mean drinking and screwing around?" Wade says out loud what I'm thinking.

Rowdy cringes. "I called him a pussy for not being man enough to just tell me."

"I understand her logic for blackmailing Boone, but surely Anna knows that you can't force someone to fall in love with you by blackmailing them."

"You heard her. She thinks Skylar brainwashed me. Anna wants to 'deprogram' me."

"That's crazy, even for Anna."

"I think I'm the only one that didn't see through her from the beginning. What a fucking idiot."

"Wanting to see the good in someone is not a bad thing."

"It is when it hurts someone you love."

I'm strapped down like a mummy with a concussion and possibly broken ribs. There's a psycho on the loose that wants me dead or in jail. She also wants my man. I know my response is inappropriate, given the dire circumstances, but I can't help it. My heart soars. "I love you, too."

Chapter Twenty-Two

Rowdy

Anna wanders into the command post while Wade and I are in the process of transferring Skylar to the paramedics on the ambulance. I need to know what she's telling everyone but I'm not leaving Skylar's side.

"Wade." I nod in Anna's direction.

"I'm on it." He trots across the parking lot and joins the group celebrating Anna's safe return.

On the way down the trail, we decided that the best course of action for Skylar was to tell everyone that she can't remember anything after she and Anna left the group to go to the bathroom. That way she won't have to change her story when it's time to go after Anna.

I'm alone in Skylar's hospital room, waiting for her to come back from an MRI scan, when Wade calls.

"*Anna's obviously aiming for a post traumatic stress diagnosis with amnesia.*"

"Shit." I glance around to be sure no one can overhear me. "Did she mention Skylar?"

"Not that I know of."

"Did you get the knife?"

"Anna refused to let go of her pack even while she was being checked out by the EMTs."

"Stay on her ass. We have to get that knife."

"She called a cab to supposedly take her home. I followed it to Denver, but lost them in traffic."

"Fuck!" I know it's not Wade's fault, but until we get that knife, Anna holds all the power.

"How's Skylar?"

"She's getting an MRI right now. They're going to X-ray her ribs after that."

"Call me when you get the results."

"Of course. Can you do me a huge favor and watch for Anna to come home? I know she probably won't have the knife with her, but I don't want to let an opportunity slip by just in case she's crazy enough to try to hide it in the house."

"Derek and I are going to take turns keeping watch. We'll both confront her as soon as she walks through the door."

"Thanks, man. I can't tell you how much I appreciate your help."

"Don't mention it."

I'm choking up, so I end the call without saying good-bye.

When they bring Skylar back to her room, it's with good news. She's got a minor traumatic brain injury but no hemorrhage or swelling. Her ribs are bruised, not broken. The rest of her injuries are minor.

She drifts off to sleep within minutes. I scoot the vinyl recliner next to her bed and hold her hand through the rails.

My phone vibrates, waking me up. I hope it's Wade with good news. It's not.

I try to keep the anger out of my voice as I answer the phone. "What do you want, Anna?"

"I want you." Anna's using her little girl voice.

I barely tolerated it before she attacked Skylar. I fucking hate it now. "Where are you?"

"Why aren't you at home?"

"I'm at the hospital."

"With her?" Anna's voice shifts from whiny little girl to raging bitch in less than a second.

"Of course I'm with Skylar."

"Meet me in your room in thirty minutes."

"It's six fucking o'clock in the morning. Can't it wait until after breakfast?"

"No. It can't." Anna pauses, breathing heavily into the phone. *"And I don't appreciate being pinned down and searched like a common criminal in my own home."*

Shit. If Wade and Derek had found the knife, they'd be calling me instead of Anna. "If you don't want to be treated like a criminal, don't act like one."

She gasps.

I know it's a mistake to antagonize her, but I'm exhausted and stressed out beyond imagining.

"I want you to leave right now. That bitch is toxic. The longer you're exposed to her poison, the harder it'll be to get her out of your system."

"I'll be there in an hour."

"Thirty minutes."

"Goddamnit, Anna. At least give me some allowance for traffic."

"Call me when you're in your truck."

"I can't." I laugh, even though nothing about this situation is funny. "I rode in the ambulance with Skylar. Old Blue is still at last night's staging area."

Anna huffs. *"Fine. I'll pick you up."*

"I thought your car wasn't running."

"I fixed it."

I'll bet she did. "What'd you do, reattach the distributor cap?"

She sighs dramatically. *"You better be waiting for me at patient pickup when I get there."*

"Or what? Are you going to burn your one ace just to punish me for being late?"

"I have more than one ace."

Shit. "Oh, yeah? What are they?"

"I don't like your attitude."

"I don't like being threatened."

She's panting now. *"Just remember that you asked for it."*

"Asked for what?" A feeling of dread sweeps through my body. "What are you planning?"

"You'll see."

"Anna, don't. Whatever it is, just don't. I'll do whatever you want."

"Too late."

Fuck. I brace my hands on the bed rails and lean over to kiss Skylar's forehead. "Hey, beautiful. I have to go."

Her eyes flutter open. She starts to stretch then gasps and freezes. "Ugh. I can't believe my ribs aren't broken."

"Bruised ribs can be just as painful, but they don't take as long to heal."

"Where are you going?"

"Anna called. She wants to talk."

"She wants you to break up with me."

"I know." I swipe the tears off Skylar's cheek with my thumb. "We won't be able to see each other when she's around, but she has to sleep and go to work. And I'm going to do everything in my power to be sure we aren't working the same shifts."

"I hate this." Skylar wipes her other cheek.

"I don't like it either, but this situation is temporary." I lean over her and press a kiss to her lips. "You and I are forever."

~***~

Anna is waiting for me in the patient pickup zone when I get there. I jerk open the passenger side door of her crappy little Ford Mustang and slide in.

She leans across the console and tries to kiss me.

"What the fuck?" I dodge it.

Anna's mouth lands on my shoulder. Her eyes flash. "You need to kiss me."

"You know I don't do that."

"You kiss your little whore all the time."

"Skylar's not a whore. I'm the only man she's ever had sex with."

"Use your phone and go to Youtube." Anna glares at me then smiles as she puts the car in gear.

I prefer the glare. "Why?"

"Type in Rowdy Daletzki, all one word, capital R, capital D."

My hands shake as I wait for the page to load. It's a Youtube channel with a photo of me on the banner. There's only one video. It's titled *My Girlfriend is a Whore*. "What the fuck is this? I don't have a Youtube channel."

"You do now." Anna's smile creeps me out. "Play the video."

I can tell by the thumbnail that it's a video of me and Skylar in bed. I'm not visible, but Skylar is. She's straddling me, wearing nothing but her lacy thong. Her birthmark is plainly visible. "How did you get this?"

"I have my ways."

She must have planted a camera in my room. My stomach churns when I see the video's already been played a hundred and eight times. I try to delete the file, but it doesn't work. "Goddamnit, Anna. What's the password?"

She laughs and shakes her head. "I don't think so."

I flag the video as inappropriate and hope that Youtube will take it down before Skylar or anyone else besides the one hundred and eight people that have already seen it... wait... there's *one hundred and seventy-six* views now? This thing's going viral.

"Anna, please. Take it down. I'll do anything you want."

"Will you kiss me?"

My throat squeezes shut. I feel like I'm going to pass out. "Yes. Now give me the fucking password."

"I'll take it down when we get home."

She's not going to give me the password. She's going to hold this over my head, too. If I don't do what she wants, all she has to do is repost the video.

She pulls into the driveway and cuts off the engine then reaches for me.

I fight the instinct to recoil and kiss her cheek.

She grabs a fistful of hair on the back of my head and pulls me closer. "Kiss me on the mouth or that video won't be the only one on your channel."

I keep my lips closed as I press them against her open, slobbery mouth. She tries to force her tongue past my lips. I tighten them even more.

Anna yanks my hair. "Kiss me like you mean it."

I jerk my head back. "Unless you want me to throw up in your mouth, don't push it."

She sighs and tries to press her forehead against mine. I lean back and shove my phone under her nose. "Prove you can keep your word or I'll have no reason to play along with your little blackmail scheme."

"Fine." She takes my phone then turns her back, hunching over so I can't see her type in the password.

I check the fake Rowdy channel as soon as she returns my phone. The video is still there, but it's marked 'unlisted' with an open lock icon next to it.

"No one can see it unless I send them the link." She gets out of the car, but instead of going to the house, she heads towards the garage. And my room. She turns and looks over her shoulder, wiggling her fingers. "Hurry up. I have to work today."

I have a sick feeling that Anna's going to want a lot more than a kiss. Her Youtube video gives me an idea. "Go on up. It's not locked. I'll be there in a minute."

I wait for her to start up the stairs then turn on my phone's video camera and shove it in my pocket. It won't capture any video, but all I need is sound.

I just hope it'll work through my jeans. "Testing, one, two, three. Testing."

I pull it out and hit play. But I can't hear anything, even with the volume maxed out. Shit. I turn sideways so I can lean over and try it again, this time my mouth is as close to my pocket as I can get it. Which isn't all that close. I'm not one of those freaks that can suck his own dick.

This time when I listen to the recording, I can hear it. It's not the best sound quality, but it's the best I can do. Now all I have to do is get Anna on her knees in front of me and make her confess. I have no idea how quickly video will eat up the limited storage on my phone, so I need to hurry.

Anna gasps when I storm into the room and slam the door. The little psycho is already in my bed. She has the sheet tucked under her arms. Thank god. The last thing I want to do is see her naked body. She bites her lip and pats the mattress. "Come here."

I grab a screwdriver out of the toolkit next to my bike then stomp over to the bed. I don't even bother removing my shoes before climbing on. There's only one place where Anna could've hidden a camera with an arial view of my bed.

"What are you doing?"

I ignore Anna's whiney voice and unscrew the cover of the smoke detector and find a tiny camera. The lens is poking through one of the vents. I toss the camera on the floor then jump on top of it. The crunching sound on impact makes me smile.

Anna gasps then glares at me.

I glare right back at her. "I don't want any videos of me or this bed. What happens here is private. Understand?"

She nods. "I wouldn't put us on the internet. It was only for my own enjoyment."

I taste bile in the back of my throat.

She sighs. "I just wanted to record my first time."

"What the fuck? Are you trying to tell me you're a virgin?"

"I've been saving myself for you."

I don't believe her, but if I pretend I do, maybe it can work to my advantage. I should at least be able to stall a little longer. "I had no idea."

"It's true."

I want to roll my eyes but resist. "If you really want to record it, I'll buy you a new camera."

She leans over the side of the bed and grabs her discarded jeans. "That's okay. We can use the camera on my phone."

Shit. I pace at the foot of the bed. "You need to get me hard."

Anna bites her lip then lets the sheet fall to her waist, revealing her breasts.

"Nope. Still soft." I grab my junk and give it a jiggle. "Come here."

She gets out of bed, buck naked, and walks towards me like a cat stalking a mouse. But I'm no fucking mouse. I put my hands on her shoulders and apply downward pressure. "On your knees."

"Wh...what?" She blinks at me, as if she doesn't know what I'm suggesting. But the way she's staring at my crotch and licking her lips gives her away.

"Do it."

"I love it when you take charge like this." She sinks to her knees and kisses me through my jeans.

I need to get her to talk about her sick scheme. I grab her head and guide it closer to my pocket. "I may be a sick motherfucker for admitting this, but thinking about what you're willing to do to steal me from Skylar is sort of turning me on. I get why girls like guys to fight over them."

"I'd do anything for you, Rowdy." Anna drags my zipper down. "I'd even die for you."

The first word to pop into my head is, *Promise?* But I don't say it out loud. "Would you kill for me?"

She nods.

Fuck. I need her to say it. I also need to give her some proof that talking about her attack is turning me on.

I close my eyes and think of Skylar. I try to imagine the fingers digging through my boxer briefs are Skylar's, but Anna's grappling is so different from Sky's gentle touch. I try another tactic and ignore what's going on below and focus on my memories of Skylar. I picture her hazel eyes gazing up at me with adoration and amazement after she came.

My dick swells to halfmast.

Anna's breathing picks up.

No. Don't think about her. Think about Skylar.

Anna whimpers then tugs my pants lower.

Shit. I grab them and pull them back up around my hips. "I want to come in my jeans."

"Really?" Anna's voice rises at the end of the word.

I hope the phone didn't pick up my weird, and completely false, statement. "Tell me what you did to Skylar. Make me hard."

"I smashed her phone so she couldn't call for help if she regained consciousness."

Bingo. But is that enough to exonerate Skylar? I won't get another chance. I thrust against Anna's hand. "And?"

"When she started to come around, I hit her in the head with a rock."

I've never wanted to hurt a woman before, but I have to fist my hands to keep from wrapping them around Anna's throat and squeezing the life out of her.

"Weren't you afraid of killing her?"

"I wanted her to die."

That should do it. As long as the phone picked up the confession. I need to check it. "I have to go to the bathroom."

"Right now?" The whiney edge in Anna's voice is like fingernails on a chalkboard.

"I'll be right back."

Anna smiles and slinks over to the bed. "Hurry up, okay?"

I dash out of my room and run into the house. Wade, Cherri and Derek are huddled on the couch. They all jump to their feet.

I pull my phone out of my pocket and hit play. "Listen to this and tell me if you think it's good enough to get Skylar off."

Derek grins. "That's what she said."

Cherri punches his shoulder, saving him from the blow I want to deliver. "Shut up. This is important."

It worked even better than I thought it would. You can hear everything we both said, including my remark about coming in my jeans. But if it keeps Skylar out of jail, I don't care who hears it.

Derek shakes his head. "Telling Anna that her confession was turning you on might be considered entrapment. You were bribing her with sex to get her to confess."

"Shit. Really?"

"Afraid so."

"What about the evidence we gathered?"

Derek's eyes widen. "Please tell me you didn't tamper with a crime scene."

Wade and I share a look. If I look anything like he does, our guilt is obvious.

Derek groans. "What did you do?"

His expression darkens as I tell him about all the shit in my pack. "You and Wade could go to jail for that."

"Fuck." I look at Wade and watch all the color drain from his face. "I'll take full responsibility and say that I gathered the evidence while you were taking care of the patient. You had no idea what I was doing."

Wade shakes his head. "I think it'll be more convincing with two witnesses instead of one."

Derek clears his throat. "The evidence is contaminated. It's not admissible in a court of law."

"What about the knife? Anna took it with her so it's contaminated, too."

Derek makes a face, as if he's in pain. "That's a little different. Since Anna was allegedly attacked, she can claim she needed the knife for self-defense. Whether or not it'll be admissible evidence is up to the judge. I'd say there's a fifty-fifty chance it could go either way."

I catch myself rubbing my arms and clench my fists. "I'm not trusting Skylar's fate to a coin toss. What are our other options?"

Derek sighs. "Keep in mind I'm not a lawyer yet. And even if I were, I could lose my license for recommending you break more laws."

"Pretend this is an episode of some TV crime drama. If you were writing it, what would my character do to protect Skylar's character?"

Derek rolls his eyes. "This fictional character would probably try to get the villain to make a more damning confession on video, then use it to blackmail her into turning over the knife and leaving the state."

"I need more time to set this up. Anna's already suspicious. Shit. I need to get back up there." I shudder and wipe the sweat off my clammy brow.

Cherri smiles sympathetically. "Go ahead. I'll wait five minutes then come pound on your door in dire need of comfort."

"What?"

"Wade and I broke up. I need you to console me."

"I thought things were progressing." Derek pumps his fist over his index finger in a lewd gesture.

Wade's face turns crimson.

Cherri rolls her eyes. "We didn't break up, numb nuts. It's just an excuse to keep Rowdy from having to fuck Anna."

Wade cringes.

"Don't wait longer than three minutes. Anna's already naked and waiting in my bed."

~***~

I grab a couple glasses and a bottle of cheap wine then trudge back to my room. I tuck the bottle under my arm to open the door. Anna's sprawled across my bed as if posing for a nude portrait. I barely suppress the urge to roll my eyes. I've been with a lot of different girls, but none of them have ever done that.

"What took you so long?" She rolls over onto her stomach and gives me what's supposed to be a seductive smile.

I want to vomit. I hold the wine glasses up instead. "I thought we'd celebrate the beginning of our new relationship."

Tears fill her eyes as she clasps her hands under her chin. A few days ago, that would have cracked a chip in my heart. But Anna killed the last shred of brotherly affection I ever had for her when she tried to kill Skylar.

I pour the wine and swirl it around in my glass, like they do on TV. I have no idea why people do that but it works as a stalling technique.

I hear Cherri sobbing before she's even half way across the yard.

Anna goes to the window and peeks outside. "What's her problem?"

"I hope she's okay."

"She's fine. Whatever it is, Wade can handle it."

"Row-deee." Cherri wails as she pounds on my door.

Anna bares her teeth like a wild animal. "Ignore her."

"I can't do that." I nod at the bed. "Cover yourself."

Anna puts one hand on her hip and glares at me over her wine glass.

"I'm opening the door."

"Go ahead."

With Anna's total lack of modesty, there's no way she's a virgin. Not that I care. I jerk the door open. Cherri falls into my arms and buries her face in my shoulder.

I pat her back. "What's wrong?"

"Wade broke up with me."

"I'm so sorry."

Anna sighs, loudly. "You two weren't compatible anyway. Go cry on Derek's shoulder. Rowdy and I are busy."

"Anna." I give her scathing look. "Show a little compassion."

She purses her lips and studies my face then hands Cherri her glass of wine. "Here. This should make you feel better."

Something in her twisted mind must have decided that it's in her best interest to pretend she has a soul. I can't believe I was so blind for so long. The second Anna turned eighteen, her own mother moved back to Mexico to get away from her.

Anna's face turns puce when I guide Cherri to the bed and sit beside her. I cradle her head on my shoulder. "Do you want to talk about it?"

"Noooo." Cherri wails the word. It's a little over the top, but still believable. "Just hold me."

"Oh for christ's sake." Anna takes Cherri's glass and sets it on my nightstand, next to an unopened condom. Something about the package looks a little off. I lean over and pick it up. There's a small indentation on one side and a matching peak on the other. A tiny hole in the middle. Holy fuck. Anna sabotaged the condom. It's not enough to blackmail me into fucking her. She's planning on trapping me with a kid.

Anna snatches the foil packet out of my hand. "I think this one's defective. You should probably take the whole box back and return it."

I'm speechless. All I can do is shake my head.

Cherri gradually shifts from sobbing to sniffling and eventually to talking.

"Wade and I get along great, except for the fact that he refuses to have sex with me."

"You know he's religious, right?" I can't help but wonder if they really are having sexual problems.

"So am I."

"Really?" I didn't know that. "Your church is okay with premarital sex?"

"'Course not." Cherri huffs. "But as long as you accept Jesus into your heart and repent after you sin, you'll still go to Heaven."

Any sort of discussion about religion makes my skin crawl, but it's a great time-filler. "You really believe that?"

She nods solemnly.

Anna grabs one of my shirts out of my dresser and slips it on. She jams her arms through the sleeves then yanks the hem down past her hips. "I think religion is a bunch of bull shit. How many wars have we fought over religion? How many people have died in the name God? What sort of God let's bad people get rich and live like kings while good, honest people die from horrible diseases and accidents."

I want to add murder to the list, but decide to let Anna run with it. At least it's got her mind off sex.

"Shit. What time is it?" Anna picks her jeans up off the floor then digs her phone out of the pocket. "I gotta go or I'll be late for work."

I avert my gaze while Anna gets dressed and whisper, "Thanks," to Cherri.

She winks at me and mouths, "Anytime."

Anna holds my bedroom door open and glares at Cherri. "Go find someone else to smear snot on. Rowdy's not allowed to be alone with other women."

Anna follows Cherri down the stairs. As soon as Anna's car disappears from view, I run back to the house and beg a ride back to the hospital.

~***~

Cherri and Wade drop me off at Avista then head over to Eldo to pick up my truck. They offered before I had a chance to ask.

Wade says, "We'll leave your truck in the back lot, away from the emergency room entrance so Anna won't notice it if she decides to step outside during one of her breaks."

"Hopefully she won't get any breaks today." Working as an EMT in an emergency room can be frantic or mind-numbingly boring, depending on the day. Not that I'm wishing for tragedy to strike anyone. But if it's going to happen anyway, I hope it's today.

I step into Skylar's room and lean against the wall, watching her sleep. I'm not usually affected by needles, tubes and bandages, I'm a paramedic for fuck's sake, but Skylar looks so small and vulnerable. I need to sit down. Not enough sleep and too many conflicting emotions are making me dizzy.

I'm so grateful that Sky's safe and not under arrest, but the rage I feel for what Anna did to her, and what she's trying to do to me, overshadows it.

I don't want to tell Skylar that Anna's trying to force me to fuck her, but I don't want it hanging over our heads either.

She whimpers in her sleep then murmurs my name. A warm sensation spreads from the center of my chest outwards. God, I love this woman.

"Rowdy." She turns her head back and forth on the pillow, grimacing. She's in obvious pain. Her writhing is making it worse. "Don't go."

I cross the room in two strides and take her hand. "I'm right here, babe. And I'm not going anywhere."

Her eyes flutter open. "Rowdy?"

I hand her the button for the morphine pump attached to her IV.

She tosses it aside and reaches for my face.

I don't want her straining her bruised ribs so I lean in and kiss her forehead. "Don't be afraid to use the morphine pump. It's more effective if you stay ahead of the pain."

"All I need is this." She tugs my head lower and sucks my lower lip.

I groan and take over without meaning to, thrusting my tongue into her mouth.

A nurse lightly taps on her door then enters without waiting for a response.

I stand up but not before she catches me hovering over her patient. Sky's lips are red and swollen. Her face is chafed from my stubble. Shit. That kiss must have lasted a lot longer than I thought it did. Time ceases to exist when I'm with Skylar.

I only work in the ER so I don't know this nurse or how likely she is to throw me out for messing with her patient. I flash her my best grin.

She rolls her eyes then gives in to the smile she's trying to suppress.

"Good afternoon, Ms. Layton. I take it you're feeling a lot better?"

Sky bites her lower lip and nods. "Much."

"How would you like to get out of here?"

"Right now?"

"As soon as your doctor releases you." She taps her iPad with a stylus. "He's making afternoon rounds right now so you can expect him in about an hour. Would you like a sponge bath before he gets here?"

Skylar shakes her head. "I just want to brush my teeth. I'll shower when I get home."

"Do you have someone to help you bathe?"

Skylar glances at me then blushes. "I think so."

Hell, yeah. I get hard just thinking about it, which is wrong on so many levels but I'm a sick bastard and Skylar is much more than just a patient. I press against the bedrail, trying to hide my erection from the overly observant nurse.

"I just need to check your vitals and go over a few things with you then I'll get out of your hair." She does a typical exam then hooks a foot around the rolling stool and sits beside Skylar's bed. "Your doctor will give you a prescription for pain meds. Take them as directed for the next four days whether you think you need them or not. He's switching you to an oral corticosteroid until you can handle using your Albuterol inhaler and recommending you use a nebulizer for acute symptoms. Do you have a nebulizer?"

Skylar shakes her head. "I'll just suck it up and use my inhaler if I need it."

Shit. Using any sort of inhaler is going to hurt like hell. Fuck that. "We'll pick one up before we leave."

Skylar closes her eyes. "I can't afford anymore medical expenses. I'll never pay off these bills as it is."

"Don't worry about it now. We'll figure something out." I know she doesn't want my help but I'm at least going to buy the damn nebulizer.

"To prevent pneumonia, you need to take at least one deep breath every hour, no matter how much it hurts, while you're awake. No heavy lifting or strenuous exercise for four weeks." The nurse pauses and shifts her gaze to me. "That includes sexual activity."

My ears burn as I give her a curt nod. I know what is and isn't allowed with rib injuries. At least Skylar's ribs are just bruised and not broken or cracked.

"You also need to rest that brain of yours. No reading, studying, texting, video games or puzzles until all your symptoms disappear."

"Classes start in a few weeks."

"You'll probably be okay by then. If not, get your doc to write a note excusing you."

"I'll be sure she follows her doctor's orders." My heart sinks as I remember Anna's orders. I'll sneak over to Skylar's as often as I can and make sure Boone knows what to look out for in a patient with a brain injury, bruised ribs and asthma. It's not ideal, but it's as good as it's going to get until I can get rid of Anna.

Cherri and Wade stop by with a get well card, a bouquet of helium balloons and a sack of clean clothes while we're waiting around for the doctor. Those two may have different religious beliefs but they both have hearts of gold. I hope they can figure things out.

I keep my eyes trained on the floor as I help Skylar step into the sundress Cherri loaned her. It hangs loose from skinny little shoestring ties on her shoulders, perfect for her bruised ribs. She didn't even have to raise her arms to put it on. I kneel on the floor in front of her and slip my hands up under her dress to help her change her underwear. Her skin is soft as silk. My dick is hard, but all I want to do is take care of Skylar and protect her.

Chapter Twenty-Three

Skylar

Rowdy's quiet as he cleans and puts away my new nebulizer. He refused to tell me what happened with Anna until I was hooked up to the machine he insisted on buying.

He kneels beside my bed. "Can you ever forgive me?"

"There's nothing to forgive. Anna basically tried to rape you."

His eyebrows shoot up. "I didn't think of it like that, but you're right."

"I just wish you hadn't tampered with the evidence." I was prepared to go to the police and tell them everything. But not if it means getting Rowdy and Wade into trouble. "I think we should destroy the evidence. According to Derek, it's useless anyway. We can pretend we have no idea what happened to it. Let the cops assume Anna came back and tried to clean up the crime scene. There's bound to be a few bits and pieces left over."

"An investigation of the scene will just as likely turn up evidence that Wade and I messed with shit."

"What are we going to do?"

"Whatever we have to."

"Anna's going to want you to sleep with her tonight."

"I know." Rowdy's voice cracks.

I take his hand and tug him closer. "Do everything in your power not to, but if there's no other way…"

"I'd rather die." Rowdy buries his face in my mattress. His head nestles against my waist, opposite my bruised ribs.

"Don't say that. Don't even think it." I comb my fingers through his hair. "It's just sex. I know you don't love her."

"Love her?" Rowdy lifts his head. "I fucking hate that bitch."

Rowdy has the strongest sense of loyalty of anyone I've ever known. He could have turned Keith in for abuse when he was a kid and saved himself from a lifetime of beatings, but his mother begged him not to. He openly claimed Boone as his best friend all through high school, even though doing so was social suicide. He stayed faithful to me for two years after I disappeared. He's put up with Anna's dramatics for years.

But once his trust is broken, it's all but irreparable. The only reason he's giving me a second chance is because leaving was never my choice. I'm not surprised he hates Anna.

Rowdy's phone alarm goes off. He groans. I want to cry, but I don't want to make it harder for him.

He kisses my forehead then stands up. "I have to go."

"I know." I take his hand and give it one more squeeze.

As soon as the front door closes, Boone clomps up the stairs. He's off crutches, but still has to wear a walking cast. He puts his hands on either side of my doorframe and leans into my room. "Hey, are you okay?"

Tears pool in my eyes. "Have you ever wanted to kill someone?"

"Besides you, Wade and Rowdy?"

"What?"

"Why didn't someone call and tell me you were hurt?"

"I'm sorry. There was just so much going on all at once. Were you worried?"

"I thought you were rolling around in Rowdy's bed. I had no idea until he brought you home." Boone grabs the desk chair and scoots it next to my bed.

"So, who do you want to kill?" He holds up a hand, palm out. "No, wait, let me guess... *Anna*."

"I can't get the image of her forcing herself on Rowdy out of my head. And I can't come up with a plan to get us out of this mess." I rub my forehead. "It's giving me a headache."

"You're not supposed to be trying to solve problems with your bruised brain, remember?"

"I need a distraction."

"Want me to tell you a story?"

"What? Like a fairy tale?"

"Exactly like a fairy tale." Boone clears his throat. "Once upon a time a handsome young prince lived in a beautiful canyon."

"Canyon? Not kingdom?"

"Do you want to hear the story or not?"

"I'd prefer to hear the real version. The one where you're not a prince."

His knee bounces like a sewing machine needle. "Can I still be handsome?"

Boone's always been vain about his looks. I decide to appeal to that vanity in hopes of calming him down.

"I can't imagine you as anything but."

His leg slows down but doesn't stop bouncing completely. "I have a secret."

"Do you want to share it?"

"Yes...and no." He takes a deep breath then lets it out slowly. "It's my fault that Mom and Dad died."

"It was a car accident, Boone. You weren't even driving."

"They shouldn't have been on the road." He swipes a tear off his cheek. "I was at a friend's house up the canyon. We had too much to drink and got into a horrible fight. I wanted to leave, but was too drunk to drive so I called Rowdy. He didn't answer so I left a voice message, begging him to come get me, then I called everyone else I could think of." He rolls his eyes. "Which, as you can imagine, was a pretty short list."

Unless things changed dramatically after I left, there wasn't a list at all. I'm surprised Boone was actually at someone else's house. That means he had another friend besides just Rowdy. "Who was the friend you were visiting?"

"It doesn't matter. What we had is over."

Sounds like it might have been a girl.

"Anyway, my fucking heart was shattered so I ended up calling Dad and asking him to come get me."

Definitely a girl.

"Dad had taken some cold medicine earlier that made him too drowsy to drive."

"Was it dark?" Aunt Lori had horrible night vision and never drove after sundown unless it was an emergency.

Boone nods. "It was about two o'clock in the morning and raining. Dad couldn't drive, but he came with her."

Now I understand where the guilt is coming from. I take Boone's hand and hold the back of it against my cheek, like I used to do when we were kids and someone had been mean to him. "You can stop if you want."

Boone smiles through his tears. "It actually feels sort of...I don't know? Freeing? To talk about it."

"Okay." My heart hammers my sore ribs but Boone's pain is obviously just as agonizing so I ignore mine.

He stands up and paces in front of my bed. "Rowdy didn't answer because he was out on a rescue call. He got my message and tried to call me back but my phone had died. He knew where I was and could tell I was upset so he decided to just come get me, not knowing that Mom and Dad had already picked me up.

"I was in the back seat with the window down, trying to keep from puking. Dad was in the front with Mom. We were coming down the canyon while Rowdy was driving up."

Blood roars behind my ears, but it's not loud enough to block out the words I don't want to hear.

"Mom took a corner too fast. We skidded off the wet pavement and rolled down the embankment into South Boulder Creek." Boone stops pacing. His eyes glaze over.

"We rolled over and over. It went on forever. When we finally stopped, we were upside down in the creek. It was running high with spring melt-off. The force of the water pushed the car upright. Mom was obviously dead but Dad kept patting her face and shaking her, begging her to wake up. Water rushed into the car. I managed to get my seatbelt off, but I couldn't fight the current. I was trapped in the back seat."

The corners of Boone's mouth curve up in a heartbreakingly sad smile. "And then, out of nowhere, Rowdy stuck his head in the front passenger window and shoved a rope at Dad. But Dad refused to take it. He said, 'get Boone out.'"

A broken sob escapes Boone's throat. I reach for him, but he shakes his head and steps back, as if he doesn't feel worthy of my comfort.

"Rowdy crawled halfway through my window, cutting himself on the broken glass. He slid a rope around me, under my arms and somehow managed to fight my drunken ass and the current to get me out of the car. He hauled me onto the bank then went back for Dad. But the car rolled over again and disappeared before he got there."

Tears stream down my face as I picture the scene.

Boone sits back down and wipes the tears off my cheek with his thumb. He smiles at me through his own tears. "When they finally pulled the wreckage out of the river, Dad was still holding Mom. He died with her in his arms."

Boone and I sit in silence, lost in our own thoughts and our own grief.

He takes a deep breath then slowly exhales. "I found out later that Rowdy broke all sorts of rules to rescue me. They even considered kicking him out of BMR because of it. It's a miracle he didn't get tangled up in the wreckage and drown. I'd never be able to forgive myself if he had. It's hard enough knowing that Mom and Dad died because I was too drunk to drive myself home."

"Is that how Anna blackmailed you?"

"What?" Boone frowns then rolls his eyes. "No. She found out that I'm gay."

"You are?" I feel my eyes widening and blink in an effort to disguise my shock. "Since when?"

Boone chuckles. "My whole life."

"But…you don't act gay."

He crosses his knees and plants a palm on his cheek. "Not all gays follow the stereotype."

He uncrosses his legs and relaxes back into his normal slouchy posture. "I fought it for years, but it just got to be too hard."

"Are you out?"

"I'm working on it."

"How did Anna find out?"

"The only thing I can think of is that she overheard Rowdy and me discussing it. He's the only straight person I've ever told. Except for you."

Chapter Twenty-Four

Rowdy

I make it back to the house five minutes before Anna does. She must have skipped out of work early. I'll have to be more careful in the future. I'm sitting in the living room, sipping on a much needed Coors, when I hear her tires crunching on the gravel out front.

She doesn't even get all the way inside the house before she starts making demands. "Put the beer down and let's go."

I take another long pull. "Go where?"

She puts her fists on her hips. "To your room."

I tip my head back and belch, loud and long. Maybe if I'm gross enough, she won't be so eager to get in my pants. "I'm a little old to be sent to my room."

"We need to talk."

I need to stall. "How about we go out to eat first?"

"Really?" She clasps her hands under her chin and grins. "Like on a date?"

I stand up and grab my keys off the hook by the door. "Call it what you want but let's go. I'm hungry."

I take her to The Sante Fe Grill in Louisville and order their cheese and onion enchiladas with extra cheese and onions.

Anna scowls at me. "You're lactose intolerant."

"Life's short. I want to live a little before I die." And if I get the runs, there's no way she'll be able to get me hard. She hasn't forced an erection yet, but friction is friction and I don't trust my dick to obey my heart. It's got a mind of it's own. I'm still in charge of when and how I use it, but it'll be easier to avoid fucking Anna if I just stay soft.

My stomach's gurgling before the check comes.

When we get home, Anna tries to pull me upstairs to my room.

I jerk my hand out of hers. "I need to stay close to the bathroom."

"I told you not to order that cheese burrito."

"Whatever."

Anna grabs her keys. "Don't go anywhere. I'll be right back."

"Where are you going?" Not that I care, but I'd like an estimate of how long she'll be gone so I'll know if I have enough time to go check on Skylar.

Anna narrows her eyes at me. I swear that bitch can read my mind. "I'm going to Walgreens."

"For tampons?" Please, please, please say 'yes.'

"I'm going to pick up a bottle of Immodium."

Shit. Well, there's goes that plan.

As soon as the front door swings shut, Wade sits down beside me and opens his laptop. "Look what I found online."

He pulls up a home security website and shows me an extensive array of secret agent type hidden cameras. There're ink pens, wall hooks, power adapters, watches and even a smoke detector like the one Anna used on me. "Awesome."

"I ordered one of each of the stationary cameras but I got pens and watches for you, me, Cherri, Derek, Boone and Skylar." He grins like a kid on Christmas morning. He's definitely getting off on this spy shit. "I'm having it sent by overnight express. Most of it should get here by tomorrow."

I had no idea he was so devious. This is going to cost a fortune, but if one of us is able to catch Anna saying something incriminating, it'll be worth it.

A pink flush spreads across Wade's cheeks. "Do you think you can avoid having intercourse with Anna until we find a way to stop this insanity?"

"God, I hope so." I'm tempted to tell Wade about the video Anna's got on Youtube. I trust him to not go looking for it, but he might let something slip in front of Cherri, or god forbid, Derek, who definitely would try to find it. Just knowing that over a hundred strangers watched it before Anna disabled it makes me want to hit something. Or someone. I can only imagine what it would do to Skylar if she knew. I don't like keeping secrets from her, but this one would only cause her grief and pain.

As long as I can keep it off the internet, there's no reason for her to ever find out.

The anti-diarrhea medication kicks in about two hours after I take it. I fake a few more bathroom runs but if I keep this up, Anna will make me take another dose. I'll be stopped up for a week. Maybe I can plead exhaustion.

She gets up from the armchair and marches over to the couch, where I'm sitting with Wade and Cherri, and reaches for me. "It's time for bed."

I ignore her outstretched hand. "It's nine o'clock."

Wade puts a hand on my shoulder. "You've been sick for the past two and a half hours. I strongly recommend you take it easy tonight."

Anna glares at him. "And I strongly recommend you stop trying to practice medicine without a license."

"He's not the one pouring Imodium down my throat." I stand up and head for the door.

Anna chews my ass out as she follows me outside. Even if I didn't hate her, I don't think I'd ever be able to handle the nagging.

She pauses beside her car. "Go on upstairs and get into bed. I'll be right up."

My feet drag as I trudge up the stairs. I take my shoes off and crawl onto the bed with a heavy heart. I don't usually sleep in my clothes, but the more barriers between me and Anna's wandering hands the better. I roll onto my stomach and pretend I'm asleep.

I can hear Anna wandering around my room. I want to see what the fuck she's up to but if she catches me with my eyes open, it'll ruin my 'don't bother me I'm asleep' strategy. Besides, I don't want to risk seeing her take her clothes off. But when I smell smoke, I don't have a choice.

Fuck. She's lighting candles. She's also wearing a white, filmy nightgown that floats around her body as she moves. It looks like the bedtime version of a wedding gown.

The bed dips. She digs her hands into my shoulder muscles and starts massaging them. It only makes me more tense.

She straddles my ass and runs her hands up and down my back. "I know you're not asleep."

"I don't feel well. Please get off me and let me rest."

"I'm not stupid, Rowdy." Her voice quivers. "I know what you're doing."

"What do you expect?"

"I expect you to act like you did this morning before I had to go to work."

I groan and bury my head under my pillow.

She yanks it off. "I took half a day off work so I could prepare everything. The least you can do is look at me."

I open my eyes and groan again. She's got rose petals strewn all over the place, enough candles to give the local fire department nightmares and a fucking video camera on a tripod.

"I thought I told you no more video."

"You said it was okay, just this once…because it's my first time."

"Are you really a virgin?"

She bites her lip and nods.

I still don't believe her but an idea forms in the back of my mind. "Don't you want your first time to be special?"

"It will be since it'll be with you."

"I don't want to waste your virginity on one night of passion." That sounds like a line from a cheap romance novel. "I want you to come to our wedding bed pure and untainted."

"Wedding?" Anna's eyes widen, sparkling in the candlelight.

But she looks like a demon to me. "Isn't that what you want?"

She launches herself at me and pounces on me. "Yes, yes, yes. A thousand times yes. I'd be honored to be your wife."

"I'll only marry you if you're a virgin."

"Why?" The whiney voice is back.

"If you're not, what's the point? Might as well just shack up like a common whore."

"But you're not a virgin."

"I'm a man." I doubt a chauvinistic attitude will make her change her mind, but it's worth a try. "The rules are different for men. How many grooms have you seen wearing white?"

She frowns, as if considering my argument. But then she nods. "I see what you mean."

Un-fucking-believable.

"Okay. I'll wait for our wedding night."

"You better sleep in your own room until the wedding. I'd hate to fuck you accidentally and ruin everything."

"You don't have to be so crude." She blows out the candles.

I close my eyes until I hear the door close then grab my phone and call Skylar. It goes straight to voice mail. Fuck. I forgot that Anna smashed Skylar's phone. I call Boone.

He answers on the first ring. *"How are you holding up?"*

"I just bought us six to nine months to find a way out of Anna's trap."

"I'm going to put you on speaker so Skylar can hear you. How'd you get Anna to back off?"

"I asked her to marry me."

~***~

"You what!" Skylar's voice comes over the speaker, loud and clear.

"Calm down, babe. Getting upset is not good for your brain injury."

"Did Anna hit you in the head, too? Why the hell would you ask her to marry you?"

"I have no intention of going through with it." I can tell she's more confused than angry. "I told her that my bride has to be a virgin to keep her out of my bed for the foreseeable future. As soon as we find a way to dismantle her blackmail scheme, I'm breaking it off."

"I don't like it."

"Would you rather have me fucking her every night?"

"Of course not." She's quiet but I can hear her breathing over the speaker. "When's the wedding?"

"There isn't going to be a wedding."

"Did you give her a ring?"

"This just went down a few minutes ago. I didn't have time to plan it out much less buy a ring."

"I'm sorry." Skylar's voice catches. "I know it's stupid, but the idea of you getting down on one knee and—"

"It wasn't like that." Is she jealous? "I didn't get on my knees. I didn't give her a ring and I sure as hell didn't mean to upset you."

"I know." She sighs. "I just hate the way she's manipulating everyone. I miss you."

"I miss you, too. I don't want to keep you from resting, but would it be okay if I come over once I'm sure Anna's asleep? I'll leave Old Blue in the driveway and ride my bike so she won't get suspicious if she looks out the window."

"Would you?" The vulnerability in Skylar's voice wrenches my heart.

"Get some sleep. I'll head over as soon as Anna's light goes out." I turn my own light out in case she's watching.

I have no idea what the fuck Anna's up to, but she doesn't turn her damn light off until two in the morning. I don't want to wake Boone up so I climb the tree next to Skylar's room and crawl in through her second story window.

She's on her back, propped up with pillows. "I was afraid you fell asleep and weren't going to come."

"I got here as fast as I could. Anna just went to bed." I pull up a chair and sit beside her.

"Could you do me a huge favor?"

"Anything, babe. All you gotta do is ask."

"Help me take a shower?"

"Are you sure you feel up to it?"

"I stink."

"I can give you a sponge bath."

"I'd rather have a shower."

It takes her five minutes just to get out of bed. I follow her into the bathroom and have to grind my teeth to keep from swearing when Sky turns on the light and I see the bruises covering her body. I thought I was prepared for it. I saw them forming during my initial exam at the scene but the blue and purple patches covering her now are so much worse.

I can't help but notice that Skylar keeps her back turned away from me and out of the mirror's view. She's still self-conscious about her birthmark. "Skylar?"

She looks up and bites her lip.

"You don't have to hide anything from me."

She ducks her chin, letting her dark brown hair fall forward, partially obscuring her face. "I know you've already seen it, and so has Wade, but…"

"But nothing. You're beautiful." I skim my fingers over a bruise on her shoulder. I hate the marks Anna's attack left on her. Not because of how they look, but because of what they represent.

I sit on the edge of the tub and turn on the water.

"Join me?" Skylar's voice is so quiet I barely hear it over the shower spray.

"It would make it easier for me to wash you. But I'm already sporting a boner."

"That's okay. I like it when you're hard."

"We can't do anything, understand?"

She nods then watches me undress. Her eyes widen when my cock springs free.

"I mean it. No shower sex until you heal."

"How about if I just watch?"

Holy fuck. "You want to watch me jerk off?"

She bites her lip and nods. "I'm supposed to take deep breaths so I don't get pneumonia. It'll help with the pain if I have something else to focus on."

"Let me take care of you first." I grab the bottle of Skylar's shampoo and squirt some in my palm. The scent alone could make me come. But this isn't the time for that shit. "Turn around so I can wash your hair."

"Just do it." She tips her head forward, refusing to show me her back.

"I don't want to get shampoo in your eyes."

Her forehead puckers up as she pulls her eyebrows together.

"I've already seen your birthmark."

She squeezes her eyes shut.

"Skylar, look at me." I reach behind her and rub the shampoo onto the back of her head. "I know you don't like it, but I think it's beautiful."

Her eyes fly open. "You do?"

I slide my hand down the left side of her back then hold it over the spot where I think her birthmark is. "It looks like an abstract painting of a butterfly sipping nectar from a rose."

"Seriously?"

"I wouldn't lie to you."

She blinks three times then slowly turns around.

My hand slides around her body as she turns. From her back to her waist to her lower abs.

She trembles as if she's cold or going into shock.

I know this is hard for her and I'm so fucking proud of her I want to squeeze her—not the best thing for bruised ribs. I squirt more shampoo in her hair and massage her scalp, carefully avoiding the spot where Anna tried to bash her skull in. The cut didn't require stitches, thank god, so it's okay to wash it. "Tell me if it stings or hurts in any way."

"It feels good." She moans in obvious pleasure.

My dick twitches but all I have to do is look at one of her bruises to get myself under control. I turn her around to rinse her hair. She has me do it again, once more with shampoo then once with conditioner. I could play with her hair all day but I don't want to run out of hot water before I get the chance to wash the rest of her.

Her body wash is the same organic brand and natural, chamomile scent as her shampoo and conditioner. I'm glad she doesn't use the perfumey shit. I'd still bathe her no matter what she used but I appreciate not having to suffer fragrance induced migraines.

I lather up a washcloth and start with her shoulders. I try not to spend extra time on her breasts, ass and pussy but it's hard. In more ways than one. Especially when Skylar's obviously enjoying the attention. I kneel to wash her calves and feet.

She tugs on my hair. "Stand up."

"I'm not done." Kneeling in front of Skylar has my face exactly where my dick wants it to be.

"It's my turn."

"Not until your ribs heal."

"It won't hurt me if I use my hands."

I stand up and kiss her forehead. "It will if I get carried away and thrust hard enough to knock you off balance."

Her pupils dilate. "I can't wait to feel you move inside me."

"Fuck, babe, don't say things like that. Not until I can make it happen."

"I want to watch you get off." Her chest heaves with each breath.

I know it's got to be painful but I don't see any sign of it on her face. This actually could be therapeutic. For both of us. I turn off the shower then get her dried off, wrapped up in a towel and seated on the closed toilet.

Skylar's gaze travels all over my body as I get back in the tub.

I pick up her body wash. "Is it okay if I use a little of this?"

She licks her lips and nods. "Of course."

I brace myself against the tile wall over the faucet with one hand, giving her a good profile view of my already throbbing cock. "I'll try to make it last, but I'm so fucking turned on after washing you, I'll probably blow my load pretty quick."

"It's okay. Do whatever feels best to you."

I've never considered myself an exhibitionist, but fuck, this is fun. I form a tight 'O' with my index finger and thumb around the base of my cock and tease my balls with my fingers. I keep my gaze locked on Skylar's face as I slide my hand up my shaft and roll my palm over the head. I count backwards from one hundred in an effort to hold on a little longer.

Skylar's thighs drift apart, drawing my gaze lower. She's trembling again.

"Sky? Are you okay?"

She nods.

"Can you take a deep breath for me?"

She keeps her gaze locked on my dick as she inhales.

I can tell from the way her jaw tenses that it hurts, but she doesn't complain. I have an idea to further distract her. "Open your towel."

Her eyes widen, but she does it.

I maintain my slow, lazy pace up and down my shaft as I watch her unwrap the towel. She's obviously overcome whatever modesty issues were holding her back before. Maybe it was all tied to her birthmark and now that she knows I like it, she's more confident about the rest of her body. Whatever the reason, I'm just glad she's willing to share it with me.

"Slide your hands up and down your thighs, keeping pace with me." Her knees fall open, exposing her glistening pussy.

"Fuck." I grab my balls and pull them away from my body. "Keep taking deep, cleansing breaths."

"Okay."

"Run your hands over your breasts, but don't touch your nipples." I tug a little harder on my balls to keep from coming when she immediately obeys.

"Slide one hand slowly down your stomach. Feel how soft and smooth your skin is?"

"Um-hum." Her eyelids drift half-closed. She takes a deep breath without me prompting her.

"Now pinch your nipple with one hand and touch your clit with the other."

Skylar teases her perky nipples then slides her hand lower but she stops just above her clit.

"How are you doing, babe?"

"I'm going to come."

"Are you in pain?"

"A little. But so far, it's worth it." She stares at my cock as it thumps against my stomach. "Don't stop."

"If I start up again, I'm going to explode."

She parts her fingers and slides her hand lower, still avoiding her clit. "I want to come when you do."

Holy fuck. "Are you close?"

"I think so." She tugs on one nipple then the other.

I let go of my balls and pump my dick three times then shoot my load.

Skylar's legs shake as she slides her middle finger over her clit. She lets go of her nipple and grabs the edge of the sink. "Fuuuuck."

I've never heard her say that word before. It's hot, cute and a little bit funny but I know better than to laugh if I ever want to see her do this again. And I definitely want to see her do this again.

~***~

I'm just stepping out of the tub when Boone knocks on the bathroom door. *"Rowdy? Are you in there?"*

Skylar answers, "He's helping me take a shower. What do you want?"

"Someone's been blowing up Rowdy's damn phone for the past hour. He left it in your room."

"Goddamnit." I wrap Skylar up in a clean towel and yank my jeans on over my naked ass. "Is it Anna?"

"What do you think?"

Why can't she just leave me alone? I open the door and step into the hall. "Hey, Boone Dog, can you drive yet?"

He averts his eyes from my naked chest. "Yeah, but it's not pretty."

I know Boone's attracted to me, but he usually does a better job of hiding it. "Can you load my bike on your car and drive me to North Boulder?"

He grins. "You sneaky bastard. You're going to tell Anna you were out riding your bike all night and have her come pick you up."

"I hate playing these stupid games, but there's too much at stake not to."

I tuck Skylar in bed, trying to get her as comfortable as possible before I leave. My heart sinks to the soles of my feet as I kiss her good-bye. "I'll come back the first chance I get."

She squeezes my hand. "Be careful. Just because Anna's obsessed with you doesn't mean she won't try to hurt you if she thinks you're cheating on her."

I ride up Broadway a couple miles before I call Anna. I need to be a little bit out of breath when I call her and more than a little sweaty when she arrives.

Anna picks up on the first ring and starts screaming at me immediately, spewing threats to repost the video, go to the cops with the knife and castrate me if I'm with Skylar.

I hold the phone away from my ear until she winds down. "Are you done yet?"

"Where the fuck are you?"

"Broadway and Iris."

She's blessedly silent for almost five seconds. "What are you doing in North Boulder?"

I can't resist throwing a little guilt her way. "I couldn't sleep so I went for a bike ride."

"You're on your bike?"

"Yeah. I got a little carried away and didn't realize how far I'd gone. Can you come get me?"

"Your bike won't fit in my car. I'll need to drive your truck."

Fuck. I swear under my breath. "I don't let anyone drive Old Blue."

"We're going to be married soon. What's mine is yours and what's yours is mine so you might as well get used to me driving your truck."

I can't fucking believe this. "There's a spare set of keys on the hook by the door in the main house."

"I love you, Rowdy." Her voice is syrupy sweet.

I want to puke. "Meet me at the Starbucks on the corner."

The first thing Anna says when she sees me is, "You rode all this way in jeans?"

"I wasn't thinking."

"How badly are you chaffed?"

"Bad enough." I pick at my crotch, pulling my jeans away from the boys.

"We better pick up some ointment on our way home so I can take care of you."

Oh, hell no. Even if I weren't trying to hide a fake rash, I wouldn't want her playing around down there. "I can take care of it myself. Virgin bride, remember?"

"Medicating your genitals won't take my virginity."

"It's the idea of it. I want to keep you as pure as possible."

"I've already touched your penis."

I fight the urge to shudder. If Anna herself weren't enough to turn me off to sex, her clinical description of my man parts would. "I said no. If you're going to be my wife, you better learn to respect my decisions."

A woman sitting at the table next to ours glares at me. She stands up and puts a hand on Anna's shoulder. "You don't have to put up with that. No man has the right to put himself in a position of power over his wife."

I'm tempted to tell her to mind her own business, but I actually agree with her. Keith used to give Mom orders then *punish* her if she didn't follow them exactly.

Anna smiles sweetly at her then places her hand over mine on top of the table. "It's okay. He's not usually like this. He's just stressed out."

"No shit." I pull my hand out from under Anna's then stretch and yawn.

Anna moves her hand to my knee. "We're getting married in a week."

I freeze. Every muscle in my body clenches. "No, we're not."

Anna pats my knee. "I've arranged everything. Plane tickets, hotel, chapel, flowers, marriage license, and reception dinner. All you have to do is get the rings."

"You can't plan a wedding in seven days."

"You can if you get married in Vegas."

Ordinarily, I would have insisted Anna hand over my keys, but I'm in no condition to drive. The cumulative stress of the past thirty-six hours has seriously affected my ability to think. Anna jabbers about the wedding non-stop on the way home. I can't deal with this shit right now so I rest my head against the window and close my eyes, tuning her out.

Anna digs her fingers into my bicep and shakes me. "Wake up, sleepy-head. We're home."

I wasn't asleep but I feel no need to enlighten her. I reach over and pull the keys out of the ignition then get out of the truck and slam the door.

"Hey!" Anna runs around the front of the truck and puts a hand on my chest. "What's wrong with you?"

"I hope you can get a refund on the plane tickets and all that other shit because we are not getting married in Las Vegas."

Her lip quivers as her eyes fill up with tears. "I thought you'd be happy."

For a split second, I feel sorry for her. It's a knee-jerk reaction. "What the fuck, Anna? You make all these plans without ever mentioning any of it and expect me to be happy? You don't know me at all."

I shove her hand off me and stomp up the stairs to my room. Anna follows, but I slam the door in her face.

She pounds on it, rattling the frame. "Open this door right now, Rowdy Daletzki, or you'll be sorry."

I jerk the door open but stand my ground, refusing to let her in. "My shift at Avista starts in four hours. I can't deal with this shit right now. We can talk when I get home from work."

"Call in sick." She tries to squeeze through the door, ducking under my arm.

I grab her around the waist and set her back on the landing. "You are not coming in here."

"If you don't take me to Vegas next weekend and marry me, I'll repost that disgusting video of your little slut."

"Really? You want the whole world to see your future husband making love to someone else?"

"You aren't visible on the screen. All anyone can see is the ugly birthmark on that whore's back."

I dig my fingers into the door frame to keep from shoving Anna down the stairs. "You need to leave, right now, before I do something we'll both regret."

Her expression softens. She lifts her hand and reaches for my cheek.

I jerk my head back. I can't tolerate her touch.

She sighs. "You're just tired. Things will look better after you've had some sleep."

"You are so fucking delusional." I pull the door shut and lock it then slide the deadbolt into place. I pull my phone out of my pocket and send a group message to Wade, Cherrie, Derek, Boone and Skylar, even though her phone's no longer in service.

Anna trying 2 force me 2 marry her in Vegas next weekend. Ideas?

It's four fucking o'clock in the morning so I don't expect anyone to reply. My phone buzzes, alerting me to an incoming call. Boone's face pops up on my screen.
"Are you shitting me?"
"I wish I were. God, Boone, what am I going to do?"
"The plan's the same, it's just a lot more urgent, that's all."
"How's Skylar doing?"
"I just checked on her a few minutes ago. She's asleep."
"I'm supposed to work tomorrow, but I'm going to call in sick. Do you think we could all meet somewhere and try to come up with a plan?"
"I'm still on sick leave at the gym so I'm free. I have no idea what everyone else's schedule is but I'm sure they'll find a way to make it. Where and when do you want to meet?"
"I'm so fucking exhausted, I can't even think straight. Can you set it up and get back to me?"
"You got it."

~***~

I wake up with a jolt. Someone's knocking on my door. I'm still wearing yesterday's clothes. I check my phone for the time, seven forty-five. Shit. I'll bet that's Anna at the door. I need to call in at work and tell them I'm sick but I don't want her to know I'm not going in.
"Hey, Rowdy, you awake?"
It's Derek. I heave a huge sigh of relief and open the door. He wrinkles his nose. "Dude. You look like shit."

"Thanks." I step back and wave him in. "Did you get my text about Anna's plans for a Vegas wedding next weekend?"

"Yeah. That is so fucked up."

"Are we having a meeting sometime today?"

"Not exactly."

My heart sinks.

"Cherri and Wade talked Anna into postponing the wedding until spring."

"How'd they do that?"

"Cherri riffed off that whole 'my bride has to be a virgin' thing and told Anna that only strippers and whores get married in Vegas. She also claimed that we all wanted to be there to witness the marriage of our best friends.

"Wade suggested moving it to Costa Rica and making it a destination wedding. He insisted on paying for everything as a wedding gift."

"And she believed him?"

Derek grins and shakes his head. "She did when he reserved the hotel and bought plane tickets for all of us online right there in front of her."

"Holy shit." I sink onto the bed and brace my elbows on my knees. "That had to cost a fortune."

"Seventeen thousand, eight hundred and forty-three dollars to be exact."

"Can he get his money back?"

"You do know he's got a trust fund worth millions, right?"

"When is this fake wedding supposed to take place?"

"Spring break." Derek grins. "Dude, we're all going to Costa Rica for spring break. Can you believe it?"

"I'm not marrying Anna so you can get a free trip."

"By the time spring break rolls around, that bitch'll be history. The first thing Wade did after she went to bed was buy a ticket for Skylar."

I wish I had Derek's enthusiasm. And his faith that it was all going to work out. But right now, I'd settle for a few hours of sleep.

"Later, Dude." Derek bounds down my stairs two at a time then jogs to his car and takes off.

I flop onto my bed and call my supervisor to tell her I'm not feeling well.

"Do you have the same virus as Ms. Jones?"

"Probably." I have no idea what excuse Anna's been giving for missing work, but if it worked for her, it'll work for me.

"Get well quick. We need you. Oh, and congratulations on your engagement."

Goddamnit, Anna. "Thanks." I nearly choke on the word.

I feel as if I just fell asleep when my phone goes off. But it's been five hours. It's Boone.

"Hey, do you wanna come over and hang out?"

I was wrong. It's Boone's phone but Skylar's voice.

"I'd love to, babe, but this is Anna's day off. We can't risk it."

"Actually, we can. Cherri took her shopping in Denver for wedding gowns. They'll be gone all day."

"I'll be right there."

Skylar meets me at the door. She wraps her arms around my waist instead of shoulders and gives me a gentle hug. The fact that she can squeeze me at all is good sign.

I run my fingertips up and down her spine. "Feeling better?"

"Much." She pulls away and takes my hand. "I got some great news today."

"Please share. I could use some good news."

She tugs me into the kitchen. Her laptop is on the table with her email account open. "Read it."

I pull out a chair and sit down then pat my thigh. "If it doesn't hurt, I'd love for you to sit on my lap."

She grips my shoulder and lowers herself slowly until her cute little ass is suspended over my lap. "It hurts to use my abs."

I palm her ass with both hands. "Give me all your weight. I'll bring you down easy."

She looks over her shoulder and smirks at me. "You'll use any excuse to feel me up, won't you?"

"Do I need an excuse?"

"Nope." She slips her hand under my shirt and snakes it around to my back. "Neither do I."

I like where this is going, but Sky wanted to share her good news with me so I read the email message on her laptop. It's from *Rock and River*, a local outdoor magazine.

Dear Ms. Layton,

We would like to feature the photo you submitted on the cover of Rock and River's fall edition. Please read the terms of the attached digital contract and if they are acceptable, sign and return the contract...

There's more to the message, but I think I got the important part. "You sold one of your photos?"

She grins and nods. "They're paying me four hundred dollars for the one I shot of Boone, right before he peeled off The Bastille."

"That's great, babe. I'm so proud of you. I want to hug you, but I'm afraid you wouldn't enjoy it very much."

She offers me her cheek. "I'll take a kiss instead."

My damn phone dings just as I'm kissing Skylar's cheek. "It's a text from Anna."

I hold my phone in front of Skylar so she can read it, too.

Check out your Facebook page.
Don't have one.
You do now. It's RowdyDaletzki all one word pw is Cowboy.

"Jesus." The last thing I want to do is go look at some lame-ass webpage.

Skylar whimpers as she scoots her ass around so she's facing her laptop. I know every little movement hurts like hell. She pants for a few seconds then pulls up the bogus page.

There's a bunch of shit that makes me want to hurl, including the profile status that I'm engaged to Anna Jones. But it's the photo album that stops my heart. The first row is pictures of Anna in half a dozen different fluffy wedding dresses, looking like a damn cupcake. But the first photo in the second row isn't a photo at all. It's a video titled "My ex is a f***ing Ho-bag." The thumbnail image is blurry, but Skylar's back is visible. So is her birthmark.

I know the exact moment Skylar sees it. Her whole body tenses then starts trembling. She's panting, gasping for air. Shit.

"Sky? Where's your nebulizer?"

She doesn't answer.

Fuck. "Is it still in your room?"

Still no answer.

"Boone!" I yell his name at the top of my lungs.

The house is so quiet I can hear his door creak open upstairs. "What the fuck, man? I'm trying to sleep."

"Get Sky's nebulizer and medicine and bring it to me, now."

I can tell by the staccato clunking overhead that he's racing around. But it's not fast enough. "Hurry the fuck up."

My training kicks in and I make the shift from terrified observer to paramedic. "Babe, I need you to stand up so I can get your nebulizer set up. Okay?"

She doesn't react to me at all.

I slide my hands under her ass and lift her off my lap.

She whimpers. I'm sorry she's hurting, but relieved she's at least responsive to pain stimuli.

I scoot out from under her then set her on the chair as gently as I can.

Her gaze is locked on the laptop's screen.

Fuck. I close it then run to the stairs. Boone meets me on the landing and shoves the nebulizer into my arms. "Is she okay?"

"No."

Chapter Twenty-Five

Skylar

It takes a second for my brain to catch up with what my eyes are seeing. And even then I don't want to believe it. Rowdy shuts my laptop, but the image is burned into my skull like a brand. My birthmark's on Facebook. Everyone can see it. Full frontal nudity wouldn't feel more humiliating than that.

"Okay, Skylar. I need you to open your mouth."

I do it without thinking. Rowdy puts the nebulizer mouthpiece between my teeth. My lips automatically close around it.

Boone's voice echoes out of the return air vent in the family room. He's yelling, swearing and pacing. The thump-clunk of his cast accents his words. *"Take it down, Anna, or I swear to god I will fucking kill you!"*

Rowdy kneels in front of me and cups my cheeks in his palms. "I need you to breathe with me. Can you do that?"

I stare into his pale, blue eyes and nod.

"Thank god." He takes a deep breath then lets it out in a rush.

I try to mimic him, but it hurts too much.

"Sorry, babe. That was just a sigh of relief. Keep breathing nice and slow."

Nice and slow isn't easy with so many different emotions warring inside me.

Boone's still on a rant. *"Only a skanky slut would post a video like that. You better take it down before Rowdy sees it."*

I take the mouthpiece out for a second. "You didn't see the video?"

"I saw it when it was on Youtube." Rowdy tries to guide it back into my mouth but I grab his wrist.

"Youtube? It's on Youtube?"

"Only for a couple of hours." He pokes my lips with the plastic tube. "We'll talk when your treatment's done."

I turn my head then bury my face in my hands. "I want to die."

Rowdy pries my hands off then cups my cheeks. His long fingers wrap around the sides of my head. "Don't say that. Don't ever fucking say that again."

I remember telling him the exact same thing a few hours ago.

"I know you're embarrassed. But that video is only one out of thousands of humiliating clips that get posted on the internet every day. We'll get through this, Sky. I promise."

I gaze into Rowdy's eyes and find my strength, my courage, my reason to fight until my dying breath.

"If you promise to finish your treatment, I'll call Wade and ask him if that spy shit came in yet."

I can tell by his grin that at least some of it has been delivered. "If you don't mind, that'd be awesome. The door's unlocked."

Rowdy tucks his phone into his pocket. "Wade and Derek are going to install the stationary cameras then bring the pens and watches over here when they're done."

As soon as Wade walks through the door, his phone dings phone dings. He gives me a sympathetic smile. "That was a heads up from Cherri. She and Anna are done shopping. They'll be back in about half an hour, depending on traffic."

Rowdy groans and presses his fingers against his eyes. "I don't want to deal with her shit tonight. Someone give me an excuse."

"I don't want you anywhere near her, but I think you're the one most likely to get her to say something incriminating."

"Actually," Derek hands me one of the spy pens. "You probably have the best chance of getting admissible evidence."

Rowdy looks at Derek as if he's crazy. "Absolutely not."

"Think about it. Skylar won't need to bait her. Her presence alone is enough to set that crazy bitch off."

"Anna's already tried to kill Skylar. I'm not giving her the chance to try again."

I agree with Derek, but I know better than to argue with Rowdy when he gets in his overly-protective alpha male mood. I'll just have to wait for the right moment. "Can I at least have one of those cool gadgets? Just in case Anna runs into me at the grocery store or something?"

"She's not going to say anything in public." Rowdy narrows his eyes at me. "I know what you're thinking and the answer is, no."

"Fine." I'll just borrow Boone's stuff.

~***~

After just a few weeks, the novelty and excitement of playing spy turns into frustration for all involved. Apparently all Anna wants to talk about is her 'dreamy, tropical wedding.'

Either she got smart and figured out she was under surveillance or she's just so blissed out by her fake engagement that I simply dropped off her radar.

Rowdy avoids Anna as much as possible by picking up extra shifts at work but he can't dodge her twenty-four seven. He never complains about it anymore, but I know it's stressing him out. I can't imagine having someone I hate pawing at me all the time.

He came up with a way to keep from kissing Anna by telling her he was saving their first kiss for the altar. Which was freaking brilliant.

He said it pissed her off at first, but she's one hundred percent onboard with it now.

She's really playing up the purity angle, dressing modestly, not drinking or swearing or trying to kill people.

Rowdy and I continue to meet secretly whenever we can. Cherri became Anna's fake BFF so she could help keep her occupied. She and Wade deserve medals for all the sacrifices they've made for Rowdy and me.

We still haven't made love. I don't want to until this Anna fiasco is over. It's not so much that I'd feel guilty for having sex with a falsely engaged man. It certainly hasn't stopped us from making out. I just don't want anything to tarnish the experience. I know it's not our first time, but it'll be the first time in four years. I don't want to be worrying about whether or not Anna's going to find out.

We aren't any closer to a solution than we were three weeks ago. Rowdy is still adamantly opposed to letting me confront Anna, but I'm sick of all the sneaking around. It's time to shut this show down. And it needs to be tonight.

Rowdy and Derek are working, Wade and Cherri are at the Louisville Street Fair, Boone's bar hopping in Denver. Anna's shift ends in ten minutes. With all of my self-appointed protectors otherwise engaged, it's now or never.

I put on my shortest skirt and my lowest cut tank then check myself out in the full-length mirror hanging on the back of my door. Not too bad. A firm tug on the hem of my tank reveals the lacy top of my fire-engine red push-up bra. Hey, look at that. I have cleavage.

A pair of stilettos would complete the outfit, but I don't own any. Even if I did, I think I'd rather wear my ass-kicking, Tony Lama boots for this little rendezvous. Or my Nike running shoes. This will definitely be a fight or flight situation.

I decide on the boots.

I use the key Rowdy gave me to get into his room. He had to start locking his door to keep Anna out. I turn on all the lights so Anna will think he's home then lie down on his bed to wait for her.

The crunch of gravel in the drive stops my heart. But it makes up for lost time when I hear footsteps racing up the stairs.

"Rowdy? Are you okay?" Anna's eyes bug out of her head when she sees me. "What the fuck are you doing here?"

So much for her cleaned up vocabulary.

"Ending this stupid charade."

"Get out." Anna flings her arm to the side, pointing at the open door.

"I'm not letting you steal Rowdy."

"He's my fiancé." She holds her hand out, showing off the tacky cubic zirconia she bought for herself. "You know what'll happen if you try to interfere."

"Why don't you refresh my memory."

"Did you forget about the evidence I have?"

I swing my legs off the bed and sit up. "I've been doing a little research and since you removed it from the scene of the crime, it's no good."

"You're lying."

"Did you know I'm left handed?" I'm not but she doesn't know that.

"What does that have to do with anything?"

"Come on, Anna, think. Which one of my hands did you grab and wrap around your knife before cutting yourself?"

Her face turns chalky but she doesn't say anything. Neither confirming nor denying my accusation. Damn it.

"Go ahead. Take your fake evidence to the cops. I don't care. I'm not letting you ruin Rowdy's life."

She grabs fistfuls of hair on the sides of her head and screams at me. "Why didn't you just die like you were supposed to!"

Now we're getting somewhere. "Rowdy's my soul mate. We're destined to be together forever. Do you really think the universe is going to let you screw with fate?"

"You stupid, lying bitch." Spit flies out of Anna's mouth.

Hopefully, the neighbors won't call the cops until after I get indisputable proof that Anna's homicidal as well as crazy. The original plan was to get her to confess to what she's already done, but I think a video of her actually trying to kill me will be even better. As long as she doesn't succeed.

She dumps Rowdy's trash on the floor, picks up an empty bottle of Coors and smashes it against the foot of the bed.

Oh shit. I back up but I'm trapped between the bed, the wall and a crazy person with a deadly weapon. I grab Rowdy's pillow and hold it in front of my chest. "Calm down. You don't want to do this."

She laughs like a freaking maniac in a B movie. "I've been dreaming about all the different ways I can kill you."

"Care to elaborate?" I really hope all the spy crap Wade and Derek installed in here is working.

She waves the broken bottle back and forth as she creeps closer. "Adding a little powdered drain cleaner to your Advair dispenser is one of my favorites."

My stomach clenches.

"Do you have any idea what that would feel like?" Anna's smile is pure evil. "The burn as it sticks to the soft, moist tissues in the back of your throat. The agony as it eats through your vocal chords. You wouldn't even be able to scream."

"Stop." If she continues, I'm going to hurl.

"You're looking a little green around the mouth. Feeling a bit woozy?"

If I puke, I won't be able to defend myself or run.

"I'll bet you can almost taste the blood as it leaks from your ulcerated trachea, can't you?"

I press my lips together and breathe through my nose.

"I wonder how long it would take for you to drown in your blood?" She takes another step closer. "Cutting your throat won't be nearly as entertaining, but the results will be the same."

My back is already pressed against the wall, but that doesn't stop me from pushing harder, as if I can squeeze myself into the sheetrock. "Stay away from me."

Anna swings the broken bottle as she lunges at me.

I block it with the pillow, saving my throat, but the jagged edge slices the back of my hand. It takes a second for the pain to register. Then another for the blood to flow. It pours down my forearm then drips off my elbow.

Anna licks her lips and shivers as if the sight of my blood is turning her on. Maybe it is. She's a sick, twisted piece of work.

I don't dare take my eyes off her to check the injury. The *splat, splat, splat* of blood hitting the hardwood floor makes me dizzy.

I need to get some distance between us. Rowdy's bedside light is a cheap floor lamp on a lightweight metal stand, but it's the only thing close enough for me to grab. I edge to the left and wait for Anna to strike again. When she does, I dodge to the right, grab the lamp and yank it hard enough to pull the plug out of the wall. The base is heavier than it looks. I use the momentum to swing it up in an arc, hoping Anna will back up.

But instead of trying to avoid the weighted base, she lunges at me again. It catches her under the chin, snapping her head back. She slams into the floor with a room shaking thud, but doesn't so much as whimper.

I keep my gaze locked on her limp body as I crawl back over Rowdy's bed, dragging the lamp with me. A pool of blood spreads out from beneath Anna. Oh shit. Did I kill her? I was only trying to defend myself.

I pull my new phone out of my skirt pocket and dial nine-one-one.

~***~

The cut on the back of my hand isn't as bad as I thought, but it hurts like hell. I run to the main house and bang on the door. "Derek, open up! It's an emergency."

He opens the door, wearing nothing but a pair of black boxer briefs. His mouth and chin are smeared red. At first, I think he's injured too, but it's only lipstick.

I rush inside and slam the door behind me. My knees refuse to support my weight. I slide down the door, but Derek grabs me before I hit the floor and guides me to the kitchen.

"What the fuck happened?" He hands me a wad of paper towels.

I press them against the back of my hand. Blood soaks through all of them in a matter of seconds. "Anna."

Derek's normally ruddy complexion turns to chalk. He lifts the hem of my tank and scans my bare stomach. "Are you okay? Any other injuries?"

"No. Just this." I keep pressure on my hand as I lift it above my heart. The throbbing lessens.

"Where's Anna?"

"In Rowdy's room." Tears fill my eyes. "I think I killed her."

Derek looks over his shoulder and yells, "Call nine-one-one."

His bedroom door swings open. A girl with smeared makeup and messy, red hair leans her head and shoulders into the hall. It's obvious she's naked. "What happened?"

"Just do it!"

"It's okay. I already called it in." I lower my bloody hands and drop my new phone on the table. I forgot that I was still holding it. I hope all the blood didn't ruin it.

Derek closes his eyes for a moment and sighs. "What did you say when you called emergency services?"

"I think I said 'Anna is trying to kill me, I need help.'"

"That's all?"

"My phone died. I think some blood got inside it."

The girl disappears back into Derek's room then emerges a few minutes later, fully dressed. She pulls her hair into a ponytail as she edges around the kitchen's perimeter, towards the front door. "I um...need to go."

"In a minute. Keep an eye on Skylar while I get dressed."

"Sorry." She gives me an apologetic glance then darts out the door.

"Shit." Derek pulls out a chair and sits beside me.

"I'm okay."

"No, you're not. Keep pressure on that." He nods at my hand. "And keep it above heart level."

He watches me for a couple minutes then goes to the sink and grabs a pair of dish gloves and more paper towels then wipes my phone off.

"What are you doing?" My first thought is that he's trying to get rid of my fingerprints but that doesn't make sense.

He shrugs. "Mine's back in my bedroom and I don't want to leave you alone."

"I told you I'm fine." The tremor in my voice and violent shaking of my body aren't very convincing.

"Your phone's not working. I'm going to go grab mine. I'll be right back."

"Grab some pants while you're at it."

Derek returns with his phone, still wearing nothing but his underwear.

"What's up, man? I'm at work."

The sound of Rowdy's voice, even through the tiny speaker on Derek's phone, calms me.

"Anna attacked Skylar."

"What the fuck? Goddamnit. Is she okay?"

"She's got a nasty cut on the back of her hand, but other than that, she's fine."

"Does she need an ambulance?"

I lean in closer to the phone. "I'm fine, Rowdy. But..." My voice cracks. "I think I killed Anna."

"I'll be right there, babe. Don't say a word to the cops. Understand?"

"Yeah."

Derek lowers his voice. "It went down in your room so the whole thing's recorded."

There's a long, silent pause before Rowdy speaks. *"Is that a good thing?"*

"Don't know yet." Derek puts a gloved hand on my shoulder. "I'll see that Skylar protects all her rights."

"Are you asking if it was self-defense?" My voice is shrill with disbelief.

"No, babe. I know it was without even asking. But sometimes what shows up on a video doesn't quite match reality."

Derek says, "I'll go grab my laptop right now so we can look at the video."

"Are you okay with that Sky? Or would you rather have Derek stay with you?"

"I'm fine. But I don't want to watch the video." I've already got the whole thing burned into my brain.

"I understand. But I think it's important for Derek to see it before the cops get there."

"I agree."

Derek gives me a quick dip of his head then jogs down the hall and disappears into his room.

I tell Rowdy everything that happened while Derek's gone. I'm just wrapping it up when the front door bursts open. My heart stops. Time stands still. My blood runs cold. It's Anna.

~***~

"Derek? Anna's here." My voice sounds amazingly calm as if I'm announcing the arrival of a guest instead of a psycho intent on killing me.

He tears down the hall and darts in front of me, nearly knocking me out of the chair. He takes a wide stance and holds his arms out at a forty-five degree angle, fingers splayed. "Stay back, Anna."

"Or what?" Her words are slurred and hard to understand.

I stand up and look over Derek's shoulder.

Anna's jaw hangs open one side lower than the other. Blood and spit leak out of both corners of her mouth. A trail of bloody footprints stains the floor behind her. And she's still got that damn broken bottle. She swings it around as she talks like she's directing an invisible orchestra. "Get out of the way, asshole."

"I'm not going to let you hurt Skylar."

She limps forward. "Then I guess I'll just have to hurt you first."

Derek reaches behind his back and pushes me towards the hall. "Go lock yourself in my room."

"No. Two against one are better odds. Besides, the cops will be here any second." The sound of distant sirens floats through the open door. "Do you hear it?"

Anna holds the broken bottle in front of her and kicks the door shut. Time moves in slow motion as the sirens grow louder. They're getting closer. Red and blue lights flash through the window, but they don't stop at the house. They don't even slow down.

Anna's grin is horribly lopsided, as if she's had a stroke. "What'd you do? Give them the wrong address?"

My stomach falls to my feet. I didn't give them any address at all. The phone died before I got the chance. I was only on the line for a few seconds. That must not have been enough time for them to get my exact location.

"They won't get here in time." Blood and spit dribble out of the corner of Anna's mouth.

"Anna!" Rowdy's voice blares out of Derek's phone. *"Don't do anything stupid. I'm almost there."*

She blinks and cocks her head to the side. "Rowdy?"

"If you hurt Skylar or Derek, they'll put you in jail and we can't be together. We won't be able to get married."

"It's too late. I've already hurt her."

"No!" His anguished cry breaks my heart.

"I'm okay, Rowdy. She's just talking about the cut on my hand."

His ragged breathing is loud and uneven. *"Anna, please, I'm begging you. Put down the weapon."*

"You still love her." It's a statement, not a question.

"I... love you more." I know he's lying and only trying to save my life, but it still hurts to hear him say it.

His headlights fill the window, casting long shadows across the floor. Anna drops the bottle then jerks the door open.

Rowdy tackles her and slams her against the wall, pinning her arms to her side.

"What are you doing?" Anna uses her little girl voice.

Derek runs to Rowdy and tries in vain to pry him off Anna. "She's unarmed. You need to back off before the cops get here."

I try to turn Rowdy's head towards me, but he doesn't budge. It's as if he's carved out of stone. His eyes are glassy and dilated. He wraps his fingers around Anna's neck. "You aren't ever going to hurt Skylar again."

I wedge a hand between Rowdy's and Anna's bodies as Derek wraps his arms around Rowdy's waist.

Rowdy screams. It's a raw, primal sound. "Your father killed my mother. I'm not going to let you kill Skylar."

"Rowdy, let go." I dig my fingernails into his bicep. "If you hurt Anna, they'll put you in jail. I need you."

He shakes his head in rapid, jerky movements then blinks and looks at me.

I heave a huge sigh of relief. "Let go of Anna and hold me."

He drops her like a sack of potatoes then wraps his arms around my waist and jerks me against his chest.

Anna slides to the floor and whimpers. Her eyes roll into the back of her head as she falls over sideways.

Rowdy and I hold each other as the sirens get closer. Derek puts a hand on my back. "Go ahead and give your statement tonight but don't answer any questions about the original attack. And don't say anything about the surveillance in Rowdy's room."

"Why not?" I went to a lot of trouble, not to mention personal risk, to get Anna's confession on video.

"I don't think we'll need the extra evidence. You mentioned the knife Anna's using for blackmail."

"So?"

"Instead of reporting the attack after it happened, you claimed amnesia. It's just simpler if we focus on what happened tonight. If we need the videos, we'll use them."

Blue and red lights flash through the window and open door. The sirens stop.

Derek leans in closer. "Anna left a trail of blood from the garage to the house so expect them to come in with guns drawn. Don't make any sudden moves."

Rowdy clings to me when they try to separate us. The sheriff and his deputies call him by name and treat him gently, but it's obvious they're losing patience with him. I tell him the only thing I can think of that might convince him to let go. "My hand needs stitches."

Works like a charm. He loosens his grip then slides his hands down my arms. I take half a step back and am immediately escorted outside to an ambulance where I once again refuse treatment and transport. Rowdy can take me when we're done.

The sheriff takes my statement. He doesn't mention the original attack and neither do I.

The EMTs roll Anna— arms flailing, legs kicking, head thrashing— past me on the way to the ambulance. It's a good thing she's secured to the sides of the gurney with restraints.

She lifts her head and screams at me. Her words are nearly unintelligible but I can fill in the gaps. "Stay away from Rowdy or I'm going to kill you."

~***~

Rowdy's chest presses against my butt as we climb the rope ladder to the tree house. It's the only way for me to do it one handed. He keeps his arms locked on either side of me as an extra safety measure. It took fourteen stitches to close the gash on the back of my hand but there was no damage to tendons or nerves. It's a small price to pay for getting rid of Anna.

"Are you sure this can't wait until you have full use of both hands?" He's such a worrier.

"Nope." I'm done waiting.

Rowdy and I were so exhausted last night when we got home from the ER that we fell asleep as soon as our heads hit my pillow. Rowdy hit the snooze icon on his phone alarm twice this morning before rolling out of bed. He gave me a pain pill and a kiss then left for work without breakfast.

While he was gone, Boone helped me set up the tree house so that it looked just the same as it had the night Rowdy and I gave ourselves to each other four years ago.

After work, Rowdy and I took Wade, Cherri, Derek and Boone out for dinner to thank them for their help and to celebrate our victory. But now, it's time for us to enjoy a private celebration.

He gives my butt a gentle push to help me get through the trap door. I spin around so I can watch his face.

His eyes widen then drift to half-mast as his lips curve up in a slow, seductive smile. "If I check The Hole, will I find a bottle of non-alcoholic sparkling cider?"

"Maybe." I'd considered buying a bottle of champagne, but decided to keep everything exactly the same, as much as possible. Besides, mixing pain meds and alcohol is never a good idea. "But you aren't allowed to check. Not yet."

I scoot onto the sleeping bag so Rowdy has enough room to squeeze through the trap door. I take the necklace out of my back pocket. "I have something for you."

He arches his eyebrows. "Oh yeah? What is it?"

"It's nothing really." My cheeks heat up as I drop the necklace into his palm. "It's just those old glass beads I made with Aunt Lori. The ones she gave you after I disappeared?"

His Adam's apple bobs as he strokes each bead.

"I filed down the sharp edges and added some spacer beads between them to protect the string. But you don't have to wear it or anything."

"Are you kidding me?" He slips it on, fastening the bead and loop closure in front then sliding it around to the back. "I'll never take it off."

"You like it?"

"I love it." He crawls over me on his hands and knees. "You fixed these beads the way you're fixing me."

"You don't need fixing." I lie back as he kisses a trail up my body. My legs fall open.

Rowdy settles between them, the hard ridge of his erection pressing against my thigh. "I still have a few rough edges that need softening."

He runs his hand up my ribcage, his thumb sweeping across my nipple. He kisses my neck, just below my ear. "How's your hand?"

My arm's bent at a ninety degree angle, propping my hand up off the floor. It's throbbing but he doesn't need to know that. I rock my hips. "As long as I keep it above my heart, it's fine."

"God, Skylar." Rowdy groans and lets a little more of his weight press down on me. He claims my mouth, sucking and nipping at my bottom lip. His tongue sweeps over mine then retreats. He pulls back and rests his forehead on mine as tremors rock both our bodies. "Are you sure?"

The question takes me back in time. We were so sure of our future, of each other and of ourselves. We had our whole lives planned out. Rowdy was going to start working for Uncle Will full-time as soon as he graduated from high school. Then when I graduated a year later, we were going to get an apartment together. He'd continue to work while I went to CU on my grandfather's grant. Then I'd get a job so he could go to college. After that, we'd start a family. It all sounds so simplistic and naive now.

I have no idea what the future holds for either of us. No one does, really. But I know what I want. And it's right here in front of me. Or more accurately, on top of me.

"I'm sure, Rowdy."

He rocks back on his knees and pulls his shirt off then slides his hand under the hem of my light pink tank, skimming the bare skin next to my waistband. "You wore a shirt just like this last time."

"It's the same shirt." I never wore it again, but I kept it. I kept the black denim shorts I'd worn too, but they, unlike my top, are not made out of extremely stretchy fabric.

He slips the front clasp of my bra between his thumb and index finger but lets go without undoing it. He adjusts himself in his jeans then lies down, half-on half-off my body, keeping one knee tucked between mine.

Tears fill my eyes when I realize he's also recreating the past.

He kisses my breast, over my bra. I trail my fingers over his bare chest, gradually working my way lower. Rowdy takes my wrist and moves my hand to his shoulder. I smile. He's got a lot more control now, but this is how we were before. One step back for every two steps forward.

He slides down and takes one of my lace-covered nipples into his mouth. Gently at first, then sucking and tugging with increasing vigor as he kneads my other breast. His stubbled cheek raises goose bumps as he drags it across my upper chest to take my other breast in his mouth.

I slide my hand down his torso again. This time he lets me caress him over his jeans. He murmurs, "God, Skylar. I want you so bad," then thrusts against my palm.

"I can tell."

He fingers the front clasp of my bra again. "May I?"

"Please."

My nipples are already hard and aching for his touch. He licks a circle around one before flicking it with his tongue. My back arches.

He lifts his head, breaking contact as he moves his fingers to the button on my waistband. "Is this okay?"

I nod.

He flicks it open. "Are you sure?"

"Wait."

He freezes then lifts his chest and frowns at me. "Wait?"

"If you touch me now, I'll come and that didn't happen the first time."

"Babe, I'm all for being sentimental, but there's no way I'm letting you out of this tree house without giving you at least one orgasm."

"Okay." Our reenactment is over. And it really is okay. It's better than okay. I'll always treasure the memory of our early years together, but what we have now is so much better. I'll always love the shy, awkward boy that I first fell in love with, but I love the strong, confident man that he's become even more.

Rowdy tugs on my shorts. "Lift up."

I raise my hips.

He slides my shorts and panties down my legs then kisses his way back up.

He rises to his knees and pulls a condom out of his pocket then tosses it on the floor, next to the sleeping bag.

My heart skips more than just one beat when he flicks the button on his jeans open. I sit up and cup my palm over his bulging fly. "Let me."

He gazes at me with hooded eyes and gives me a quick, single nod.

I barely tug on his zipper. It slides down effortlessly, the pressure of his pulsing erection forcing it open. I hold my injured hand out to the side and slip the other one inside his boxers. He makes that chest-vibrating, animalistic growling sound that never fails to liquify my joints and steal my breath.

I struggle to pull his jeans down with one hand.

He rocks back on his heels then stands up with the grace and power of a mountain lion. His gaze locks on mine. "Lie down."

I lie back on the sleeping bag and watch him lower his jeans and boxers. When he gets them below his knees, he steps out of one leg then the other without so much as a wobble. His balance is perfect. Everything about him is perfect.

He sinks to his knees and applies the condom. He pinches the tip then rolls it down his shaft, just like they taught us in health class back in high school. But this is so much better.

Rowdy chuckles, drawing my gaze up to his face. My face burns when I realize he caught me watching him. "Sorry."

"Don't be." He slides his hands slowly up my legs, spreading them as he covers my body with his. "I love how fascinated you are with my dick."

"Oh, god." I hide my face behind the crook of my elbow.

Rowdy takes my wrist and pins it above my head. "Look at me, Skylar."

I open my eyes.

His gaze locks on mine as he slides up my body. He stops with the tip of his erection pressed against me, poised at the brink. "Last chance. Is this what you want?"

I hook my heels around his waist and arch my back. But Rowdy lifts his hips. "Tell me what you want."

I know that how I answer will dictate whether he takes me slowly and gently or with unrestrained abandon. I want both. "Make love to me...then fuck my brains out."

His eyebrows shoot up. He blinks then closes his eyes and laughs. "Oh my god."

His laughter is contagious. I giggle then smack the side of his arm. "Stop laughing at me."

"I'm not laughing at you. I'm laughing with you." He presses a kiss to my forehead. "You're amazing, you know that?"

"Right now, all I am is embarrassed."

"Don't be." He slides in a fraction of an inch, stretching me. I gasp.

He pulls out. "Are you okay?"

"I'm just surprised. I wasn't expecting it to hurt this time."

"It's been four years and this is only your second time." He brushes a wisp of hair off my face. "Do you want to stop?"

"Hell, no." I dig my heels into the hard muscles of his butt. "Just take it slow."

Rowdy rolls off me onto his back.

"I said I didn't want to stop." I take a deep breath to clear the whine out of my voice. "Please? Don't stop."

"We aren't stopping." He sits up and grabs my waist then lifts me onto his lap. "We're putting you in charge."

"But, I don't know what to do."

"Tab A goes into slot B."

I laugh and smack him again. "You know what I mean."

He lies back and laces his fingers behind his head. "Just do whatever you want, babe."

I play with him for a few minutes while I gather my courage then rise up onto my knees.

He's not laughing now.

There's a slight stinging sensation as I lower myself onto him.

"Take your time, Sky. There's no rush."

I nod and ease down a little more.

"Breathe, babe. Slow and deep. Try to relax."

I notice his breathing isn't slow or deep. He's not exactly relaxed either. He moves his hands to his sides and clenches his fist but remains perfectly still.

I take his advice, even though he's not following it, and focus on relaxing all my muscles. I open up and slide the rest of the way down his shaft. "Ah..."

Rowdy squeezes his eyes shut and bites his lip.

I try to crawl off, but Rowdy digs his fingers into my hips and holds me in place.

"Are you okay?" Ohmigod. What if I broke it? "Did I hurt you?"

"No, babe." He opens his eyes and gives me a tight smile. "It just feels so fucking good."

"Oh. Okay." I rock my hips forward, rubbing my clit against his patch of black curls. "Oh!"

Rowdy loosens his grip but keeps his hands on my hips. "You like that?"

"God, yes." The full sensation inside me, combined with the friction outside, is indescribable. It's better than what he does with his fingers or even his mouth. Which, as Rowdy would say, is pretty fucking amazing.

I lean forward and put my good hand on his chest to brace myself.

Rowdy grips the front of my shoulders. "I got you."

I let him hold my weight as I rock and grind against him. "I'm close."

"Do you want to come now? Or do you want to make it last?"

What a question. I want to come now, but this is our first time in four years. This is a memory I'll treasure for the rest of my life. "Make it last."

He lowers me to his chest then rolls us over. He holds most of his weight off me, but keeps enough pressure so I can feel every inch of his body on the surface of mine. How's this supposed to make it last?

He pulls out.

Oh. That's how. Not quite what I had in mind.

He suckles at one breast then the other. It feels just as good as it did earlier, but I want him inside me.

As if reading my mind, Rowdy enters me again. This time he keeps all his weight off me, so the only place we're touching is where we're connected. His movements are slow but deliberate. Each thrust goes a little deeper, filling me a little fuller, bringing me closer to the edge.

He pulls out just before I climax.

I groan in frustration.

Rowdy kisses my jaw, right below my ear. "Patience, babe. It'll be worth it."

He brings me to the brink so many times I lose count. I'm so close. I try to stifle my moans and keep my muscles from clenching so he won't know. If he pulls out again, I'll die.

He picks up the pace and rocks into me harder. I dig my fingers into his shoulders. If I didn't have such short nails, I'm sure they'd draw blood.

Rowdy growls and grips my chin, holding my head still. "Open your eyes. I want you to look at me when you come."

Thank god, he's not going to stop me this time. I open my eyes and gaze into his.

He pulls back until just the tip remains inside then slams into me burying himself completely. His rhythm is frantic, like waves crashing onto the beach. He reaches between our bodies and presses a finger against my throbbing clit as he continues to pound into me.

My whole body spasms. I keep my gaze locked onto Rowdy's face and scream his name as I shatter into a million pieces.

I'm just starting to float back to earth when Rowdy's thrusting loses its perfect rhythm. His movements are jerky and unpredictable. He straightens his arms, lifting his chest and arching his back, as he rams into me one last time. His body shudders. I orgasm again as he pulses inside me.

Rowdy shifts to the side as he collapses on top of me. "That was fucking amazing."

"It was, wasn't it."

He chuckles then pulls me onto his chest as he lies back, still maintaining our connection. I want to stay like this forever, but when Rowdy starts to soften, he pulls out. A quiet whimper slips out before I can stop it.

Rowdy kisses my forehead. "I'd stay buried in you all night if I could, but I don't want to risk getting you pregnant."

I listen to his heart as it gradually slows down and settles into a steady rhythm. He's so quiet, I think he's fallen asleep until he kisses the top of my head and whispers, "I love you so much."

"You're the only boy I've ever loved. And the only man I ever will."

"You're it for me, too, babe. Always have been. Always will be. This is a forever thing."

We drift off to sleep for a couple hours. I wake up with the moon in my eyes and find Rowdy gazing at my face. "Were you watching me sleep?"

"No. I was staring at you, hoping you'd feel it and wake up."

"Why?" I yawn and stretch. "What time is it?"

"Time for round two."

Chapter Twenty-Six

Rowdy

Eldorado Canyon has always been a sanctuary for me. A place to escape the relentless drama of my life. A place to hide when Keith's drunken rages turned violent. A place to brood when Sky left at the end of every summer and winter stretched out before me like an endless desert. A place to grieve after Mom died and Skylar disappeared without a word.

As soon as I got out of jail, I fled to the canyon. I was so consumed with rage and grief I couldn't contain it. Skylar and I had climbed The Naked Edge together the day before she disappeared. I wanted to climb it again. It was an undeniable compulsion. For some reason, I thought that climbing The Naked Edge would give me some relief from the unbearable pain.

And it did. As long as I was climbing.

Back then, I couldn't afford my own gear, so I free soloed the five eleven route. The eagles, hawks and falcons, floating eye-level in the turquoise sky, were the only witnesses of my grief. And my foolishness. They watched without sympathy or censure.

I hid my suffering from everyone else. The only evidence of my despair was the salty, white residue of dried tears amongst the lime green and yellow lichen.

I shudder now as I think about the risks I took. I'm lucky to be alive. I haven't attempted to climb The Naked Edge since that day, but I think, maybe, it's time.

It's also time to move on from the trauma that drove me to such extremes. Time to replace the memory of that climb with something else. Something better.

If we're going to climb The Naked Edge and still have time to make our six-thirty reservation at The Flagstaff House restaurant, we need to get started. I shift my hips back, away from Skylar. If she wakes up with my morning wood poking her in the ass, we won't get out of bed for at least another hour. Any other day, I'd trade the climb for a morning romp, but not today.

My gear's already packed. So's Skylar's. I get dressed then wake her up with a kiss.

She groans and turns her face. "Morning breath."

"Hey. I brushed my teeth."

"Not yours." She covers her mouth. "Mine."

"How many times do I have to tell you, I don't give a fuck." I pounce on her and steal another kiss then hop off the bed, taking the covers with me.

Skylar grabs at the down comforter but I yank it out of her hands.

"Come on, sleepyhead. We have a mountain to climb."

She buries her head under her pillow.

"I'll let you lead the third pitch."

She peeks at me. "Third pitch of what route?"

"The Naked Edge."

She squeals and jumps from the bed straight into my arms, wrapping her legs around my waist. She hangs onto my shoulders and leans back. "Can I lead the first three pitches?"

Skylar's climbing skills have improved over the summer. I feel comfortable letting her lead almost any route we climb. But this is The Naked Edge.

"How about you lead the first and third?" The second pitch is hard to protect. A lead fall could have fatal consequences.

"Okay." Before Boone's accident, she would have argued to lead the entire route.

She does a great job, cranking up the first pitch, pulling the crux like a pro. I lead the second, as planned, then let Sky take the sharp end on the third with a reminder to stay alert. "Don't let the relative ease of this pitch fool you. There're some runout sections you need to watch for."

The fourth pitch is the crux of the entire route. We double check each other's gear after swapping leads. Sky's helmet taps mine as she kisses my cheek. "Be careful."

"You too." Following is much safer than leading, but there's always the potential for disaster.

I question my sanity as I struggle to back up the old, fixed pin in the overhang just below the chimney. I'm so pumped by the time I get myself scrunched into the narrow space that I'm forced to rest for a few minutes, even though my back and neck are screaming in pain. As soon as I get the lactic acid shaken out of my arms, I crank right around the roof and clip into the three bolt anchor.

This hanging belay—with nothing but six hundred feet of empty air between my ass and the ground—is fucking outrageous. I take a moment to enjoy the view then yell, "Off belay."

Skylar replies, "Belay off."

I lean back in my harness to keep an eye on her as she approaches the crux. It's already been a long, hard climb. Will she be able to pull it? I struggled with it and my wingspan is at least ten inches greater than hers. I protected it as much as possible with some small stoppers and a blue Metolius TCU. But I'm still nervous.

I keep as much tension on the rope as possible and still allow enough room for her to maneuver. If she peels off here, she'll have a hard time getting back on route.

I don't know how she does it, but she dances through the crux moves like a ballerina. She clips into the bolt on my left with a wide grin. "That was freaking amazing! I can't wait until I've got the skills to lead that pitch."

"Try to calm down, babe." I don't want to kill her buzz, but I don't want her adrenaline to spike and then leave her depleted. "Save some energy for the final pitch and descent."

"I'm good." Her grin widens. "You look exhausted. Do you want me to lead it?"

"No way." I reach across my body and start moving the pro she cleaned onto my rack. "I've got this."

The fifth pitch isn't technically as difficult as the fourth. It just seems harder because of the full-body workout I just endured. Skylar makes it to the top and joins me. "Thank you."

"For what?"

"For climbing The Naked Edge with me, for letting me lead a couple pitches, for letting me back into your life. For everything."

"You're welcome." My voice cracks.

Skylar crinkles her brow, obviously wondering why I'm so emotional.

I swallow, trying to clear the lump out of my throat. "This climb is sort of symbolic for me."

She tucks a knee up and hugs it against her chest. "How come?"

"Lots of reasons." I consider telling her about my solo ascent, but I don't want to tarnish this day with bad memories. I also don't want to give her any ideas about free soloing this route. "Our relationship up to this point has certain similarities to this climb. We were so young when we first got together. We believed we were invincible. We thought our biggest challenge was the long separation between summers."

Skylar nods. "What do you think was our crux? My disappearance or Anna's blackmail?"

"That shit with Anna was scary. It still is." She's locked up in the state mental hospital in Pueblo, but all she has to do is convince an overworked shrink that her meds are working and they'll let her out. "When you disappeared, I lost my mind. I don't know how I made it through that." I bump Skylar's shoulder with mine. "Don't ever do that again."

"I'm so sorry." Her eyes catch the afternoon sun. "That was my crux, too. I thought I'd never see you again."

I take her hand and trace the scar on the back. "I know we'll have lots more challenges. New untried routes with cruxes of their own, but I hope that's the worst thing we'll ever have to face."

"Me too."

"Whatever problems life throws at us, I know I can handle it as long as I have you." Sweat beads across my brow and runs down the back of my neck. I unzip the top pocket on my pack and pull out the little blue velvet box. "You're my lifeline."

Skylar's eyes widen. A quiet gasp slips past her parted lips.

I pop the box open. The small solitaire diamond catches the afternoon sun, throwing sparks of rainbow light across our bodies. "I know we're young and you still have three more years before you graduate. But I've got a good job and we don't have to get married right away. We can have as long of an engagement as you want and—"

"Yes."

"Yes?"

She extends her left hand.

My own hands shake as I pluck the ring out of the box. The last thing I need to do is drop it six hundred feet to the ground. I slide it onto her finger then kiss the back of her hand. "Thank you."

"You're welcome." Her eyes sparkle brighter than the diamond on her finger.

I know that as long as I live, I'll never tire of gazing into those hazel depths. It won't matter if they're dimmed by time and hooded with wrinkled skin, they'll always be beautiful.

She grins at me in true Skylar fashion. "I'll race you to the bottom."

Acknowledgements and Author Information

Want to know what happens when the gang goes to Costa Rica for spring break? Curious about whether Cherri and Wade can overcome their differences? Wondering if Derek will ever settle down with someone special? Will Boone find the courage to come out to the rest of his friends? And what about Anna? Will that crazy bitch get her act together or continue to cause problems? These questions, and more, will be answered in future stand-alone books of the Rocky Mountain Romance series.

If you'd like to know when the next book is available, sign up for my newsletter at www.charliwebb.com

I want to take this opportunity to thank a few people that have been such a huge part of this incredible journey. My husband, even though he doesn't condone 'sexually explicit books' he didn't judge me or try to censor this story.

Carol for hiking through Eldorado Canyon with me and sharing her awesome photos.

Scott, for sharing his expertise as a former member of Rocky Mountain Rescue (the *real* volunteer organization that I used as a model for Boulder Mountain Rescue). Any errors or inaccuracies in the story are mine.

I also want to thank my editor, mentor, and dear friend, Kris at Final-Edits. Without her support and encouragement I'd still be writing fan-fiction.

My beta readers for their insight and suggestions. The story is stronger because of them.

But most of all, I want to thank everyone that's read, recommended or reviewed any of my stories. You make my dreams come true on a daily basis and I adore each and every one of you! *Mwah!*

If you enjoyed **Naked Edge,** please recommend it to your like-minded friends. I read every review I receive on Amazon, so if you'd like more of Rowdy, Skylar, Wade, Cherri, Derek and Boone, that's a great place to mention it ;-)

I love to hear from readers, so drop me a line at charliwebbbooks@gmail.com

Follow me on Twitter @CharliWebbBooks

Find me on Facebook

Other books by Charli Webb (writing under Charlotte Abel)

The Channie Series: An award-winning young adult paranormal romance series that will make you believe in magic.

Enchantment (Book One): Channie Belks is trying to hide the fact she's a witch. Sorta hard to do after her parents slap a chastity curse on her for flirting with "dirty-minded, non-magical, city-boys." She can't even walk by a hot guy without zapping him. There's a way to break the curse; but one mistake could kill her. It's not worth the risk...until she meets a certain BMX champion named Josh. Suddenly, the threat of death isn't such a deal-breaker.

Taken (Book Two): Bound by love and magic. Betrayed by those they trust. Not everyone survives. In this second installment of The Channie Series, Josh and Channie are tested physically and emotionally as the tough choices they are forced to make affect not only their future together but their very existence. The risks are high but the rewards are even higher.

Finding Valor (Book Three): Josh awakes with no recollection of the previous six months of his life, including his relationship with Channie. Not only is it hard for him to believe that he's married and his wife was kidnapped, but accepting that he is a mage and prophecies of the Book of the Dead are almost impossible. Will he be able to save Channie from her mother's dark magic before she is sacrificed? And more importantly, will he live up to his power-name and find Valor in time to save all the clans?

The Sanctuary Series:
River's Recruit (Book One): A beautiful, young shape-shifter discovers a lost backpacker trespassing in her territory during a blizzard. She has two choices: recruit him into her cult-like tribe, or kill him.

River's Remorse (Book Two): Coming in 2014

Glossary

Anchor - Protective gear set up to support a belay.

Belay - The act of protecting a roped climber with the aid of a friction device.

Biner - Climber slang for "carabiner."

Bolt - Permanent protection drilled into the rock.

Cams - A spring-loaded protection device that expands when placed into a crack.

Carabiner - D shaped metal rings with spring-loaded opening used to connect rope and equipment.

Chimney - A rock formation with somewhat parallel sides. A climber ascends using outward pressure of arms, legs, hands, feet, back and sometimes even the head.

Clean - The act of removing protection from a pitch. Usually performed by the second climber.

Crux - The most difficult part of a climbing route or pitch.

Free solo - Climbing without a rope.

Gumby - A derogatory term for a climbing novice.

Lead - The first climber to ascend, placing protection and clipping the belay rope as they climb. Falling while leading is more dangerous since the lead climber will fall at least twice the distance between the climber and the last piece of protection.

Nut - A metal wedge attached to a wire loop that is inserted into cracks for protection.

Peel - Fall.

Pendulum - A lateral swinging fall that occurs when the last piece of protection is placed far to one side.

Pitch - The part of a climb between two belay stations.

Protection - Climbing equipment used to stop a fall or set up an anchor for belaying. Often referred to as "pro."

Prusik - (Noun) A knot used for ascending a rope. (Verb) The act of ascending a rope using a prusik knot.

Pumped - A build up of lactic acid in the forearms, making it difficult to hang on.

Rack - The protective equipment taken on a climb. Also, part of the climbing harness where equipment is hung.

Roof - Overhanging rock.

Route - The predetermined path of a particular climb. Often made up of several pitches.

Runout - A long distance between two points of protection.

Scree - Loose gravel.

Second - A climber who follows the lead.

Sharp end - The end of the rope attached to the lead climber. "Taking the sharp end" refers to lead climbing.

Sport Climbing - Climbers clip into pre-placed, permanent protection or "bolts" whether outdoors or in a climbing gym.

Talus - Larger rocks and boulders that are sometimes locked together to form a stable surface.

TCU - Three Cam Unit.

Traditional or **"trad"** climbing - Climbers place their own protection as they climb.

Traverse - To climb in a horizontal direction.

Made in the USA
Charleston, SC
04 February 2014